"HARD ABOUT!"
ADMIRAL KIRK SHOUTED.
"RETURN FIRE ON MY ORDER!"

"Fire, Admiral? On *Recovery?*" First Officer Pulver of the *U.S.S. Paladin* questioned. "But our own people are on that ship!"

"I know," Admiral Kirk said grimly. "We simply have no choice." He turned back to the viewscreen.

"Mr. Sandover!" he said to the weapons officer. "You heard me! Prepare to fire!"

And twin beams of energy shot out toward the ship carrying two of James T. Kirk's closest friends. . . .

Look for STAR TREK Fiction from Pocket Books

Star Trek: The Original Series

Star Trek: The Next Generation

Star Trek: Deep Space Nine

Star Trek: Voyager

STAR TREK®
RECOVERY

J.M. DILLARD

POCKET BOOKS

New York   London   Toronto   Sydney   Tokyo   Singapore

This book is a work of fiction. Names, characters, places and incidents are products of the author's imagination or are used fictitiously. Any resemblance to actual events or locales or persons, living or dead, is entirely coincidental.

An *Original* Publication of POCKET BOOKS

POCKET BOOKS, a division of Simon & Schuster Inc.
1230 Avenue of the Americas, New York, NY 10020

Copyright © 1995 by Paramount Pictures. All Rights Reserved.

STAR TREK is a Registered Trademark of Paramount Pictures.

This book is published by Pocket Books, a division of Simon & Schuster Inc., under exclusive license from Paramount Pictures.

ISBN: 0-671-88342-9

First Pocket Books printing March 1995

10 9 8 7 6 5 4 3 2 1

POCKET and colophon are registered trademarks of Simon & Schuster Inc.

Printed in the U.S.A.

For Kathy, with love and gratitude

Acknowledgments

Let's get right down to it: this book exists because of my collaborator, the divine Kathleen O'Malley. Kathy wrote a huge portion of the first draft *and* provided emotional hand-holding for me during a very difficult year. (And, since we live on opposite coasts, we have the phone bills to prove it!) For those of you that don't know, Kath is an author in her own right; run, don't walk, to your nearest bookstore and pick up copies of her two collaborations with Ann Crispin, the *Starbridge* books *Silent Dances* and *Silent Songs*. (And while you're at it, buy the rest of the Starbridge series, too.)

Thanks, Kath. I couldn't have done it without you.

The next person that deserves long-distance hugs and kisses is editor Kevin Ryan, who has been incredibly kind and incredibly patient in waiting for this book. Thanks, Kev. I won't forget it.

I'd also like to thank every STAR TREK fan who read *The Lost Years* and who is now holding this book. Without you, I wouldn't have had the opportunity to write about some of my favorite characters and their continuing adventures in the Lost Years series. . . .

Prologue

"You're really going through with it, sir?"

Admiral James T. Kirk turned away from his office window and its sweeping view of the San Francisco Bay; above the choppy, leaden water, dark clouds sailed swiftly in an ever-changing panorama.

Kirk released a silent sigh and faced his questioner. Beneath his trimmed golden brown beard, Lieutenant Commander Kevin Riley still had enough of an Irish baby-face to give the appearance of a man much younger than the thirty-odd years Kirk knew him to be. People often underestimated Riley because of it. But when Kirk looked at his aide, he could see the hard-won maturity etched around his blue eyes and the corners of his mouth.

Over the past year and a half, Riley, likewise, had come to know Kirk. Maybe not as well as Leonard McCoy or Mr. Spock had . . . but well enough. They'd watched each other change as they worked together at

Starfleet Headquarters. For Riley, the changes had meant real growth, a burgeoning strength of character, but for Kirk . . . the adjustments had not nearly been so positive.

"You don't think I should do it?" Kirk asked his aide. Not that another opinion would make a difference at this point—he had made his decision, and nothing could shake him. But over the past several months, he had come to value Riley's input; a friendship and trust had developed between the two.

"Now, that's a true Irish answer, Admiral," the younger man said with a slight smile. "A question for a question. I know you, sir. Once your mind is made up . . ."

Kirk shook his head, wanting Riley to believe he wasn't shrugging him off. "I respect your opinion, Kevin. You should know that by now."

Riley glanced shyly away as if embarrassed by Kirk's high regard, and the unexpected use of his first name.

"Tell me," Kirk insisted quietly. "You don't think I should do this? When you, more than anyone at Starfleet, knows what's happening to me here? You've watched this *job,* this 'exciting opportunity' they promised me dwindle into nothing but a bureaucrat's dream. You've seen the work—the *paperwork*—pile up and up until we've both been buried under it. You, even more than my *wife*—" He paused abruptly, his voice catching on the last word.

It had been two months since his one-year marriage contract had expired. Two months since Admiral Lori Ciana had stoutly refused to renew that contract. Two months since she had moved out of his home, his life, his bed.

Kirk swallowed, gritted his teeth, then nodded at his own error. "—that is, my *ex*-wife . . . even more than Lori, *you've* watched what they've done to me. It's been more than six months since I've been out of this office. Six months since I've done something, *anything,* even remotely worthwhile. And a year since . . . I've been in space. . . ."

He paused, that phrase almost whispered, and left it hanging there between them. He smiled at Riley conspiratorially. "Do you remember, Kevin? What it was like? Six months . . . on the *Enterprise?*" He couldn't help himself. His voice dropped into an almost reverential hush when he mouthed her name.

"I remember," Riley murmured.

Kirk turned back toward the view of the windswept sky. "In a year we might've discovered two new class-M planets, mapped a couple of solar systems, contacted two or three alien races. Spock would've found time to translate four new languages, improve five computer programs, write two new ones, and author half a dozen scientific papers. And Bones . . . Bones would've discovered a handful of vaccines, isolated a bunch of unknown organisms . . . and found a dozen new ways to get under Spock's skin." He was smiling now, in spite of his melancholy, until he turned back and caught sight of his aide's pitying expression.

Damn, Jim thought disgustedly, as Kevin lowered his eyes to spare him. *I must sound like the ancient mariner! But the only albatross around my neck is this* job. "Don't you miss it at all, Kevin? Don't you miss working in space?"

"I don't know, sir," Riley admitted honestly. "For a long time I thought I'd never go back. But lately . . . maybe because I've been working with you . . . I find myself wondering. . . . Are you sure it's really *space* you miss so much, Admiral, or is it the *responsibility?* All those people under your command, a million decisions to make a day—you thrived on that, sir. It

3

was the responsibility I couldn't handle for a long time. But now . . . I think maybe . . . yes. I guess I do miss it. The responsibility of working in space."

Kirk pointed a finger at him as if his aide had just pinpointed the problem. "And that's where we're going, Riley. Into space. You and I. We've done our bit for God and country. We've written enough reports and refitted enough ships to satisfy anyone." He'd even had to oversee the refitting of the *Enterprise*. He'd done it, too, knowing all the while he was refitting her for another captain—Will Decker. "We deserve a better assignment. And today, I'm going to tell Admiral Nogura just that. Let the chips go ahead and fall."

Jim could see both admiration and fear warring in Riley's eyes. A confrontation with the old man, the most powerful figure in Starfleet, was quite the calculated risk. Kirk could very well have to live with whatever ultimatum he delivered. But did that matter any longer? *I've lost Lori. I've lost the* Enterprise. *Lost Bones, Spock, and the only work I ever cared about. What else have I got to lose?*

Just Starfleet. He remembered the day, almost two years before, when he'd been on leave at his mother Winona's home in Iowa, and Nogura had come, determined to talk him into the admiralty. Jim had been just as determined not to give up the *Enterprise.*

"Make your pitch," he'd told the old man. *"I'll go ahead and refuse the promotion . . . and if you want to, you can drum me out of the Fleet. But I won't be kicked upstairs."*

And Nogura, his tone as smooth and brittle as glass, had said quietly, *"God knows, I don't want you to resign if I can help it. But I can't stop you from leaving the Fleet."*

It might very well come to that; having to resign, to walk away from his years in Starfleet, to become . . .

what? A commercial pilot hauling cargo and passengers? Captain of a crew of thirty on the border patrol?

No matter; he could not envision what his future might be without Starfleet. But he had seen what it was in the Fleet, without a ship, without the exhilaration of being in space—and *that* future he could live with no longer.

Perhaps he could not reclaim the *Enterprise*—but at the very least, he would force Nogura to make good his promise that Kirk would be a diplomatic troubleshooter, not a deskbound bureaucrat . . .

Or he would resign.

"Wish me luck," he said softly, and strode toward the exit.

"Admiral!" the younger man called after him.

Kirk paused in the doorway, knowing that, whatever Riley might say, he would not be swayed.

"Just make sure he knows, sir," Riley said firmly, "that this decision . . . goes for both of us."

Kirk blinked, taken aback.

"I'm not willing to spend my life pushing anyone else's papers, sir . . . with all due respect."

Kirk gave his aide a questioning glance; but Riley's gaze was unwavering, his jaw set with a determination that matched the admiral's. Jim did not smile, but his expression warmed with admiration and gratitude. He nodded, and headed silently for the staircase that would lead him to the lion's den.

The short flight up wasn't so brief that Jim didn't have time to remember in vivid, exasperating detail every warning both Spock and McCoy had given him about allowing Nogura to promote him.

His first day as a new admiral at Starfleet Headquarters, he'd reported to Nogura's office and discovered McCoy there, chewing out the Starfleet head. McCoy's voice had been carried clear out into the corridor:

". . . he doesn't belong here. I told you, and every one of your damnable psychiatrists told you . . . but you don't care, do you? You don't care about what's best for him, you only care about what's best for you."

Kirk had been furious at the doctor; now he remembered the incident with painful gratitude for his friend's concern. McCoy had been right; and now Jim didn't know if he'd ever forgive the old man for the way he'd manipulated both Kirk and Lori to get exactly what he wanted out of them. In his head, Kirk knew that to Nogura, Starfleet was worth *any* price, but in his heart, Jim felt too used to be able to sympathize with his superior's priorities.

He entered Nogura's aide's office, fully prepared to bully the young Vulcan male into gaining admittance into the old man's well-protected lair. But the aide caught him up short.

"Admiral Kirk," the Vulcan said smoothly. "Admiral Nogura is waiting for you, sir." Efficiently the tall, slender aide moved around the desk and opened the connecting door into the senior officer's quarters.

Kirk tried not to feel nonplussed—a reaction he'd had much too often to suit him since working for Nogura—and entered the admiral's spacious office warily.

Behind his desk, Nogura rose, smiling. The head of Starfleet was silver-haired, golden-skinned, diminutive; yet despite his unprepossessing appearance and demeanor, the small, elderly man radiated power, presence, unshakable calm.

As Jim entered, Nogura moved around his desk to greet his subordinate. "All those years with Spock must've given you a dose of telepathy, Jim," the admiral said pleasantly. "I just called down to your office to find you were already on your way up. I wish the rest of my officers were able to anticipate my needs as well as you do."

Kirk said nothing, sensing Nogura's flawless timing was again at work. How often, in the last year, had he tried to argue for better assignments, only to have the old man head him off at the pass? *Not this time, Admiral.*

"Jim, do you realize it's been over a year since you've been in space?" Nogura's deep-set black eyes furrowed in concern even as Kirk had to keep from grinding his teeth out loud. "Too long, way too long for a man like you. I know you, Jim, you're not happy planetbound." The aged admiral shook his head as if it were somehow *Kirk's* fault for not bringing the subject up sooner.

"That's exactly why I was coming to see you, sir," Kirk interjected. "It *has* been a year. . . ."

"A very productive year, I must say," Nogura reminded him. "Your work on those starship refittings has changed the very shape of the fleet. Just wait till you see the *Enterprise* again, you won't recognize her. Our engineers tell me the expected efficiency of the new designs . . ."

"*Thank* you . . . sir . . ." Kirk interrupted bluntly. "Those are kind words . . . but they're no longer enough. This job hasn't turned out to be what I expected."

"And that's my fault completely, Jim, I know," the admiral agreed, too willingly. "But Starfleet needed your expertise. No one else could've given us your knowledge, your ideas. I don't know if you'll ever really understand how much your work this past year and a half has meant to Starfleet."

Is this what they tell all paper pushers? Kirk wondered bitterly. It didn't matter. He wasn't going to let the old man talk him into any more bureaucratic exercises. He deserved better. "I was *supposed* to be using my expertise as a troubleshooter. . . ."

"That's what I promised you, and that's what you'll

be," Nogura agreed, but Kirk no longer believed him. He'd heard the promise too many times. "That's why I was calling you. To discuss a new assignment."

Kirk's eyes narrowed. "In space?"

"In space. A very *interesting* part of space. Near the planet Zotos Four." Nogura moved over to his wall screen and activated it, showing the mapped coordinates of the sector.

Jim recognized it at once, and, despite himself, his interest level picked up. "That's right where Federation, Tholian, and Klingon space intersect."

In spite of the nearness of the Klingons, it was actually the Tholians that were the bigger problem. A paranoid and territorial spacefaring race, they were known to declare wide-ranging neutral areas as "theirs" and then defend them by obliterating unsuspecting ships that wandered into them. They'd had a number of skirmishes with the Klingons and one with the *Enterprise* herself.

"Are the Tholians showing any signs of admission?" Kirk asked. Old reflexes kicked in and he began formulating strategies for dealing with the belligerent aliens. If he could only talk to Spock! The Vulcan had actually communicated with the Tholians while handling the ship's crisis. Kirk had been trapped in a space-time continuum, and his only direct experience with the Tholians was from what he'd learned from his first officer's logs.

"No," Nogura assured him. "Nothing like that. The Tholians and Klingons both have been very respectful of the boundaries lately. Do you remember that lengthy report you spent a month reviewing and writing a rebuttal to?"

Kirk stared blankly. There'd been *dozens* like that.

"Myron Shulman's report on the ship he designed, the *Recovery,*" Nogura prodded.

Oh, Kirk recalled irritably, that *one.* "Yes. The

Recovery, according to her designer, would be a fully automated, high-speed rescue vessel capable of evacuating large populations without needing to call in dozens of starships or risking Fleet personnel. It was an ambitious project, and a well-researched, well-written report."

"Which you trashed," Nogura recalled.

"I gave my *opinion,*" Kirk corrected. "You told me to be honest, to spare no one's feelings."

"An order you've never had trouble obeying," the admiral remarked, looking decidedly amused. "Your response was exactly what I expected, as did Shulman. That's why he asked for it. After all, you were the man who'd lived through, and defeated, Daystrom's M-Five fiasco. Shulman was particularly interested in what you had to say about his project. He took every one of your suggestions to heart. They refitted the *Recovery* from stem to stern as per your recommendations—and now she's ready for her maiden run. And you'll be there."

Kirk saw right through Nogura's hype. "You're talking about a simulation. . . ."

"That's true, but the *scale* of the simulation is . . ."

"A *simulation,* in space. With all the appropriate bells and whistles. This is my *troubleshooting* assignment? In the report, you stated you'd be sending the vice-chief of operations, Admiral D'nuba, to the initial simulations."

"I did," Nogura assured him. "The ship had ten different trials under ten different scenarios and performed flawlessly each time. Right down to the pinpoint accuracy of the transporters. Think of the changes to space travel, Jim, with intraship beaming a possibility—"

"Then why do I—" Kirk tried to interrupt.

Nogura held up his hands. "Hear me out, Jim. Zotos Four has been used as a science station for the last ten years. There are maybe two hundred scientists and staff there. The planet is largely inhospitable but, because of its evolutionary stage, was valuable as a working lab. But the project that'd been set up there is complete now. We need to pull those people off, and all their belongings, equipment, everything, so that Zotos can continue to develop without interference. Sure, a starship or two could do the job in a few hours, but we want the *Recovery* to handle it. Evacuating Zotos, or planets with even larger populations, is exactly the job she was designed for. Zotos has a difficult atmosphere, communications are a problem, homing in on coordinates is tricky—just the kind of conditions she's going to face in a real evacuation scenario. This will be her real test, her true maiden run."

Nogura paused, as if wanting to be sure he had Kirk's full attention. "Because of the size and the scale of the *Recovery* and the nature of this evacuation —there'll be several starships on hand, mock distress signals being sent, even a simulated attack—we felt it necessary to warn our 'neighbors.' Moving that much hardware close to a border could make anyone nervous. Ambassador Sarek has handled that part of things for us, and his suggestion was, due to the humanitarian nature of the *Recovery*'s mission, that we invite the Tholians, the Klingons, and the Romulans to watch the exercise at a respectable distance, so that there could be no misunderstanding about what we are doing. I don't really think he expected them to accept. But they did. Once that happened, Shulman and Sarek both insisted *you* be there."

"The Tholians, the Romulans, *and* the Klingons are all going to be present?" Kirk was amazed. The *Recovery*'s completely automated nature made him wary right from the start. He'd been skeptical about a rescue ship that worked on its own, without human direction. He'd been particularly nervous about the humanitarian vessel's need for defense capabilities—which felt as wrong to him as a twentieth-century Red Cross transport's being armed with cannons—and he'd said so. His report had posed a host of what-ifs that came straight from his vast experience with computers which needed no mortal hand. "What if something goes wrong?"

"Shulman will be there, ready to intercede. Sarek will remain in touch, through onscreen communications, with our neighbors, and—"

"When did the Klingons, the Romulans, and the Tholians become our *neighbors?*" Kirk demanded to know. "They're our *enemies,* sworn to overrun us, or destroy us."

"Which is why this goodwill gesture is so important. It's the first time these four groups, all sworn enemies of one another, have agreed to participate, however marginally, in a peaceful activity. This could be a pivotal moment in Federation history, Jim."

Kirk found his arguments strangling in his throat. Finally, he could only ask again, "What if something goes *wrong?*"

"That's why you must be there," Nogura assured him. "Who better to find solutions on the spot, solutions Shulman will be too busy to think of, solutions Sarek will be too removed to suggest? If something goes wrong, I want you there, Jim. You. The one man who, no matter what happens, will never forget where he is, what is happening out there, and *who his enemies are.*"

Kirk contemplated that for a moment, even as his mind told him he'd heard this speech before. "Admiral—let me be candid." He forced his tone to be as even, as calmly controlled, as Spock's would have been in the same situation. "I came this morning to remind you of your original promise to me: that I was to be a troubleshooter. It was because of that promise that I accepted the promotion to the admiralty. Frankly, sir, you haven't kept your promise. If you do not intend to, tell me—because in that case, I resign."

Before the last word was out of Kirk's mouth, the older man countered, "But this is exactly what I'm offering you, Admiral; a fresh troubleshooting assignment."

"Is it, sir? Sounds more like I'm going to be twiddling my thumbs along with all the other observers. With all due respect: No more evasions, Admiral."

A long silence passed between them; Nogura looked toward the window, and his own view of the Golden Gate Bridge beneath dark, swift-moving clouds, and sighed.

"I know you're unhappy, Jim," he said at last. "I'm sorry about that. I can't make you understand how important it's been that you be here doing what you've done for me. Get through this simulation, and we'll talk again. If this goes right, I'll owe you."

Now, *that* was something Jim had never heard before. He stiffened slightly; by the time he came back, the *Enterprise* refitting would be finished. Maybe he could go out with her on her maiden run. . . .

"You'll owe me," Kirk repeated, looking hard into Nogura's dark, unreflective eyes. When the older man did not flinch from that statement, he yielded. "All right, Admiral. I'll pack my dress uniform. And I'll remember this conversation."

Nogura nodded, and Kirk was surprised to see that the old man actually looked *relieved.* "Take Riley with you. He needs new experiences. He can't spend his whole life nursemaiding you, even if that's what you'd like. Besides, he's one of the *Enterprise*'s original crew. I expect his career to move forward, as all the others have."

Kirk nodded and, as he left the admiral's office, tried to squelch the traitorous thought, *All the others . . . except their captain.*

Myron Shulman sat before his computer and blinked the sweat out of his eyes. He was tired, too tired, really, to be trying to finish up this programming. But it had to get done. It had to be right. There had been some slight hesitation in response time in the last simulation. He wasn't happy with it, not happy at all.

He blinked again, trying to focus on the program even as the symbols, abbreviations, and special codes swam before his eyes. What was the problem again? For a moment, the tall, lean, brown-eyed man couldn't remember.

He had worked so long on this, so hard. That was all right. He was a marathon runner, he was used to going the distance. Myron ran a hand through his longish, curly black hair. The program was so important. So important. Why couldn't he focus?

He blinked and stared again at the screen, where his program shifted and changed until it reformatted itself into a three-dimensional image. Myron shook his head. Now he could see the problem. It was there, in the safety margins. He manipulated the images, nudging them, moving their edges, reformatting them into new shapes. She had to protect herself, the *Recovery*. Kirk didn't understand that; he was paranoid, and rightly so, after his experience with the Daystrom computer.

But Daystrom had been too involved with his machine, had put too much of himself into it. To Myron, the *Recovery* was nothing more than a superhuge ambulance. She wasn't his, she belonged to

J. M. Dillard

the universe, to anyone who needed her services. She would be a true emergency vessel, equipped to handle anything.

Once he got the programming right.

No, not right. *Perfect.*

She had to be able to defend herself, and all the people she held in her cavernous holds. Once aboard the *Recovery,* people had to believe they were absolutely, positively safe.

Safe.

Myron manipulated his program, unwilling even to blink, until it was completely reformatted, reshaped into its new, improved, configuration.

"Now," he murmured, "now she'll be safe. Kirk will see. He'll see and understand. She'll keep her wards safe now. . . ."

As Shulman worked amid tottering piles of cassettes and shifting stacks of flimsies, his program codes grew into more and more complicated patterns —patterns based on a language Shulman had never learned, built in a matrix he couldn't understand. But he kept at it—to show Kirk, to insure *Recovery's* success . . . and to give honor to the holy triad.

Chapter One

"WELCOME ABOARD, DR. MCCOY!" Dr. Angelina Mola greeted the civilian physician warmly.

"Why, thank you, ma'am," Leonard replied as he stepped aboard the massive rescue vessel *Recovery*. It was the first time in eighteen months that he'd set foot on a vessel larger than a ten-passenger shuttle, and the sensation was rather overwhelming. "I consider this invitation quite an honor."

"The honor is ours, Doctor," the stately, eighty-year-old matron declared, with a soft Spanish lilt. She was a head taller than McCoy, and stood as straight as a tree.

An oak, Bones thought, admiring her.

The dark-skinned, black-eyed woman seemed, to him, to be the consummate professional, from her cap of close-sheared, tightly curled black and silver hair, to her trim, austere FDRA uniform, to her no-

nonsense work shoes. Not a hair out of place, not a seam out of line, that was Dr. Mola. She hadn't changed a bit from the stern, all-business professor who had first introduced Leonard McCoy to the idea of joining Starfleet when he had taken her course, Medicine on the Cutting Edge—Practicing in Space, as a premed student. *That was about a hundred years ago, wasn't it?* he thought wryly. Yet despite her perfectionistic demeanor, there was an irresistible warmth in her voice.

"I almost didn't recognize you, Leonard," Mola said, with a hint of fond disapproval.

"Ah." McCoy's smile grew sheepish as he stroked the beard covering the lower half of his face. It had grown faster and more thickly than he'd anticipated, a fact that made him quite proud. But he couldn't get used to the silver hairs that were beginning to out-number the black. "Well, it was just one more thing I had to try, now that I'm a civilian."

She lifted a thin black brow, but made no further comment. "The suggestions you made to Dr. Shulman," she continued as they walked down gently curved corridors, "regarding the setup of sickbay and some of the more advanced medical equipment, opened up a whole new area for us to explore as we worked on this ship. Because of your input, Leonard, *Recovery* now carries the most complete—and *automated*—medical facility in all of Starfleet. It will be possible for rescued personnel to be able to diagnose and treat *one another,* regardless of the severity of their ailments, even if there is no doctor among them."

"Now, *there's* a scary thought!" McCoy quipped, bringing the slightest of smiles to the dour face. "This place could put old country doctors like myself right out of business!"

She hmphed at him. "I don't think there's much

concern there, Leonard. If anyone's in danger of being put out of business, it's *Recovery;* that is, if your old *compañero* had half the chance."

McCoy glanced at her. "Now, Angie, come on. Shulman asked Jim for his opinion, and got just what he asked for. You can't damn a man for having his say. Besides, you told me the ship had been vastly improved by his suggestions."

She nodded, acquiescing. "You're right. The ship has been improved, thanks to both Kirk's and *your* input. Here, Leonard, look at this." She stopped beside a wall panel that had a computer screen set into it. "Computer, where are we?"

A map of the ship suddenly lit up the screen. The huge, elliptically shaped vessel was shown overhead; then the image was rotated so that the viewer could see a cutaway section.

"You are located on deck seventy-five, in the central core," the feminized voice of the computer intoned as a place marker lit up in red on the map. "You are seventy meters from the entrance to the primary sickbay." Another twinkling light, this one in blue, marked the place and the direction to travel. "You are eight meters from the nearest food and beverage servitor." A green marker blinked, revealing its location. "You are twelve meters from the nearest relief station." McCoy lifted an eyebrow as that marker showed up in yellow. "Are you in need of any services?"

"Not at this time, computer," Dr. Mola said, and the screen instantly went blank.

"Pretty nice 'you are here' sign, Angie," McCoy drawled.

"That's not all there is to it," she told him. "If a person reaches a screen and then passes out and can't ask for help, the computer automatically beams the victim to an empty cot in sickbay and begins diagnostics." She must've interpreted his questioning expression. "And yes, the computer can definitely tell the difference between an unconscious state and normal sleep."

"But . . . intraship beaming! That's enormously dangerous—"

Her lips pursed in a small smile. "Not aboard *Recovery*. Shulman has perfected the transporters; they have pinpoint accuracy and numerous safety features. His improvements will revolutionize space travel."

"Yeah? Well, I'll let someone else try them out. Those things scare me enough without my having to worry about materializing inside a wall."

"They've been tested countless times, Leonard—more times, in fact, than any other system on this ship. I've used them myself, with complete confidence." Ignoring the disbelieving glance he gave her, she indicated the now dark wall viewer. "These screens are located every thirty meters throughout the ship. They are accessible by *anyone* aboard the vessel. Eventually, I believe stations like these will become standard throughout the Fleet. The computer will tell the questioner where they are, answer their needs, help them find their way to their quarters, help them obtain food and equipment from the replicators, almost anything. The computer will even be able to tell those aboard how to manage certain repairs, should the ship develop a problem. She can suggest various rescue remedies, even defense plans, should she come under attack. Once inside *Recovery,* those who've been rescued can be given the means to handle anything that occurs."

"If you say so," the doctor remarked amiably.

"You sound skeptical." Mola raised a coal black brow.

"Well, I've seen more than one of these 'answer to

all your prayers' machines," he told her. "In my experience, the reality often falls far short of the dream."

"That's what tests and simulations are for, *mi amigo.* And that's why I insisted you come along as our honorary civilian observer. I know if you see, firsthand, the ship in action, I can convince you of *Recovery*'s value. If I can do that, then I can convince anyone. Even *Kirk.*"

"Yeah, well, convincing me is one thing. Convincing the *admiral . . .*" McCoy made a sound of fond exasperation. The mention of Jim made him homesick for his old friend, and the *Enterprise.* For the past year and a half, the doctor had lost himself in researching the Fabrini and applying their medical expertise on far-flung planets. Being on a huge ship again brought back memories of another ship, another time. . . . "I mean, to him this'll be just another report that crosses his desk. It's not like he'll actually *see* the ship's performance."

She smiled, as if she'd anticipated his argument. "Oh, yes he will. Nogura's sending him. There was too much pressure on them; Kirk had to come."

McCoy's eyebrows furrowed. "To a *simulation?* That hardly sounds important enough—"

She glanced about them as if to insure their privacy. "No, not just for the simulation. *Recovery*'s already been through the paces on testing. This . . . is different. There are other factors involved."

He glanced at her sideways. There was something she was holding back.

"Por favor, Leonard, forgive me," she said softly, "but I cannot say what they are. It is hard for me to refuse you, but . . . you are, after all, a *civilian* now."

He grinned, clearly surprising her. "Oh, don't apologize, old friend. I'm just your average, retired space dog, and glad of it. I had my fill of classified information when I was in uniform. You can keep your dark, disturbing secrets. I get more sleep at night these days then I ever did when I was in the Fleet."

"Thank you for understanding," Dr. Mola said. "You always were the perfect *caballero.*"

Looking away from her, he asked as casually as he could, "So, Jim's coming out to watch the show, huh?"

"Yes. We'll be there before him, of course. I'm sure there'll be some free time before the evacuation actually gets under way. Certain . . . things regarding the scenario must be set up ahead of time. It would be a simple matter for me to call him, and let him know you're here."

"No!" McCoy said, a little too quickly. "We . . . haven't seen each other since we left the *Enterprise.* Jim beams over to the *Recovery,* and before you know it, it'll be old home week. Both of us will be expected to write reviews of the test. If people see us together, and if our reviews agreed . . ." He trailed off, hoping she'd pick up the thread. The fact was, the thought of seeing Jim again unnerved him; he was not so sure his old friend *wanted* to see him. Not after the way McCoy had burst into Admiral Nogura's office and chewed him out for talking Jim into that promotion. But he hadn't been able to help it. Nogura had gone over his, McCoy's, head, ignored his recommendation that Jim be permitted to keep his command, and kicked Jim upstairs.

He wondered vaguely whether Jim was happy— then forced his attention back to Dr. Mola, who was nodding.

". . . could make the test look tainted," she was saying. "You're right, of course. We can't risk even a hint of collusion. That's noble of you, Leonard. I'm sure you would've liked to have seen your friend. I'll make sure there's no mention of your name. Of course, after the test is run, he'll no doubt want a tour of the vessel. . . ."

"It's a big ship, Angie. I'll manage to avoid him."

She looked at him oddly. Before she could comment again, a tall, ascetically thin man approached them. Dr. Mola's face brightened. "Dr. Shulman! Are we about to depart for Zotos Four?"

"Yes, Dr. Mola," the soft-spoken man replied. "We'll be under way within the next ten minutes. I'll be watching the computer reports from my quarters. Have you checked the guest register? Is everyone aboard and ready to go?"

McCoy watched the man with a doctor's eye. He was olive-skinned, but there seemed to be a flush about his color, as if he were slightly feverish. The barest hint of sweat stood out on his brow. *Well, after all,* the doctor reminded himself, *this ship's been his life's work. He wouldn't be human if this voyage didn't have him in a complete lather.*

"Absolutely, Dr. Shulman," Angelina assured him. "All sixty-four invited guests are on board. The planetary delegations of the FDRA arrived an hour ago, and Dr. McCoy, our civilian guest, was the last to arrive."

"Excellent," Shulman muttered. "Then I'll set the programming in motion and we'll be on our way. It won't do to be late. Not at all. Good evening, doctors."

The tall man nearly jogged away from them in his urgency, and McCoy found himself staring after the designer.

"Don't mind Myron," Angelina explained. "He's been twitchy ever since he heard Kirk would be there. He'll be fine once the ship goes through her paces."

"No doubt," McCoy murmured distractedly. "Didn't I read somewhere that Shulman is a long-distance runner?"

"That's right. Won the bronze in the Federation Olympics five years ago."

McCoy nodded and turned back to his guide. "That explains it. Those marathon runners always seem as hyper as greyhounds to me."

Dr. Mola laughed. "As laid-back as you usually are, Leonard, your reaction doesn't surprise me." She stopped them before a pair of sliding doors with a medical symbol beside them. As the doors whooshed open, she waved him inside. "Ah, here, finally, we arrive at sickbay. I can't *wait* to show you my favorite toys!"

Sarek gave a single nod to dismiss his white-robed guide, a young Vulcan female with downcast eyes, and stepped out onto the balcony that overlooked the horizon. To the east, Mount Seleya, black, jagged, and impenetrable, spiraled upward against the darkening purple sky. The last rays of the fiery sunset had faded, leaving the thin air cool; within minutes, the temperature would drop some thirty or forty degrees, and the burning desert would metamorphose into a cold wasteland. He had purposely timed his journey to avoid crossing the plain of Gol during the most intense heat.

For a moment he stood motionless, save for the lock of wavy silver hair lifted from his forehead by the breeze, and gazed out at the mountains.

Silence permeated his surroundings. The young postulant who had led him to the balcony had glided noiselessly upward over the black steps, leaving Sarek intensely conscious of the echoing ring of his own bootheels against the stone. Hewn millennia before from the dark mountains, the retreat housed some few hundred students of *Kolinahr,* the pursuit of nonemotion; but Sarek had seen no one save the student who had greeted him at the great stone archway, and in the deep silence on the balcony, it was simple to imagine that he was entirely alone in the desert.

It was, to Sarek's mind, the most quintessentially Vulcan place on Vulcan. The retreat at Gol had existed even before Surak's peaceful revolution, when *Kolinahr* adepts were much-feared practitioners of the art of mind-control: the mind-lords, who ruled through terror and manipulation. After Surak, the adepts turned their control inward, and mastered their own minds and emotions rather than those of others.

Adepts were now held in reverence; Vulcan families were privately proud to count a *Kolinahr* student among their members.

But in this hallowed and quiet place, Sarek found himself struggling to suppress not pride (though he did feel an inkling of that emotion, at the thought that his son had chosen such a consummately Vulcan life) but concern.

More than a Terran standard year before, when James Kirk had been promoted to admiral and relinquished command of the *Enterprise,* Spock had resigned his Starfleet commission and returned to Vulcan to accept a teaching position at the Science Academy. Sarek had been pleased, especially when Spock had announced his engagement to a much-respected Vulcan scientist, T'Sura. Sarek felt certain that his son would become comfortable among his own people at last.

And then Spock had taken two human friends on a visit to Gol. Such a thing was not uncommon; the *Kolinahru* welcomed visitors seeking a quiet retreat. But one of those friends, Dr. Leonard McCoy, was kidnapped under bizarre circumstances, and the other, Keridwen Llewellyn, accompanied Spock and the *Kolinahr* High Master, T'Sai, on a successful rescue mission and was killed.

Sarek knew little of the details; Spock remained resolutely taciturn on the subject. But when he returned from the mission, he immediately called off his marriage to T'Sura and retreated to Gol.

Sarek had at first assumed that Spock's sudden interest in Kolinahr was due to his short visit with its practitioners, and the subsequent mission with the High Master. But Amanda, Spock's mother, insisted that her son's decision must have been somehow related to the human woman's death. Sarek was now beginning to consider whether his wife's all-too-human instincts were correct.

He had put off this confrontation for almost a year, until it could be avoided no longer, because of his growing conviction that *Kolinahr* was the wrong path for Spock. Perhaps, many years ago, he would have approved—just as he had disapproved of Spock's decision to join Starfleet and work among humans. But years of reflection had caused him to alter his original assessment; Spock was, after all, half-human, and to deny that fact was to deny Spock himself, and the heritage given him by his mother.

Kolinahr would require Spock to utterly reject that part of himself.

Yet until that moment, as Sarek stood waiting in the cooling, desert-scented breeze, he had not fully acknowledged his discomfort with the idea. And, in that instant, he realized what he was required to do; realized it, but did not relish it.

He turned at the whisper of footsteps against stone, and let his gaze fall upon his son.

"Father," Spock said, with perfectly neutral inflection, as he lowered the hood of his white postulant's robe.

Sarek's mind returned involuntarily to an encounter of some twenty years before, when he and his son had disagreed intensely over Spock's choice of Starfleet.

But this Spock bore little resemblance to the one of twenty years ago. This Spock was no stubborn, passionate boy, but a gaunt, severe *Kolinahr* adept. He had grown thinner on a spartan diet, so that the sharp angles of his jaw were even more pronounced; in the dimming light, shadows gathered in the hollows beneath his cheekbones. His dark hair fell midway between his jaw and shoulders—quite straight, Sarek noted, like his mother's, and the ends had taken on a faint reddish cast from the same pitiless sun that had browned his skin. His bangs were long and brushed to one side.

And beneath his upswept brows were eyes whose gentleness had been replaced by a depthless, disturbing cold.

Sarek heard that same chill in his son's soft voice.

"You have come to take your leave?"

In the context of Gol, the question had a deeper meaning. Before the great Ritual, in which the student's mind was joined to that of the High Master and all emotion was obliterated, the student was encouraged to sever all emotional bonds with family and friends. This was most easily accomplished through mind-touch. Shared memories would be acknowledged, all attachments and obligations dissolved.

Amanda had already grudgingly acquiesced, and taken her leave several months before—though she had made her disapproval clear to her husband, if not her son. It was Sarek's turn now, for Spock would undergo the Ritual in a matter of weeks. This Sarek knew not because he had been in contact with his son—Gol permitted no communication with the outside world—but because traditionally, the Ritual was performed after a year's study and preparation. Spock's year was almost up.

Sarek drew in a breath and replied, "No. I have come to explain why I will not."

Spock said nothing, only remained consummately still, awaiting the promised explanation; his muscles did not tense, nor did his rate of breathing change. But he blinked once, swiftly.

"I cannot approve of your decision," Sarek continued. "And, unlike your mother, I cannot be party to that of which I disapprove." He paused, searching for words as Spock remained as still and unreactive as the black stone surrounding them. "You are half-human, Spock. While I commend your choice of the Vulcan way, I cannot condone a path which requires the utter denial of that fact."

"I do not follow your logic." Spock spoke in the same soft, passionless tone. "You disapproved of Starfleet; and approved of my return to Vulcan, and the bonding with T'Sura. It was my assessment that you preferred I 'deny,' as you put it, my human half."

"I . . ." Sarek heard the faint heat in his own voice, and forced himself to adopt the same calm intonation as his son. ". . . merely do not wish for you to deny either heritage. It is very simple logic. And it is not coincidence that both I and your mother disapprove, Spock. Surely your friends, Admiral Kirk and Dr. McCoy, agree."

"I would not know."

Sarek's surprise did not show on his face. "They have not come to take their leave of you?"

"I have not requested it of them," Spock said, and Sarek thought he heard the faintest trace of contempt as his son continued: "They are, after all, human."

"And closer to you than I or your mother," Sarek countered. "If you do not dissolve your ties to them, then the achievement of true *Kolinahr* will be extremely difficult, if not—"

"I have noted your opinion," Spock interrupted swiftly, with a hardness that made Sarek lift an eyebrow and fall silent. "However"—and his tone grew soft once more—"I am determined to achieve *Kolinahr*. With or without your assistance."

Sarek paused at the faint, distant keening of a bird; he inclined his face toward the sound, away from his son, and felt the evening breeze, now cold, upon his cheek. He turned back to Spock. "Then further discussion is unwarranted."

"Agreed." Spock lifted a hand, parting third and middle fingers to form a V. "Live long and prosper, Sarek."

And with those words, he proclaimed them no longer father and son, but Sarek and Spock; even though Sarek had not agreed to take his leave, Spock was stating that, in his own mind at least, the relationship had been formally dissolved.

Sarek raised his own hand in salute. "Live long and prosper, Spock." For a few seconds, no more, he remained gazing on his former son for what, according to *Kolinahr* tradition, would be the last time. The encroaching gloom had muted the details of Spock's face; his skin appeared silver-gray, his eyes and brows and hair had begun to fade into the black stone behind him, just as the jet mountains on the horizon were disappearing into the backdrop of night.

And then Spock turned and disappeared silently through the archway, a flash of white swallowed up by darkness. Sarek remained outside in the cold for a few moments more, then slowly, reluctantly, followed.

Back in his cell, Spock sat cross-legged on the floor in front of an old-fashioned oil lamp.

Gol was just as it had always been from the time of Vulcan's earliest history—free from the comforts of civilization. Spock's cubicle, like that of all Gol residents, consisted of a room of just sufficient dimensions for a tall Vulcan to lie down without head or feet touching the walls. It was unadorned, without furniture save for a small closet carved into one corner. Postulants slept and sat upon the floor, yet Spock had come to consider it quite comfortable. The chill of night was countered by the warmth held by the glittering black rock that formed walls, ceiling, floor; by morning, the rock had grown cold, and retained a pleasant coolness during the worst of the daytime heat.

Night had fallen completely. Without the glow of nearby cities, the sky was black as the jet-colored stone; impossible, save for the glowing stars, to tell where the window—a simple hole carved in the wall—ended and the sky began.

From his pocket, Spock drew out a palm-sized, circular disk with an esoteric geometric design etched onto its burnished metal surface. He set it respectfully down in front of the oil lamp and fixed his gaze upon it. The meditation mandala had belonged to an accomplished adept, now deceased, who had followed custom and willed the mandala to the Gol retreat, that it might be used by another aspirant to achieve the enlightenment and freedom of *Kolinahr*.

The mandala's precise age was unknown. It was, at the very least, several centuries old, its original pink-gold surface long tarnished to a dull greenish bronze by the fingerprints of generations of adepts.

Spock released a long, slow breath and paused before beginning his meditation to examine his thoughts.

He had believed, after so many months at Gol, that

he had nearly succeeded in purging all emotion; but Sarek's arrival had brought with it a revelation to the contrary. Perhaps in the purified, controlled atmosphere of Gol it was easy to maintain equilibrium. But Sarek had brought with him memories of life outside, and his stinging refusal to take leave of his son had released in Spock the recollection of another bitter encounter—the day Spock had informed his father that he intended to join Starfleet.

Sarek had insisted that life among humans would damage Spock's ability to control his emotions.

"Every time your control falters, you reflect poorly on all of Vulcan. . . ."

And Spock had hotly countered, *"I wonder how my mother would react if she knew you were warning me against being contaminated by her species."*

But Sarek would not be reasoned with; he had proclaimed Spock *vrekasht,* an outcast—no longer his son.

Spock could not help seeing the curious parallels between this evening's encounter and that of twenty years before. Except that this time he, Spock, had been the one to willingly sever the father/son relationship; and now it was Sarek who argued that Spock ought not deny his human heritage.

Could it be possible, Spock pondered, staring intently at the mandala's design as if seeking an answer there, *that my desire to achieve* Kolinahr *sprang from a desire to please my father?*

A year ago, he would likely have suppressed such an embarrassing, distressing thought. But *Kolinahr* demanded extreme introspection, extreme self-honesty. Unexamined emotions and memories could not be purged.

Yet he knew that he had come to *Kolinahr* for a different reason: because, just as his father had warned twenty years before, Spock's control *had* faltered—and caused the death of an innocent woman.

Or so he had believed at the time. Now, after months of intense contemplation, he had come to realize that she might very well have died despite his failure; indeed, perhaps he and Dr. McCoy and High Master T'Sai might all have died as well even had he not suffered an emotional lapse. It was impossible to know such things, and guilt was illogical and unproductive. He had overcome it after a great internal struggle.

Now, he knew, he would have to overcome a fresh welling of anger at Sarek, for refusing to assist him in releasing all emotion associated with the memory of his father proclaiming him *vrekasht*. Such anger would not be easy to overcome, for his conflict with his father had been one of the most painful incidents in his life.

And he would also have to overcome a troublesome doubt provoked by Sarek's words: *"If you do not dissolve your ties to your friends, then the achievement of true* Kolinahr *will be extremely difficult. . . ."*

He had not thought of Jim Kirk and Leonard McCoy in many months. He had not considered that he had many issues to resolve concerning his former shipmates. True, he had felt some faint stirrings of betrayal when Kirk had revealed his decision to give up command of the *Enterprise,* and to accept a promotion to the admiralty; but Spock had long ago overcome that emotion. He had focused instead on freeing himself from the emotional bonds to his family, and his sense of insecurity concerning his identity as a Vulcan.

Yet (though, Spock noted with irony, it was difficult to admit) Sarek had been correct in stating that Spock had been closer to James Kirk and Dr. McCoy than he had been to his own parents. Perhaps it would be wisest to investigate his father's claim.

Spock closed his eyes and summoned a mental image of his friends.

First came Dr. Leonard McCoy. Spock had last seen the doctor a year before, shortly before the Vulcan's retreat to Gol. Their last encounter had been overshadowed by the recent tragic death of McCoy's associate, Dr. Keridwen Llewellyn.

An aura of sadness surrounded the memory; sorrow had been etched on McCoy's haggard, unshaven face, in his red-rimmed, bloodshot blue eyes. But he had shown no sign of blaming Spock for Llewellyn's death; indeed, he had accepted Spock's decision to pursue *Kolinahr* with grace and compassion.

"Maybe those Kolinahr *folks have the right idea. Maybe we'd all be better off without emotions."*

To his astonishment, Spock found himself repressing a fond inward smile at the mental sound of the doctor's voice. Impossible; he had relived the memory completely many months ago, had used the mind-control techniques to banish all emotion associated with Leonard McCoy.

And yet . . . affection for the doctor stubbornly persisted. And if he still possessed fondness for Dr. McCoy . . .

Spock drew a breath and evoked the image of James Kirk, as he had been on his first day as an admiral at Starfleet Headquarters in San Francisco.

To Spock, who had called from Vulcan, the admiral had seemed curiously uncomfortable in his new uniform and office, though his face had been alight with typical Kirkish enthusiasm at the thought of conquering something new, something unknown.

That brightness had faded quickly when Spock revealed that he had resigned his Starfleet commission.

"I'll miss you, Spock. You've been a damn fine officer—and a good friend."

So. Sarek had again been correct. There were still emotional bonds that needed to be broken. The memory had brought with it a glimmer of pain.

And more: As he contemplated his friends, Spock felt a sudden unmistakable curiosity.

Where are you now, Dr. McCoy?

And you, Jim—are you still at Starfleet Headquarters? Still convinced that you made the right decision?

Spock opened his eyes and rose—a reflexive reaction to the faint but unmistakable sensation of contact, as though another mind had attempted to contact his across the ocean of space.

The sensation had been too weak to identify the source, but Spock immediately considered whether the few mind-melds he had accomplished with Kirk and McCoy had produced a subtle mental link.

Impossible.

Impossible, yet Spock stepped over to the window and gazed out at the stars—at Sol, the source of light and life for Earth, where Jim Kirk dwelled—and sensed unmistakable danger . . .

Chapter Two

THE SCENE BEFORE Kirk's eyes wavered a bit as he materialized, then gradually solidified into clearer view. For a heartbeat, he imagined he had just beamed aboard the *Enterprise*. The thought triggered a wave of homesickness for his own ship, his own crew; it had been nearly two years since he had last set foot aboard her.

But this was a different ship, a different transporter room; her crew was not his to command, but that of the woman standing alongside the transporter console before him.

Dressed in sedate Starfleet gray, *Starhawk's* captain was not a tall person, but she nonetheless projected the illusion of height by holding herself perfectly erect. Her shoulder-length black hair, shot through with silver, the exotic tilt of her eyes and high cheekbones all spoke of Tatar ancestry.

For a glimmering instant, Kirk got the impression

of extreme dignity, extreme serenity that was almost Vulcanlike; and then the captain grinned broadly, dispelling the illusion.

"Admiral," she said with unfeigned warmth, moving forward to extend a hand as Kirk stepped from the transporter pad. "Welcome aboard. I'm Captain Zhanya Akhmatova."

"Captain." Kirk clasped her hand; her grip was delicate, determined. "A pleasure."

She hesitated, peering at the empty transporter pads behind him. "Is your aide arriving later?"

"Commander Riley will be helping Captain Romolo coordinate his part of the simulation," he answered smoothly. In truth, when Kirk had realized that his aide's ex-wife, Anab Saed, was a security officer aboard the *Starhawk,* he had offered Riley the option of a little busywork aboard the *Paladin.* The younger man had jumped at the chance.

Akhmatova brightened at the mention of the other captain's name. "Ah. Well, he's in good company. Baldassare is an old friend of mine—we go all the way back to the Academy. I had hoped to have some time to say hello to him myself since we're in the same neighborhood, but a captain's duties don't exactly allow for reunions." She gestured toward the exit. "May I show you to your guest quarters, Admiral? My staff was fighting over who would get the honors, but I picked the longest straw."

"The privileges of rank?" Kirk asked lightly.

"Of course," Akhmatova allowed cheerfully. "I always win. Don't you?"

He gave a small grin. "Always. Lead on, Captain."

Flanking Kirk, she spoke as she led him into the corridor. "There's to be a formal dinner tonight in the officers' mess, preceded by a small reception at nineteen hundred hours. You have an hour or so to rest up, take a tour of the ship, or . . ."

"Or?" Kirk lifted a bemused brow at the sudden coyness in her tone.

"Or you could have a drink with the captain. Frankly, I'd relish the chance to sound you out privately on this whole *Recovery* issue."

"That sounds fine," Kirk said. "But I'd better warn you—my private view is the same as my public."

"Really?" She tilted her head to regard him sidewise.

"You don't sound like you believe me."

Akhmatova's outer office was equipped with the luxury of a wall servitor. She stood smiling across the small conference table at Kirk, who sat. "What'll it be, Admiral?"

"Saurian brandy."

She swiveled toward the bulkhead. "Computer. One Saurian brandy, one water."

"Water? Wait a minute, Captain. I'm not so sure about allowing this interrogation if I'm going to be the only one imbibing. . . ."

But Akhmatova did not hear. The computer almost instantly interrupted with, "Ship's stores do not include Saurian brandy. Please make another selection."

"Water," Kirk sighed. Akhmatova made a wry face.

"Now, Admiral, how do you expect me to grill you if you're entirely sober?"

Kirk laughed and felt himself relax. He liked Akhmatova—and it occurred to him that it was because she was treating him as an equal . . . another *captain,* instead of one of the brass.

"Computer, two waters."

Two frosted glasses appeared almost at once; Akhmatova set one in front of Kirk, then took one herself and sat down opposite him.

"So," Kirk said. "For some reason, you're desperate

to know my opinion about *Recovery.* So here it is: I hope it works. I sincerely do. But I have my doubts."

"Because of the Daystrom incident." She took a sip of water, all the while holding him in her careful gaze.

He gave a single, slow nod.

"Well, forgive me, Captain, but I'm not so sure I wish Myron Shulman success. Rescue missions are still one of the main duties of starships. And I, for one, am in favor of keeping starships busy."

Kirk shrugged. "They'll stay busy. They'll just be free for other missions: Peacekeeping. Diplomacy. Most importantly, exploration. That *is* their primary task."

"Yes . . ." Akhmatova fell silent and fingered her glass thoughtfully, as though debating something. Then she looked up, and, with a sudden intensity that made Kirk blink, said:

"Of course, I really didn't bring you here to talk about *Recovery.* I don't give a damn whether she succeeds or fails."

A shrill whistle interrupted. She swiveled smoothly in her chair toward the intercom and punched a toggle. "Akhmatova here."

"Captain. Ambassador Sarek's party has arrived and is being escorted to their quarters."

"Very good. Out."

She turned back to Kirk and hesitated, gathering her thoughts.

Kirk's eyebrows were still lifted in mild surprise, but otherwise his expression never changed. "You were saying, Captain?"

She clasped her hands, elbows resting on the table, and leaned forward; there was no lightness in her tone now. "I want your advice, Admiral. You've been where I'm about to be. I'm due for promotion next month. I figure I've got three choices: accept it and be kicked upstairs; refuse it and pray Nogura will let me keep my ship; or retire and be done with it." She let go a measured sigh, and for the first time Kirk saw a flicker of anxiety in her expression. "Are you happy with the choice you made?"

The final question caught him off-guard. He liked Akhmatova; her toughness reminded him of his own, and he wanted to be honest with her, to help if he could.

At the same time, his happiness was none of her damned business. Because, over the days and weeks and months since leaving the *Enterprise,* he had grown increasingly unhappy. And seeing Akhmatova now was a reminder of what he had once had, and lost.

Abruptly he saw Lori in his mind's eye, on the day she had left him.

"Just promise me one thing."

They had been embracing for a final time; his lips had brushed her hair as he asked, *"What's that?"*

"Get a ship again. It's what you want most, Jim. More than anything else. More than me . . ."

He had told himself then that she had said it because she was hurting and had projected that hurt onto him. But with the passage of time, he was beginning to believe more and more that she had been right. Her words had never left him.

He took a long drink from the sweating glass in front of him. The water was refreshingly sweet and cold going down. At last he said, "I'm not you, Captain. You're the person who has to live inside your skin. What may be right for me—"

"I understand, sir." Akhmatova's tone had grown quiet, respectful, showing that she understood what a deeply personal question she had asked a superior. "What's heaven for one is hell for another. But—I don't think we're all that different, you and I. I'd value an answer to my question."

He drew a breath, stared fixedly at a bead of moisture leaving a shiny trail down the side of the frosted glass. "All right. I think I was happy . . . at first. Nogura made me a deal—that I'd see excitement, adventure. Travel." He looked up and straightened in his chair. "This is travel . . . but does it seem like excitement to you?"

She said nothing, only nodded somberly.

"Now you answer *my* question, Captain—can *you* be happy without this ship?"

She stared at him as though he were speaking gibberish, another language. He almost repeated the question, but she finally said, "I try to imagine it, and can't. The *Starhawk* is my *life.*"

"Then fight for her," he said—and felt a shiver run through him. It was as if someone else had spoken the words to him—someone who understood Jim Kirk well enough to know precisely what he needed to do.

Akhmatova's voice grew whisper-soft. "Did you fight for *Enterprise?*"

"Not hard enough." He tried, and failed, to keep the bitterness from his tone.

He left shortly after, and found his way back to the guest quarters. Their sterility left him restless, and he had briefed himself completely on the *Recovery* trial run.

And so he wandered down to the botanical gardens. Each ship's garden had a personality all its own, Kirk realized; the *Starhawk*'s began as an English flower garden, filled with roses, camellias, tiger lilies, neatly sculpted hedges of blue-green rue. It was far different from the *Enterprise,* with its stone meditation garden designed by Spock, and the stand of bonsai trees artfully tended by Hikaru Sulu.

Kirk drew in a breath of flower-scented air as he strolled. The order quickly gave way to an untamed

Terran herb garden, with blooming clumps of rosemary, lavender, rose geranium. Beyond, a straight, motionless figure sat cross-legged upon a bench beneath a lemon verbena tree, near a small stone waterfall that filled the air with cool mist.

A Vulcan, Kirk realized, and for an unsettling moment, the figure looked uncannily like Spock. But this Vulcan was slightly older, more solidly built, with streaks of pure white in his iron gray hair.

Kirk quickened his pace as he recognized Ambassador Sarek—and stopped two seconds later, as he realized the Vulcan's eyes were closed in meditation. He hesitated, then turned to leave quietly.

"Admiral Kirk."

He turned to look behind him at Sarek, who had opened his eyes and risen from the bench.

"Ambassador." He smiled. "I didn't mean to disturb you. . . ."

"It is no disturbance. As coincidence would have it, I was just finishing my meditation." He paused; his dark eyes flickered over Kirk. "I trust you are doing well since we last met. My belated congratulations on your promotion."

"Thank you. I'm fine. And I hope you're doing far better than when we last—"

Sarek brushed any concerns away with a small sweep of his hand. "Yes, my health is far better than it has been in some years."

"And your family?" Kirk repressed the desire to ask, *Your son?*

"Amanda is quite well." Sarek hesitated. Had he been human, Kirk might have said that a shadow passed over the ambassador's face; but this was a Vulcan, Spock's father. Surely, Kirk told himself, it must have been his imagination. "As for Spock, I saw him recently—for the first time in several months."

Kirk frowned, puzzled. "I thought Spock was living in ShanaiKahr with you. Did he move?"

Again Sarek paused, as though choosing his words carefully. "Spock has elected to pursue *Kolinahr.*"

"*Kolinahr?*"

"The ancient Vulcan path of total nonemotion. It is an arduous procedure; it requires retreat, solitude, intense contemplation."

So. Spock must have felt the necessity to purge himself of the "emotional contamination" of all those years around humans. But Spock had always seemed to Jim quintessentially Vulcan; if anything, he overcompensated for his human half, trying to—as Bones had been so fond of putting it—"out-Vulcan the Vulcans." *Kolinahr* seemed like overkill; yet Kirk kept his expression pleasantly neutral. "You must be very proud, Ambassador."

Sarek looked away, at the crystalline waterfall; when at last he spoke, his tone held something far different from pride. "It is . . . a decision that will have a profound impact upon his life, his career as a scientist. For once he performs the final Ritual and achieves total *Kolinahr,* he will remain at the mountain retreat for the rest of his life, and be allowed no contact with the outside world."

Kirk stared at him, too stunned to believe he had made correct sense of the ambassador's words. "You mean . . ."

Sarek looked back at him with that dark, penetrating gaze. "He will not see friends or family again."

"I see." And yet he did *not* see—could not believe or understand that Spock would have done such a thing without saying good-bye. He had thought the Vulcan his closest friend; perhaps he had been wrong.

"His mother is, naturally, quite distressed by his decision."

"And you, Ambassador?" An impertinent question

to ask a Vulcan, perhaps; but if Sarek took offense, he showed no sign.

"I am—quite logically concerned. Spock's talents could best be utilized elsewhere."

Agreed, Kirk told himself—silently, for he knew that he and Sarek would not concur on precisely *where* those talents should be applied. Sarek no doubt felt his son belonged on Vulcan; but Jim knew that Spock belonged in Starfleet.

The image of Edith Keeler rose unbidden in his mind. She had accused Jim and Spock of seeming out-of-place in Earth of the 1930s; and Jim, smiling, had asked where she thought they belonged.

She had nodded at Spock and said: *"Him? By your side, as if he's always been there, and always will be."*

Kirk had always agreed with the sentiment. The worst thing about the admiralty—besides the loss of his ship—had been the loss of his friends. Perhaps, now, he was experiencing what Spock had felt upon learning that Jim would not return as captain of the *Enterprise:* the sting of abandonment.

To never set eyes on his friend again . . . It was as if Spock had died.

When does this ritual take place? he almost asked, but was interrupted by the appearance of a slender young Vulcan female, who had approached them so quietly that he started at the sound of her calm voice.

"Ambassador? The reception will begin shortly."

Sarek dismissed her with a brief nod of acknowledgment, then turned to Kirk. "Shall we, Admiral?"

Jim let go a slow sigh, and looked up at the face that so reminded him of his friend. "Let's go."

In a large conference room aboard the *Paladin,* Lieutenant Commander Kevin Riley sat comfortably watching the crew members who had just begun to filter in for the captain's briefing. Almost all of them

were cadets. Riley had known Romolo's ship was a
training vessel, but he had been unprepared for the
ratio of wet-behind-the-ears kids to experienced personnel. He was one of a handful of seasoned officers
aboard *Paladin,* and at the moment, the only apparent
adult in the room; obviously, the brass had seen the
simulation as a milk run.

Cadets notwithstanding, Riley felt both relieved
and unhappy to have taken Admiral Kirk up on the
all-too-obvious offer to assist Romolo—relieved, because he dreaded seeing Anab again; unhappy, because he wanted desperately to see her.

He knew that he should have remained on the
Starhawk, encountered her at the reception, and said
a polite hello, but each time he considered it, his
courage failed. Besides, he had nothing to say to her.
They hadn't spoken for six months, ever since she had
contacted him to coolly announce that she was cancel-
ing their marriage contract. The decision had left him
devastated; until then, he had convinced himself that
she would return to him.

Correction, he thought grimly. He *did* have something to say; or rather, something to prove. He'd been
a different person when Anab left eighteen months
before to serve on the *Starhawk*—an indecisive, insecure person who had remained in Starfleet simply to
please her.

The day she'd shipped out, she'd begged him, *"Get
out of Starfleet. Find out what it is you really want to
do with your life. You're not doing Kirk any favors by
working for him halfheartedly."*

"Mr. Riley?"

He glanced up at the sound of his name, and gazed
into a pair of bright blue eyes. Their owner, a pale-
skinned woman with a smooth, shoulder-length cap of
red-gold hair, extended a hand. Riley noted at once
the insignia on her gray uniform, and realized who she

was in the instant before she introduced herself in a clipped British accent.

"Commander Ruth Pulver, first officer."

Riley smiled and took the proffered hand. Pulver's alabaster features and large, heavy-lidded eyes reminded him of holos he'd seen of Victorian-era beauties; but her grip was firm, her attitude clearly no-nonsense. She did not return the smile. Riley noted at once that the cadets in the room had suddenly hushed. Perhaps Pulver's rigid demeanor was a necessity on a shipful of trainees.

"Commander," he said, instinctively straightening in his chair; something about Pulver's perfect posture demanded it. "Please . . ." He gestured at the empty chair beside him.

"Thank you." She sat with exceptional grace. "So, Commander . . . have you had an opportunity to tour the ship yet?"

Riley did not reply. At the sound of the doors sliding open once again, he chanced to break eye contact with Pulver and glance up, in the direction of the entrance . . .

. . . just in time to see Anab enter the room.

At once he understood the metaphors that related emotional pain to the heart; for the instant his gaze rested on her, it was as though someone had abruptly inserted a fine steel wire through the center of his chest, then drew it out, slowly. His breath left him in a small, involuntary gasp, and mixed in with the realization that he was still in love with her were anger and disgust with himself that he could have allowed such a thing. Surely he was stronger than that. . . .

But he had forgotten how painfully beautiful she was. Dressed in her security uniform, which blended in with the moving palette of neutral-colored uniforms, Anab herself stood out from the crowd. She was statuesque, long-limbed, graceful, her skin the color of rich brown earth, her hair shaved close to the scalp to accentuate the long, graceful sweep of her neck. She was walking alongside the chief engineer, the two of them chatting animatedly.

And then she caught his eye.

They gazed at each other in utter astonishment for a second, no more; then each looked quickly away.

Impossible. Impossible. She was not supposed to be here, but back aboard the *Starhawk,* attending the reception.

Riley tried not to watch as she took a seat behind his, out of his line of view, and forced his attention back to his conversation partner.

Pulver had finished speaking and was staring at him quizzically.

"Ah," he said, flustered. "Sorry . . . I'm afraid I didn't quite catch—"

Her demeanor grew even more coolly formal. "I was offering to take you on a tour of the ship, Commander, once the simulation was over."

"Yes," Riley responded, trying unsuccessfully to ignore the rapid-fire beating of his heart at the knowledge that Anab was somewhere behind him, watching him. "Thank you. I would enjoy that."

Pulver opened delicate rosebud lips to reply—and closed them again as the briefing-room doors again opened, and the captain entered.

Waving his hands to prevent his staff from standing at his arrival, Captain Baldassare Romolo, a portly, handsome blond Italian, moved to his seat with his usual economy of motion. "We're all here?" With an ease that was in sharp contrast to his first officer's stiffness, he gazed appreciatively at the crowd, then gave a satisfied nod. "Good, let's get started. We're approximately five hours away from Zotos Four. There, we'll rendezvous with the *U.S.S. Starhawk.* The *Starhawk*'s captain, an old friend of mine,

Zhanya Akhmatova, has pulled the short straw, I'm afraid." His lips stretched in an amiable half-moon over pearly teeth, his dark green eyes twinkling in amusement. "They have to haul the brass."

There were twitters from the cadets around the table. Riley managed a small smile—he was, after all, one of the brass himself—a fact Romolo had apparently forgotten.

"Of course," Romolo continued, "we haven't gotten away scot-free. The admiral traveling on *Starhawk* helped in the refit the *Paladin* received just before the mission, so I'm sure he'll want to come aboard and see the ship and review the crew. Expect it. We have his aide here with us now—Lieutenant Commander Riley, who has graciously offered his assistance with our part of the simulation." He gestured at Riley, who rose slightly in his chair and nodded at the crowd. Once again, he caught sight of Anab; this time, she did not look away, but managed a strained smile.

Riley returned it, knowing his own must have seemed sickly.

"What admiral will we be entertaining, Captain?" the chief engineer asked.

"They're sending the very best—the chief of operations, James Kirk."

A muffled yelp came from across the room. The captain gazed casually over at his bridge crew, and the cadets seated behind them.

"I hope there's no problem with that, Mr. Diksen," the captain said quietly, but Riley could tell he found the situation amusing.

The short brunette female blushed furiously, but managed to stabilize her voice. "No, *sir!* No problem at all. On the contrary, sir, it's quite the honor . . . sir. . . ."

"Fine, Diksen," the captain assured her. "I'm glad you see it that way. If you have any questions about the admiral, you might direct them to Lieutenant Commander Riley."

Riley felt every cadet's gaze turn to him; Diksen's eyes were as big as saucers as she stared openmouthed at him.

"Riley served under Kirk's command on the *Enterprise*'s five-year mission, didn't you?" the captain asked congenially.

Riley nodded in uneasy affirmation.

The captain turned back to the staff and outlined his plan for their immediate mission. "Once the evacuation of Zotos Four has been completed, Lieutenant Anab Saed from *Starhawk* security and two representatives from the *Paladin* will depart in a shuttle. A shuttle from the *Paladin* will be sent at the same time. That ship will fire upon you and disable your vessel. Lieutenant Saed will be in charge. Saed, I expect you to make sure your people are prepared for the attack, but the attack will be *real,* and while shields will be employed, the ship will actually be disabled. If all goes as planned, the *Recovery* will protect and rescue you, beaming your entire ship inside it."

Riley watched as Anab nodded, her expression intent as she focused on the captain's words. And then Romolo paused; the seriousness left his face and voice. "Am I correct in thinking you two know each other? Seems I remember seeing something in your files. . . ."

Anab's expression slackened with dismay; Riley glanced back at Romolo and realized that the captain was addressing him.

"Yes, sir," he said softly, doing his best to maintain a pleasant expression.

"Well, then, Riley, how about a chance to kill two birds with one stone? Get out of the office and see a little action, plus have the chance to spend some time with an old friend?"

Before Riley could reply, the captain turned toward Anab. "He's a capable officer. And he knows the simulation inside and out; in fact, he briefed me on it. Any objections?"

For a beat, Anab remained silent, her expression unreadable as she avoided Riley's gaze. At last, she replied, her voice firm. "No, sir."

And then Romolo turned his wide, smiling face toward Riley.

He could not imagine why Anab had been called over to the *Paladin* to head the simulation—unless there were simply not enough seasoned, qualified officers on board. For the briefest glimmer of an instant, Riley considered refusing, but in the surprise of the moment, he could think of no reasonable excuse. He and Anab were adults, after all; and if there was no way out of it, then he might as well be gracious.

After all, the simulation would be over quickly enough; and then he would be able to return and retreat to the safety of his quarters aboard the *Starhawk.*

He drew a breath and managed a forced smile. "I'm looking forward to it, sir."

Chapter Three

CADET REESE DIKSEN sat at the communications station and tried to force herself to concentrate on the boring, mundane duties that were required of the officer manning the board. They'd be at Zotos IV within the hour. *Within the hour.* That meant that within the hour she might find herself in the presence of Admiral James T. Kirk. She swallowed. Kirk, *himself.*

Distantly her mind registered incoming and outgoing messages, most of which the computer handled automatically. There were only a few she had to actually make any decisions about. She hated being at communications, especially during high-speed travel. She had to compensate for time differentials, and subspace interference—but to her, it was nothing but maintenance work. This was not the job she envisioned herself in when she fought to be the highest honors student in Starfleet Academy. Except for messages to the captain, how important could this job be anyway?

Messages to the captain.

It suddenly occurred to her that Kirk would have to call over for permission to beam aboard. That meant, more than likely, that *she* would have to handle the call . . . that *she* would be the first person to speak to Admiral James T. Kirk.

Admiral Kirk. Now, *that* was the biggest travesty in Starfleet history. Why he ever let them kick him upstairs, she could not imagine. A man like that driving a desk—it was a waste—no, worse than a waste: a crime.

Kirk.

What it would be like actually serving under him?

"Mr. Diksen!" the first officer, Commander Pulver, called out to her sharply, breaking her reverie. The by-the-book officer was standing right by her shoulder, looming over the daydreaming cadet.

"Uh . . . yes, sir?" Reese glanced down at her board. Every telltale was lit, blinking angrily.

"You have failed to properly correct for subspacial interference," Pulver intoned crisply, in her perfectly modulated British voice. "Communications is at a standstill. Correct your board, please."

"Yes, sir," Diksen said smartly, her ears burning with embarrassment. She could almost feel the captain's eyes boring into her back, that perpetually bemused expression on his face. In contrast to Pulver's rigidity and the Vulcan science officer's cool nonemotionalism, Romolo was so fatherly to the cadets it was downright patronizing. Diksen knew he thought the "youngsters" were "cute" in their role-playing seriousness.

"Sorry, Captain," she apologized, as her hands flew

across the board, making the adjustments in record time. She didn't relax until Pulver moved away, peering now at some other cadet's performance.

"I know the routine aspects of communications are dreary, Diksen," the captain said softly. She could hear the smile in his voice, which only irritated her further. "But in a crisis, communications can be the most critical post on a ship. It's a lot like being an emergency worker—a whole lot of sitting around until you're really needed, and then everything moves at warp speed. Don't underestimate your post, Diksen. Stay alert." He paused significantly, then added, "We wouldn't want to miss the admiral's call, would we?"

Reese knew her ears were a brilliant scarlet. "No, sir," she said respectfully.

His quiet chuckle sounded blaring among the soft noises of the bridge instruments.

Getting her board back in order helped to get her mind in similar shape. She was training to be an officer. What might happen to her career if she screwed up this simple task?

An intership call came in for the captain, and she routed it to his chair. She heard him murmur to his comm port, then was surprised when the first officer said to her, "Diksen, you're due for a half-hour break."

Her eyes strayed to the chrono. "It's a little early yet, sir."

Pulver's icy reserve never budged. "We'll rendezvous with the *Starhawk* in an hour. Once that happens, you will remain at your post for the rest of the shift. Therefore, for efficiency's sake, you, Changsom, Kjolner, and Schell will take your break now, so we can have continuity when the admiral arrives."

"Aye, sir," multiple voices replied.

"And Diksen," the captain added as she rose from

her station and was replaced by a senior officer, "Cadet Ngo has requested your presence on the hangar bay. Don't be late returning." He smiled affably, as if he were reminding his daughter about their agreed-upon curfew after a dance.

It only made Reese act more professional. Pulling her uniform in place, she replied crisply, "Aye, sir!"

His chuckle followed her out the bridge doors right onto the lift.

She fumed silently, until she noted that the other three members of the bridge crew dismissed with her were all cadets. She noticed, too, that they hung back from her a little in the confines of the small lift. But she was too annoyed to hold her tongue. "The grown-ups needed some private time," she said sarcastically. "They sent the kiddies off to play! What an insult."

Thira Changsom, a young man who had a wrestler's powerful build but a scientist's serious, gentle demeanor, glanced quickly with dark, almond-shaped eyes at the others, then responded evenly to Reese, "Of course they need some private time. Part of their job is to find meaningful assignments for us, so they can evaluate our potential. They can't very well do that with us sitting there."

Reese's lip curled faintly. He *would* come up with that. Most of the cadets were just like sheep, doing whatever they were told. But Kirk had never gone with the herd—he'd questioned everything, right down to the *Kobayashi Maru*. Reese was determined to model Kirk every way she could. And if that meant being a bit of a thorn in Starfleet's side, fine. Even as respected an establishment as Starfleet needed a little goading now and then. She thought for a moment—maybe that was why Kirk took the promotion. To be in a better position to prod that sedentary, too-comfortable establishment right in its—

"Do you want us to get something for you to eat?"

Laura Kjolner asked politely, as the lift stopped at the cafeteria.

She shook her head. "No. Thanks. I'll meet you guys back on the bridge."

As the three cadets left her in the lift—barely masking the questioning looks they threw back at her—Reese had to suppress the urge to make "baa-baa" noises at them. If they were what Starfleet considered officer material . . .

Suddenly the doors whooshed open on the hangar deck, and Diksen stepped out, refocusing her attention. Where was Josiah, and what could he possibly want with her here? She moved across the deck until she noticed his lithe, long-limbed dark figure crouched in one of the shuttles. Reese moved toward him across the spacious hangar, curious.

When she came up beside him, she realized he was running some kind of diagnostic test on the shuttle.

Nodding, Josiah gazed up at Reese with large dark eyes set in a narrow taupe-colored face, and ran long, thin fingers through tightly curled chestnut hair. Crouching over the inner works of the shuttle, with his long skinny arms and legs and large hands and feet, he reminded Reese of a nesting stork.

"I screwed up today, Reese," he said, his voice weary. "I messed up a matter-antimatter alignment by such a huge margin I could've—theoretically—blown up the whole ship. I screwed up major, but the funny thing was, right after I got lucky and found that problem with the deck plating and had the chief engineer ready to canonize me."

It wasn't like Josiah to dwell on his errors. But the last thing he needed, Reese knew, was to be coddled. "Maybe it was just the thing you needed to get your head out of the clouds!"

When he looked at her, startled, she went on more gently. "Listen, Josiah, why do you think they call this 'training'? They *expect* us to screw up. You're not the first! That's why there was a senior officer hanging over your shoulder, to save your butt—and everyone else's—if you made a mistake."

He shrugged, clearly not wanting to argue with her, but still doubtful. "Yeah, well—it's made me a little —insecure. I was assigned to safety-check the shuttles, especially the ones they'll be using for the simulation. I started worrying that maybe I'd missed something." He gestured with a huge, large-knuckled hand. "Sometime tomorrow two people are going to be locked in this box, and if I screw up the safety check—it could mean their lives."

"Come on," Diksen prodded her friend, "I watched you run those checks. You've been over this thing from stem to stern, with every diagnostic tool you have. You know very well it's got specially designed shields, that the walls are double-thick, that all the equipment has special insulators on them. This shuttle has extra fire-response units. And the people in the simulation will be in pressurized suits, just in case the ship does spring a leak."

Josiah shook his head worriedly. "This isn't school anymore, Reese. This is no simulation. This ship will be hit with phaser power. It's my job to make sure she's ready for that. I guess I started feeling—maybe I'm in over my head."

Diksen sat in front of Josiah, and stared him down. "What are you talking about? We used to stay up late at night and imagine the day when we'd get to do this stuff! I'm stuck on a communications board like some overdressed comm technician, while you're actually working in the field you always wanted to! When we got our assignments you were rubbing your hands together and gloating!"

She took her friend by the shoulders and made him lift his dark eyes up to stare into hers. "You've spent your whole life waiting for this moment! How many times did you tell me that, growing up, you never imagined yourself doing anything but serving aboard a starship? You told me 'Engineering's the place to be! The place where all the action is.' Now you've got a chance to see what it's all about. You've just got the cadet first-time jitters. You've got to snap out of it!"

Josiah blinked his large eyes rapidly and nodded briskly, as if suddenly accepting everything she'd said as faith. But that was always the way it had been between them. Reese had always believed Josiah's pep talks whenever she had those moments when it all seemed too much to handle. That's why they had been such good friends through their entire Academy years, and why they'd worked to get assigned to the same ship. They couldn't imagine starting their careers without having the other nearby to lean on.

"I know you're right, Reese," Josiah said, his angular, handsome face lighting up with his normally cheerful nature. "You always know just what to say. Maybe that's why they put you in communications!"

Grinning, she slapped his shoulder, and they both laughed.

When Reese finally slid into her station, relieving the senior officer who'd been sitting there, it didn't escape her attention that she was thirty seconds late.

"Nice to see you, Diksen," the captain said smoothly, before Pulver could say something more pointed. "I was afraid you'd decided to order out."

The bridge crew, used to the peculiar brand of their captain's humor, chuckled along with him. Except, of course, for Sonak, the Vulcan, who merely lifted an eyebrow, and Commander Pulver, who stared at her disapprovingly.

Diksen was about to apologize for her tardiness when her empty stomach growled so loudly the entire bridge turned toward her. *There go my ears,* she thought, feeling the warmth bloom in them. Even Sonak was staring at her, both slanted eyebrows lifted in an expression of curious disdain. Apparently, this managed to amuse even the stiff first officer, who, Reese noted, had to turn away to hide her expression. Diksen ignored them all and hunkered down over her board.

Then she saw the telltale to her left light up at the same time a voice spoke into the receiver nestled in her right ear.

"This is the *U.S.S. Starhawk* hailing the *U.S.S. Paladin.*" The voice was the *Starhawk*'s computer, Reese realized with some disappointment.

"Captain," she announced, "we're being hailed by the *Starhawk.*"

"Good thing you got back, Diksen," he said amiably, "or you would've missed this. They're early. Put it on screen."

Her hands moved across the board and a new image filled the huge viewscreen. The bridge of a starship appeared before the *Starhawk*'s crew, with an exotically beautiful mature woman sitting in the captain's chair.

"Zdrastvuitye, Paladin," the woman said with a smile, sweeping a lock of silver-tinged dark hair from her face.

"And to you, *Starhawk,*" Captain Romolo replied. "It's good to see you again, Captain Akhmatova."

There was something about the tone of his voice . . . Reese looked over her shoulder, but wasn't in any position to see Romolo's expression. But there was a warmth and familiarity in Akhmatova's as she looked at him that made her think these two must have had some special, long-term relationship.

She never thought about starship captains and normal, human relationships. Scanning the hours of research on Kirk she'd sifted through for her reports, she could not remember finding much about his personal life. There was, of course, information about his father, his parentage, his early life and schooling, but once he entered the Academy, there was really nothing. It was as if his whole life focused on the *Enterprise* and the five-year mission. He had been, for Reese, so long an invisible mentor, so long the one person she modeled herself after, she'd never given much time to the blanks in the records. How did starship captains develop relationships? How could they last? How did they function? Were they even possible? She'd have to do some more research. . . .

A familiar name snapped her out of her reverie.

"Admiral Kirk is sorry he couldn't be here to greet you himself," Akhmatova told Romolo, "but he's down in Engineering looking over some of the refitting we had done there."

"Perfectly understandable," Romolo agreed. "Will you convey a request to him?"

Akhmatova nodded agreeably.

"Ask the admiral if he'd allow us to show him the *Paladin.* We have a good group of cadets that would be honored to be reviewed by him."

"I'll pass that suggestion on," Akhmatova assured him.

"It's good to be working with you again, Captain," Romolo said warmly, as the two of them signed off.

Diksen sighed disappointedly and sagged back in her chair. Now, wasn't that just the most *mundane* communication possible?

As Kirk stared at the big matter-antimatter chamber while the *Paladin*'s chief engineer explained some new hardware toy, he found himself fuguing out. *I wonder what Scotty would have to say about all these new gimmicks.* *"Aye, Captain, they be lovely, it's true, but can ye rely on them under fire, I'd be wantin' to know?"* This was his second ship review in the last four hours, and when he'd learned of Captain Romolo's invitation, he'd dreaded it. In the last half hour, however, Kirk had almost forgotten his misgivings.

The captain of the *Paladin* was so laid-back, so comfortable, that in just a few moments after their meeting, Jim had felt as if he'd known the man for years. Romolo's obvious expertise, his total comfort with the responsibility of command, shone in every area Kirk visited. Yet, he could've sworn there'd been no last-minute hysteria to prepare for the inspection. All this, in spite of the fact that the ship carried a large number of totally raw cadets. Cadets who somehow didn't seem that raw under Romolo's tutelage.

They were in Engineering when that concept was really brought home to him.

"Admiral," Romolo said, introducing him to a young man, "I'd like you to meet Mr. Josiah Ngo. Cadet, tell the admiral what you found on inspection just before we left the starbase for this mission."

Slender and tall, with light-brown skin crowned by reddish dark hair, Ngo nodded at his captain, then turned to Kirk. With a bony, skillful hand, he lifted a section of what appeared to be standard deck plating from a nearby console, then with the other hand picked up a diagnostic tool—one of Scotty's favorites if Kirk remembered right.

"This piece of plating," Ngo explained, "was part of the flooring that supported the matter-antimatter chamber. Usually, anything that supports that equipment has been examined so many times you begin to take it for granted. I was assigned to review the whole area, and run diagnostics on structural integrity, which is simple enough given a Reichman analyzer. The analyzer said the plates were okay, but . . . but I wasn't satisfied with that. Something about the plating . . . well, it just didn't *feel* right. When you walked on it . . . the give was different. So, I kind of 'married' this Reichman analyzer to a Vulcan T'Pell molecular reorganizer, and decided the readouts contradicted each other."

"Those two instruments were never designed to work together," Kirk murmured with surprise.

"I know, sir," Ngo agreed, flashing a shy smile, "but making them work together showed us that there was definitely something wrong with the plating. Something that wasn't showing up under any other analyzer."

Chief Engineer Gambeta, a handsome African woman with skin several shades darker than Ngo's, stepped forward. "When Josiah brought his concerns to me, I immediately replaced the plating."

Kirk's eyebrows rose. That simple statement belied the tedious, labor-intensive, and dangerous job that was involved in working around the matter-antimatter chamber.

"I had no choice, really," Gambeta insisted, "since the safety of that chamber was involved. We almost had to scrub this mission. But once we had the plating removed, it was easier to determine that it had suffered a very subtle molecular damage, perhaps while the ship was being refitted. It would've deteriorated slowly until the plating finally disintegrated. If that had happened while we were in space, perhaps at warp speed . . ." She shot Kirk an ominous look. "We worked round the clock to keep on *Recovery*'s schedule."

Kirk nodded, looking admiringly at Ngo. "And you did all this, just on a feeling?"

Uncomfortably, the cadet shifted his weight from

one long, cranelike leg to the other. "I know it doesn't sound very scientific, sir. . . ."

"Don't apologize," Kirk insisted. "Trust your instincts, your feelings. They were right. They will be again. Listen to them. That kind of instinct can't be learned. Good work, cadet."

"Thank you, Admiral," the young man said, smiling shyly as Romolo moved Kirk on through the rest of Engineering.

"So, you didn't know we'd be showing up here for this exercise with a crib full?" Romolo asked as they left the area.

"I'm a little surprised, actually," Kirk admitted as they walked through the curved corridors. "With the presence of hostile—" He interrupted himself, then corrected, "That is, of our *neighbors*"—he was gratified to see Romolo's knowing smile—"I wouldn't think Starfleet would consider this a training exercise."

"Well, it really is only a simulation," Romolo reminded him, "and the ambassador will be interacting with our *neighbors* on the *Starhawk,* so it's not like we'll see any action. At least it's a good shake-up drill for the cadets. They'll be taking part in an important exercise, and get close enough to the neighbors to remember what they smell like. It's a good group, too."

"So they seem. I was impressed with young Ngo—even if he did look to be about twelve. Which reminds me—he should be part of the team that's on the shuttlecraft part of the simulation. I have a feeling about him." He eyed Romolo knowingly. "I suspect this assignment falls to you fairly frequently, Captain."

Romolo's lips curved easily into a smile, brightening his full, handsome face; his tone was one of distinct fondness for his young charges. "I'm not afraid of green troops, sir, that's well known. I was lucky myself coming up, to have a good captain. It can make all the difference in an officer's training."

Kirk nodded, eyeing the rotund man warmly. He suspected serving under Romolo would make quite a difference in this crop of cadets. He had a humanity that could often be lacking in a captain. With all the stress and demands of the position, it was hard to hang on to that. *Bones would've liked this guy,* he found himself thinking. Then he recalled the conversation he'd had with Akhmatova in her quarters.

Baldassare is an old friend . . . but a captain's duties don't allow for reunions.

"While we're just walking and talking here like two old friends, Captain Romolo—" Kirk began suddenly.

"If we're talking as old friends, the name's Baldassare," the affable man corrected.

Kirk nodded, pleased. "All right, Baldassare. Then I'm Jim. I wanted to mention that I've spent some time with Captain Akhmatova. We had an . . . interesting conversation. She's not afraid to put an admiral on the spot!"

"I can imagine," said Romolo with a fond grin. "Zhanya's a hell of a captain, and quite an impressive human being. We came up together in the Academy. Zhanya was the head of our class—and I must admit I wasn't even in the top ten. But whatever grades I did excel in, I did with her help. We've been friends all these years. Served on our first ships together. But then the promotions came, and time passed. And it gets harder and harder to be with old friends."

It was the first thing Romolo had said in Kirk's presence that had an air of melancholy about it. "I understand completely, Baldassare," he replied, his own tone rich with regret. "And because I really do understand, I've been wondering when you might—ask me a favor."

The captain shot him a look of genuine confusion that made Jim smile. "You know," Kirk continued, "I can't remember the last time I've been on a ship and some officer didn't have a favor to ask of me—usually having something to do with a petition to Nogura. Then, after meeting Zhanya and then talking to you, I kept waiting for you to ask something of me." Kirk gave the captain a reassuring smile, but Romolo only seemed more baffled.

"You and Captain Akmatova are old friends. You go back to the Academy. You spend very little time together these days. Lately . . . I've found myself remembering old friends I no longer see—and it really put me in your shoes. Why don't you give the conn to your first officer while I'm aboard your ship? I can stay on the bridge—just for appearance' sake. I've no doubt your first officer can handle anything that comes up. This way, you can visit with your friend."

The way I would with mine, if I could . . .

The request took Romolo by surprise. "Admiral . . . I couldn't take advantage—"

Kirk shot him a look, and the *Paladin*'s captain corrected himself immediately. "I mean—*Jim*—what about the simulation?"

"That's the point—it's a *simulation*. The last in a long series of simulations. And, I don't mind admitting to you, Baldassare, that the feel of your ship . . . well, it reminds me too much of the *Enterprise*. I don't even mind admitting that it would be a thrill to hang around the bridge again. Even for a training exercise."

"It's a very generous offer, Jim," Romolo agreed, still hesitant. "I could visit with Zhanya and be back before the demonstration with the shuttle."

Kirk shook his head. "Don't worry about it. It's just

routine. We can keep this between the two of us. I don't think Starfleet has any idea the price starship captains pay to sit in that chair. The *human* price— friendships, relationships . . ." He trailed off, thinking of Lori Ciana, of Bones, of Spock. . . . "Really, Baldassare, I know very well how rarely these kinds of opportunities present themselves. So, take advantage of it. And hope I don't ruin your cadets for you!"

Romolo chuckled. *"That* would be my least concern!"

Chapter Four

"THE *RECOVERY* is onscreen now," Commander Pulver's precise, cool voice announced from the captain's chair.

Reese turned to face the screen, and her jaw dropped just a little as the massive evacuation vessel moved into her prearranged position between the two starships. She'd seen models of the rescue vessel, but only now, with her vastness filling up the space between the starships, could the cadet really appreciate the rescue ship's scale. Both the *Paladin* and the *Starhawk* looked like a couple of hovering hummingbirds beside the monster ship. One of the senior human officers, a red-haired man with a neatly trimmed mustache, whistled appreciatively.

"An accurate assessment," Sonak, the Vulcan science officer, commented, "if I judge your reaction to be complimentary, Mr. Sandover. *Recovery* is the first of her kind, a truly unique endeavor." He paused significantly, then mentioned, "As is this opportunity. If you will turn your attention to the upper-right-hand corner of the screen, you can just see three vessels there. One of them is Klingon; one, Romulan . . . and the last is Tholian. A most unique assembly."

Reese gazed in silent awe at the sight: An ungainly Klingon Bird-of-Prey hovered near a sleeker, more elegant Romulan Warbird; flanking them both, like a reluctant sparrow trapped between two hawks, was the tiny, triangular Tholian ship. It was one thing to recognize the enemy vessels during an Academy training exercise; quite another to see them in the flesh.

"Well said, Mr. Sonak," Captain Romolo's rich voice agreed from the direction of the turbolift.

The entire bridge turned, then snapped to attention as a man wearing admiral's braids stepped out from behind their captain. Reese had been so engrossed in the image of *Recovery,* she'd never heard the lift doors open.

In the split second before Romolo could introduce the man, realization dawned on Diksen. He was wearing admiral's braids. That broad, handsome face beneath brunette hair, those hazel eyes, it could only be . . .

"Looks like our timing was perfect," Romolo remarked, checking his chrono. *"Recovery*'s right where she should be. That means the simulation will begin in about fifteen minutes. Crew, allow me to introduce Admiral James T. Kirk." Romolo moved around the upper bridge area, introducing Kirk to his officers. "At navigation we have Mr. Leandro Sandover. . . ."

The captain moved around the bridge giving the admiral the time to learn everyone's name and station.

As they did, Diksen forced herself to remain standing at attention, her knees locked rigidly, in spite of the flight-or-fight reflex her body was undergoing. She'd studied everything official on Kirk she could get her hands on, and now he was here. The greatest starship captain the Federation had ever produced. *Here.* She blinked for a moment and realized the captain had arrived at her station. That he was about to introduce Kirk to her. Her brain struggled to process the information.

"At communications, we have Cadet Reese Diksen," Romolo was saying. "This is her first assignment in deep space." The captain smiled warmly at her. "I don't know how much time you have to keep track of Academy affairs, sir, but Mr. Diksen won the Vulcan Award of Excellence this year."

Reese felt as if every molecule of blood just rushed to her head, battling its way to her eartips. *No. No. He wouldn't tell the admiral about that . . . !*

Kirk's eyebrows rose in appreciation. "Is that so? Congratulations, Mr. Diksen. You're only the fourth human who's ever won that award."

I know, she tried to say, but nothing would come out. *You were the first.*

"What was your study about?" Kirk asked her.

She opened her mouth, but for once in her life, nothing happened.

"It was on *you,* Admiral," Romolo said cheerily. Kirk turned to him, surprised, and Reese prayed to gods she didn't know she believed in that he would not look at her again. But he did, as Romolo continued, "She won for a report weighing the political value of the Prime Directive, as opposed to its practical application. She used your experiences, your difficulties in following the Prime Directive, as evidence of the problems starship captains have to face trying to marry philosophy with action."

How many times had Reese wanted to discuss that study with him? A hundred, a thousand times, she'd wanted to interview him over his record, find out why he did this, instead of that, why he chose one road over the other. But now that the opportunity was here, she just wanted to sit down, catch her breath, and try not to throw up.

"I'm *impressed,* Cadet," Kirk said as if he meant it. "I'm sorry I haven't had time to keep up with the Academy's academic reports, but I assure you, as soon as I get back, I'll look up your study. If the Vulcans thought that highly of it, it must be interesting indeed." He smiled, and it lit up his face, making his hazel eyes sparkle. "I hope you didn't choose my career because of my well-known . . . problems following the Prime Directive."

Her eyes widened. "Oh, no, sir, no, to the contrary!" She realized she was on the verge of babbling and bit her cheek to get a grip on her seesawing emotions. "That is . . . your record is the best example of the real-life difficulties facing any captain on active duty who tries to follow the Prime Directive."

Suddenly, the words *active duty* seemed to hang there between them like something unmentionable. Kirk's face seemed to cloud over for a moment, but he recovered.

"Your record, sir," Diksen said firmly, back in charge of herself again, "is one any captain could learn from—that was why I chose it."

Romolo chuckled at her forthright honesty, and she realized, too late, that another captain might've taken offense at that.

"I'm complimented, Mr. Diksen," Kirk assured her. "Perhaps we'll find time to discuss this again."

"Yes, sir," she mumbled. "Thank you, sir."

As the captain and Kirk moved away, she heard Romolo tell the admiral, "She finished first in her class in the *Kobayashi Maru* as well."

But I didn't beat the scenario, she thought disgustedly. Ever since Kirk had the opportunity to change the programming, security had been extra tight on the simulation.

Then Romolo introduced the science officer, Mr. Sonak. Sonak stood at the science station, hands clasped primly behind his back. She saw Kirk immediately mirror his position, instead of extending his hand as he had for each member of the human crew. Vulcans would handshake when they absolutely had to, but it was not their custom, and, she knew, most of the touch telepaths found contact with the unshielded thoughts of humans unpleasant, if not actually rude. Kirk inclined his head respectfully toward Sonak as the captain introduced them, but never attempted to move any closer. However, Reese didn't miss the change in his expression.

It was subtle, mostly something about his eyes, but she couldn't help but think that meeting Sonak brought back memories of all those years Kirk had worked with the Vulcan Spock. Sonak's features were so similar to every other middle-aged male Vulcan she had ever met that at times she wondered how Vulcan females could distinguish them. He had the same black hair in the bangs-over-forehead style that Vulcans affected, the same brown eyes as she'd seen in Spock's images. His height and build were similar, and Reese knew Vulcans had a body language that was so alike it was scary. Sonak was younger than Spock, but with Vulcans between the age of thirty and one hundred, that hardly mattered.

While studying Kirk, Reese also learned a great deal about the crew that had worked with him, especially his closest associates, his first officer, Spock, and the human doctor McCoy. McCoy had left Starfleet rather abruptly after the five-year mission—for reasons she could never determine—but even more baffling was the fate of Spock. He, too, left Starfleet, then seemed to disappear. She could find no information about him in any records, anywhere. She wondered if Kirk knew, and if that knowledge colored his meeting Sonak? Reese watched the men interact with a voyeuristic interest that surprised her.

"Mr. Sonak," Kirk said, "have you served with Captain Romolo long?"

"Three years, ten months, two hundred twelve days, six hours, and . . ."

"Yes," Kirk interrupted before the Vulcan could recite minutes and seconds. He smiled then, and again, the look was full of warmth, changing his face. "I . . . served with a Vulcan science officer aboard the *Enterprise.*"

"Yes, sir," Sonak replied. "You served with Spock, who was also your first officer. He had a very distinguished career. It serves as a model for the rest of us. His understanding of human beings, of their culture, and even their humor, was remarkable." Sonak sounded almost admiring—for a Vulcan.

Kirk nodded. "I will admit to you that I found serving with a Vulcan an experience that was nothing short of . . . fascinating." The merest ghost of a grin played at his lips; he wore the look of a man who'd waited his whole life to use that line.

Sonak raised an eyebrow in muted wryness as Romolo led Kirk to the captain's chair where his first officer still stood at attention. Pulver was as coolly collected as ever—not a smooth copper hair out of place, not a hint of anxiety in her ice blue eyes.

When the captain introduced the two, Kirk extended his hand and said to her, "Commander, your career is known to me. I understand you've been approached about a command of your own." Diksen had to admit Pulver seemed much more like a starship captain than the cheerful Romolo. She'd be a demanding one, too.

Pulver gave a single, solemn nod, her shoulder-length hair swinging slightly; Diksen was amazed that it could move at all, since the woman seemed chiseled from stone. "I have been approached, sir, and I've taken it under serious advisement," the first officer agreed primly.

"I'm dreading her promotion," Romolo confided to Kirk, sotto voce. "When she finally does leave me for her own ship, then I'll *really* have to act like a captain. I'm not looking forward to it!"

The two men grinned; Pulver acknowledged the compliment by allowing the corners of her mouth to lift slightly—the closest Diksen had ever seen her come to a smile.

"If you ever need to discuss your decision, Commander," Kirk assured her, "my door is always open to you."

"Why, thank you, Admiral," she said, sounding genuinely flattered.

"Well!" Romolo said congenially. "I can see, Admiral, that you and my bridge crew are going to get along famously!" Turning to his staff, he told them, "The admiral has graciously offered to relieve me for a short while."

Reese blinked as she heard those words. Kirk was taking command of the *Paladin*? Everyone seemed a little nonplussed by the action, and even the unflappable Pulver blinked several times rapidly, before regaining her composure.

"Mr. Pulver," Romolo continued, "you'll have the conn, of course, with the admiral remaining on the bridge as . . . a helpful observer."

An *observer*? Reese could barely believe it. The

greatest starship captain of all time was just going to stand around and watch Pulver give her clipped little commands.

"You all know what's expected of you in the simulation," Romolo said affably. "Let's show the admiral what a good team is capable of." He turned to Kirk, and shook his hand. "Thank you again, sir."

"My pleasure, Captain," Kirk said, and it seemed to Reese he really meant it.

Could it be she was right? Had the admiralty turned out to be less than Kirk imagined? How could a bureaucrat's job ever compare to the *Enterprise*'s five-year mission?

Romolo left the bridge quickly, and as he did, Pulver moved with a hint of wariness toward the captain's seat, eyeing Kirk speculatively.

"Please," he said, addressing the bridge crew, "it's only a simulation, but it'll be hard to get through if you all remain at attention." He smiled again, and this time it seemed to relax most of the staff. "At ease, everyone. Resume your posts."

Gingerly, the crew did as they were told. But only Sonak seemed to be able to comply with any sense of normalcy. Then again, when had she ever seen the Vulcan lose a moment's aplomb?

As Reese forced her attention back to her board, she tried not to think about the man strolling casually around the bridge, as if it were the first time he'd ever been on one. But she couldn't help herself. It was happening, really happening. She was serving under *Kirk!* Sort of . . .

She almost jumped when Josiah's voice whispered in her ear, then realized it was coming over the receiver nestled there. She touched her board, made the reception clearer. What could he want *now?*

"Have you met him yet?" Ngo hissed at her. No doubt he was still in Engineering, making an extracurricular call. He'd know she wouldn't be able to say much. And Reese knew very well which "he" Josiah referred to.

"Uh-huh," she responded softly, so as not to be overheard. It wasn't that unusual for the communications officer to communicate directly over the comm in low tones. Not everyone that wanted to get through to the captain should be given that access. Part of her job was screening.

"He was okay down here," Ngo reported. "Has he left yet?"

"Unh-unh."

"Still on the bridge, huh? Well, don't stare, and don't let your ears turn red!"

Reese glowered at the board, both bits of advice coming far too late to do her any good.

"Kirk assigned me to go on the shuttlecraft!" Josiah told her. His voice was tinged with excitement. Gone was the hesitation he'd voiced earlier.

She was thrilled for him. Quietly, she asked, "You okay about this?"

There was such a long pause, Reese felt a flash of anxiety. At last Josiah said with a sigh, "Yeah, I'm okay. We're all suited up and ready, just waiting for the word to go."

"Any feelings?" That was their own shorthand. Josiah had on more than one occasion saved them both through his instincts. He seemed to know when something, usually mechanical, was about to go amiss.

"No. Everything feels fine. I'd better go. We're on standby alert."

"Right. Good luck!" Diksen severed the communication. Feeling as though she were being observed, and fearing that if she turned, she'd find Kirk at her shoulder, she looked to see Sonak watching her impassively. She wondered if his fine-tuned Vulcan hearing

71

had picked up the word "feelings." She might've said something to him, but just then another voice spoke in her ear. Diksen sat bolt upright. It was the *Recovery*.

"Captain. I mean, Admiral . . . I mean, Commander—" She stopped, completely flustered, trying to remember just what was the proper form of address, and who she was supposed to give it to. It didn't help that he was nearby, smiling down at her.

Pulver turned in the chair and directed a frosty stare at her. "Yes, Mr. Diksen?"

She swallowed and settled herself. "Commander, we're being hailed by the *Recovery*."

"Very good, Mr. Diksen," said the British officer. "Put it on screen, please."

Dr. Mola ushered Leonard McCoy into a large auditorium-like bay that had been equipped with a podium, a huge viewscreen, and amphitheater-seating for the assemblage. Most of the fifty other representatives from the FDRA were already there, making Bones and Angelina choose seats near the back.

"Dr. Shulman will help narrate what the ship will be doing during the simulation," she explained.

Leonard nodded. He was trying not to be distracted by the knowledge that, just a short distance away—in spatial terms at least—was a man he had once considered his closest friend. A man he hadn't spoken to in over a year. A man he had thought never to see or speak to again. Why was this bothering him so much now?

Suddenly, Shulman entered, the last to arrive. He moved to the podium so naturally he seemed to belong there. But, in spite of Shulman's easy gait, Leonard thought the ship's designer looked ragged. McCoy wondered if, after the simulation, he might have a chance to run a diagnostic over the man. Of course, if anything serious was wrong with Shulman, the ship, according to Mola, should've picked it up.

"And so, we come to Zotos Four," Shulman announced from the podium without preamble, "the final test for *Recovery.*" He touched something on the podium, and the viewscreen came on, showing the view of the hazy planet.

To either side of *Recovery*'s camera, two starships hovered nearby. McCoy wondered which one Jim was currently on, then forced his mind away from the thought.

"This planet," Shulman continued, "covered by a dense, almost impenetrable atmosphere, sent out a weak distress call twenty-four Terran hours ago. Without any direction from me, *Recovery* intercepted the call and began her journey. Now, again without my assistance, she will proceed to evacuate Zotos Four."

And with that, Shulman took a seat in the front of the group that had been left vacant for him.

"Now what?" McCoy asked Mola, sitting beside him.

"You must wait and see!" she chided him.

Suddenly, McCoy heard the unmistakable sounds of a channel being opened, as if he were standing right beside Uhura's board. The feminized computer voice of *Recovery* cut through the air.

"Scientific Station Thirteen on Zotos Four, this is the rescue ship *Recovery*—are you reading me?"

There was a significant pause, so the ship repeated the hail. Finally, before it could repeat the message a third time, there was the crackle of static and the central image of the revolving planet changed. The new picture was broken, full of interference and hard to see, but there appeared to be a fair-haired Terran male at its center.

"We read you, *Recovery*."

"Evacuation can begin on your go-ahead," the ship said. "Are personnel prepared?"

The picture steadied a bit; McCoy recognized the leader of the Zotos IV scientific team, Alain Deveraux. "As ready as we'll ever be," Deveraux answered.

"Evacuation will proceed in the following order," the ship announced. "Healthy personnel first, then injured, then dead."

That made good sense, the doctor thought. Healthy personnel could assist the ill when they arrived.

"Finally," the ship continued, "we will beam up equipment, and lastly, buildings and structures. Healthy personnel will receive further instructions once they are on board."

"Buildings?" McCoy asked Mola in surprise.

"The ship can beam up buildings," she assured him, "but there's no need to reconstruct them on the ship. Their patterns are stored in a special replicator."

"This is the FDRA ship *Recovery*," the ship continued, "hailing the *U.S.S. Paladin* and the *U.S.S. Starhawk*. You are in the vicinity of an emergency evacuation. If necessary, you may be called upon to provide assistance."

Suddenly, the bridge of the *Starhawk* appeared on the left of the large viewscreen, while the center portion of the screen reinstated the view of Zotos IV. The officer in the command chair was not the captain —something that didn't surprise McCoy—but most likely the *Starhawk*'s first officer. He knew how boring captains perceived simulations to be. Jim used to make Spock suffer through most of them on the *Enterprise*.

The striking Eurasian woman in *Starhawk*'s command chair nodded at her own viewscreen and acknowledged the ship's hail. "This is *Starhawk*,

Recovery. We read you and stand ready to assist. And good luck to you, Dr. Shulman."

From his seat at the front of the auditorium, the scientist nodded an acknowledgment at the screen.

The left side of the screen changed to show the nearly identical bridge of the *Paladin*. McCoy felt the breath leave him in a gasp as an all-too-familiar figure came to stand beside the captain's chair.

Jim Kirk, dressed in his gray admiral's uniform. The doctor's eyes widened and he stared unbelievingly as Kirk grinned broadly at the viewscreen— apparently having a fine old time.

Beside him, the woman in *Paladin*'s captain's chair said in a precise voice, "And this is *Paladin, Recovery*, likewise ready and waiting your orders. We, too, wish to send our best wishes to Dr. Shulman, Dr. Mola, and all the representatives of the FDRA."

The images of the two bridges hung side-by-side on the viewscreen in front of McCoy's disbelieving eyes, as he stared at the many-times-life-sized Kirk. The sight caused a wave of homesickness to wash over him; for the first time in over a year, he realized how badly he missed his old friend—and being aboard the *Enterprise*, despite all his noise about how glad he was to be out of the Fleet. At the same time, he felt a fresh surge of the same frustration and anger he'd experienced that day at Starfleet, when he'd told Nogura Jim belonged in command of the *Enterprise*, not a desk at headquarters.

Even now, Jim looked out of place standing beside Commander Pulver. No doubt it was the closest he'd come to that chair since he'd been promoted. McCoy didn't have to wonder if Kirk's seemingly cheerful expression had to do with his proximity to the bridge —even if was only to last for this moment.

"What's he doing there?" McCoy whispered, aghast.

"He must be relieving Captain Romolo," Angelina whispered into his ear. She paused as she watched the doctor's expression, and said, "It's all right. He can't see you."

He started visibly, then turned sheepishly toward her.

"All he can see is the officials, such as Shulman, in the first row," Mola said, her expression kindly. "He won't spot you back here."

For once in his life, McCoy was at a complete loss for words. He watched his old mentor as she examined his stricken face and knew he did not have to say a single word, that she knew and understood everything.

Her dark eyes softened with sympathy. "I didn't realize things were that way between you. I'm sorry, Leonard. I know you were once good friends. And good friends are hard to lose."

He could not answer her, so merely swallowed and turned away, unable to keep his eyes off Kirk's amiable, relaxed visage.

No wonder you're smiling, Jim, he thought bitterly. *Being on the bridge was the only thing that ever made you happy. . . .*

He paused, scrutinizing Kirk. Except for the change in uniform, he might as well have been aboard the *Enterprise.* That had to be the first officer at the conn. Then McCoy blinked incredulously as he realized that a *Vulcan* sat at the science station, and fought back a dizzying rush of déjà vu.

Beside him, Angelina stiffened in her chair, no longer paying attention to his momentary angst. McCoy followed her gaze to the front of the big room, where Shulman had jumped up from his seat. The scientist's back was stiff, his whole demeanor tense.

"So, you're front and center, eh, Kirk?" Shulman called, addressing the admiral's image. "I expected you to sit this one out in your comfortable VIP quarters! Or are you here to witness firsthand your hoped-for failure of *Recovery?*"

Angelina rose abruptly. "Excuse me," she muttered, and without even glancing at McCoy, hurried to the front of the auditorium.

Several officials in the front row had leaned forward, murmuring together. What was going on? Was Shulman so upset by Jim's report that he couldn't bear the very sight of the man?

In an instant, Dr. Mola had arrived at the front row and slowed her approach, clearly not wanting Kirk to see her rush to Shulman's side. With a businesslike gait, she moved to the scientist's left, as though her very presence might defuse the situation.

Before Kirk could respond, another member of the front-row dignitaries shot out of her seat. McCoy recognized the well-known disaster-relief specialist, Dr. Chia Noon. "You're out of line, Dr. Shulman!" the petite Indian woman declared. "Admiral Kirk's careful examination of *Recovery's* early flaws kept us from making costly mistakes. And who better has the right to question this project than the man who confronted the M-5 disaster?"

The man beside Dr. Noon said, "Just one moment, Chia, now you're out of line. . . ."

Good Lord, thought McCoy, *the whole group's gonna go for each other's throats! Jim, you sure have the charm. . . .*

"Please, doctors!" Angelina begged her colleagues, but it was Kirk's voice that brought order to the quarreling assemblage.

"Dr. Shulman," Kirk said in his smoothest tone, "only a fool would not wish you well in this venture." He stepped away from the command chair as if to remove any semblance of authority it might give him. His overly reasonable delivery took the fire out of everyone's opinion as the group subsided to hear him. *"Recovery* holds out hope for the victims of untimely disasters. Why would I wish for her failure?"

Shulman's hands were balled into fists and he took an aggressive step forward, as though ready to challenge Kirk physically. "To prove yourself right, of course. There isn't a person in this room that doesn't know how you feel about self-sufficient computers, about a ship capable of functioning on her own, even of defending herself. . . ." Shulman's voice grew angrier until it shook with irrational rage.

McCoy could see that the Kirk's borrowed bridge crew seemed rattled by the discussion, as did the officers aboard the *Starhawk.* He found himself feeling sorry for his old friend. *Is this the kind of bureaucratic bull-hockey you have to put up with at Starfleet quarters, Jim? And if it is, how do you ever get anything done?*

Angelina reached out, took hold of Shulman's arm, but the scientist shook her off.

"Be fair, Dr. Shulman," Kirk insisted, still moderating his voice to a degree of reasonableness that impressed McCoy. "I'm not the only person that's questioned the need for a rescue ship to be armed with state-of-the-art weaponry."

"Defense!" Shulman shouted. *"Defense* weaponry!"

"Yes, of course," Kirk agreed calmly. "Defense weaponry."

"I'm glad you're here, Kirk," Shulman gloated. "Because Dr. Noon is right, very right. And no one has wanted you to know more than I, that without you, *Recovery* could not have become the vessel she is. Without you and your damning report, the scattered, diversified emergency-relief organizations that backed my work could not have formed the strong coalition we have."

McCoy snorted to himself. He was well aware that

Mola, Shulman, and the varied consort of organizations forming the FDRA would be forever at each other's throats. How they'd managed to ever get this ship spaceborne was a source of amazement to him.

As if answering the doctor's skeptical thought, Shulman announced, "You see, Kirk, it's easy to become organized when one has a common *enemy.*"

On the screen, Kirk set his jaw. McCoy imagined how Jim felt getting the riot act read to him not only in front of his bridge crew, the entire ship under his command, another starship that was observing—but in front of three enemy vessels! *Look out, Shulman— you've done it now! You're makin' him mad. . . .*

"I think, Dr. Shulman," Kirk said with deadly calm, "that to call someone who disagrees with you an *enemy* is a little strong."

Dr. Mola stepped in front of Shulman and faced Kirk, physically preventing the researcher from saying anything more, and holding her arms out toward the admiral in a placating gesture. "Admiral . . . forgive Dr. Shulman for speaking from his heart about a project that has taken so much of his effort. Let me assure you that I and the rest of the FDRA welcome your presence here. *Recovery*'s success today will be witnessed by her most demanding challenger—and without a challenger, how could we have developed the high standards we have? We all owe you our thanks."

"Speak for yourself, Mola," Shulman barked irritably. "Watch closely, Kirk! See how much more efficient, safe, and reliable the right machine is over the weak and ineffectual efforts of mere humans!" Abruptly, the scientist sat down, crossing his arms, his whole body rigid with anger.

His jaw still set, Kirk chose his words with painful care. "Dr. Shulman, Dr. Mola, I meant what I said. I look forward to *Recovery*'s success."

As if she sensed the time was right to interrupt the tense atmosphere, *Recovery* announced her next action. "Beginning beam up of Zotos Four personnel."

The center portion of the screen changed abruptly, and the image of the mist-laden atmosphere of Zotos IV was replaced by a picture of another large auditorium like the one McCoy was in. He forced his gaze away from Kirk's face, remembering he was here as an official observer, and studied this new, unfurnished auditorium. Suddenly, figures began materializing within it, dozens of figures, more than a starship could've ever managed at a time, even with all its transporter pads. Each figure was at least ten feet from the other so there was no danger of regenerator-beam crossover. Every figure forming in the auditorium completed its materialization at the same time, so there was no danger of someone accidently walking into another person's field. McCoy realized that he could not count the number of people who'd been instantaneously beamed up into that large room.

Dr. Mola moved to the podium, claiming everyone's attention.

McCoy had the feeling she was standing in for Shulman, who remained in his seat still glowering at Kirk. "Since Zotos only has a complement of two hundred scientists, *Recovery* has beamed them all aboard at the same time—with the exception of a few staff members who are in need of minor medical care. Had this been a fully developed planet, this scenario could've been duplicated in over a hundred such hangars, *simultaneously.*"

Even McCoy was impressed. He glanced at Kirk's face to see that he, too, seemed surprised.

The voice of the ship spoke up, and McCoy realized the computer was addressing the people it had just "rescued." "There are four individuals who require medical attention. Which of you here can assist in their care?"

Two Zotos IV scientists identified themselves as doctors.

"Then both of you," the computer intoned, "and the individuals in question will be beamed directly to sickbay."

No sooner had the computer announced that than those two people, a man and woman, were beamed out. The screen changed once more, showing the sickbay where six people materialized. Amazingly, four of them materialized directly onto diagnostic beds. *Talk about precision work!* McCoy mused.

For a moment, he forgot about Jim looming up there on the screen as he watched *Recovery* diagnose, prescribe treatment, and provide care for the four different people with four different ailments that had been brought into her sickbay. Then Jim turned to speak to the Vulcan behind him, and that simple act brought back too many memories for the doctor.

There seemed no point in suffering through any more auld-lang-syne fantasies; McCoy rose and headed for the rear exit, knowing he'd be far better off experiencing this scenario in the one place he actually belonged: sickbay.

In hangar bay four, Riley stepped toward the shuttlecraft with a mixture of anticipation and dread. Despite his discomfort at seeing Anab again, the process of suiting up and preparing for the drill brought back his days aboard the *Enterprise*—not the fear- and guilt-ridden days after one of his command decisions had resulted in the death of a colleague, but the early days, when he had been full of optimism and exhilaration.

At the same time, Anab's presence made him acutely self-conscious. As he moved toward the shuttlecraft *Grace Hopper,* Anab fell into step beside him, her helmet under one arm. Behind them, the cadet accompanying them approached; she spoke quickly, softly so that only Riley could hear.

"K.T. . . ."

He looked at her, trying to ignore the pain evoked by hearing the special nickname only she used.

Her full lips curved in a faint, wry grin. "This is what comes of us both trying to avoid each other. I volunteered to be the experienced officer aboard the shuttlecraft, since they're at a premium aboard *Paladin.*"

He let go a small gust of air that was not quite a laugh, thankful for her attempt to break the tension. "So . . . we wind up together. I just wish Romolo would read his files more *carefully.*"

"Well, even though it's awkward . . ." She lowered her lashes, not quite meeting his gaze. "It's good to see you again."

"It's good to see you, too," he said, half-truthfully, then fell silent as the cadet, a young man, as tall and willowy as Anab, with the same graceful, long Somalian features and dark chestnut skin, caught up to them at the shuttle's entrance.

Anab's tone grew abruptly professional. "Commander Riley, this is Cadet Josiah Ngo. Ngo will be serving as your navigator." She gestured toward the pilot's seat.

Riley turned to her. "No, thanks . . . I'll let you do the honors, Lieutenant. This was your assignment; I'm just here as an observer. As far as I'm concerned, you're still in charge."

"Well, if I'm to be in charge—with all due respect, sir," Anab said formally, as though their relationship had never been more than that of an officer and her superior, "our original plan was that I would oversee two cadets, one who would pilot and one who would navigate. The captain hasn't reversed his order, and with your permission, I would like to continue this simulation as we had rehearsed it."

"Fine. Best to stick as closely as possible to the original plan." Riley climbed into the shuttle and the pilot's seat; Ngo took the seat next to him, and Anab sat behind them both. The three of them secured their helmets in place.

Riley started at the fleeting touch of a hand upon his shoulder.

"Thank you, sir," Anab said softly, then leaned forward to speak into the comm. "This is shuttlecraft *Grace Hopper*. We're ready, Commander."

Pulver's cool, precise voice filtered into the small craft. "Very good, Lieutenant. Prepare for takeoff."

"Aye, sir."

She nodded to Riley, who discovered, to his surprise and pleasure, that none of his Academy training had deserted him. With an ease that felt as if it had been days, not years, since he had last piloted a shuttle into space, he touched the controls that would void the air inside the hangar bay and open the airlock doors.

The great hangar doors rose, and the infinite starlit darkness of space yawned before them, in stark contrast to the brightly lit shelter of the hangar. Riley pressed a few more controls; the tiny ship lifted gently, then silently left its home.

As the *Grace Hopper* followed her preplanned trajectory and its mothership fell farther and farther behind, her inhabitants were finally able to view the true size and scope of the vessel they were about to test.

Riley let out a silent gust of air; beside him, Josiah

Ngo's lips parted in amazement. *Recovery's* shape was rectangular, much like that of her infinitely smaller cousin, the *Grace Hopper,* but sleeker, smoother, and enormously vast.

"Heads up," Anab snapped behind them.

Riley glanced up to see the *Starhawk's* "enemy" shuttle approaching just as Ngo spied the ship and squawked, *"Unknown vessel approaching at two o'clock!"*

Caught up in the sudden immediacy of the simulation, Riley searched his instruments. "Scanners say they're arming photon weapons. Shields up."

"I'm hailing them," Ngo announced. His voice had calmed down a notch, but the excitement and tension could still be plainly heard. "Friendship messages in all languages."

"Changing trajectory to avoid collision course," Riley announced; oddly, Ngo's excitement calmed him, made him appreciate the value of his years of experience aboard the *Enterprise.* "Maintaining shields."

"They're going to fire!" Ngo announced, clearly trying hard not to shout. He sounded like he couldn't believe it was going to happen, in spite of the fact that it was all part of the planned simulation.

"Swerving to avoid—" Riley began, but his voice was cut off by the photon blast.

He knew it was just a fraction of a real photon hit, but it still jarred the little ship badly, bouncing them all around. Each of their pressure suits immediately went into self-diagnosis, automatically checking and reporting on itself so that the wearer could be sure it was ready if the ship was suddenly breached.

"Wow! Shields are down thirty percent!" Ngo announced in amazement, then, as if realizing his unprofessional outburst, amended it with a subdued "sir." He hesitated, glancing down. "There's something wrong with my suit. I think it's the pressure. . . ."

Riley leaned over to help Ngo check out his suit diagnostics.

"No!" Anab leaned forward, her expression one of frustration and alarm. "This isn't the time or place to worry about that! Send the distress!"

Riley straightened at once. She was right of course; he shouldn't be helping Ngo, but should have taken over his duties—checking the instruments, supplementing the shields, and, more important, sending the distress signal.

But before he could do so, they were hit again, suddenly, and his awkward position caused Riley to careen forward wildly against the console, smacking his head inside the helmet hard enough to daze him. His teeth came down on his lower lip with a clack; the metallic taste of blood filled his mouth. *Damn! The distress call! The ship . . . !*

The last blast had hit the small vessel at an odd angle and sent it spiraling wildly like a poorly tossed football. Riley tried to fight the fog in his mind and reach for the controls to restabilize the ship.

Dimly, he was aware of Commander Pulver calling, "Lieutenant Saed? Commander Riley? Shall I pull you in? Transporter room, can you get a lock?"

He was aware of Anab reaching past him, grappling for the instruments. But before she could reach the control, the *Grace Hopper* suddenly slowed her out-of-control spinning, then righted herself, seemingly of her own accord. A computer-generated voice spoke.

"This is the FDRA vessel *Recovery*. We are in control of your ship. Do you require assistance?"

Before anyone could utter an affirmative, the second shuttle answered for them by firing another round of photon fire. Riley watched it emerge, a small firestar of red tumbling almost slowly their way, and automatically braced himself for it. He glanced at the board; shields were down sixty percent. Beside him, Ngo gaped, mesmerized, at the bolt of power coming their way. This one would breach the ship. Ngo's suit—

When the torpedo fragment hit, instead of being blasted, the tiny shuttle just rocked slowly, as if the powerstorm of the photon blast had somehow been absorbed.

"You are in no danger," the *Recovery* told them. "You are being protected by a projected forcefield. Your attacker is being subdued by the same technology. They will not be able to fire on you again. They will be brought aboard this ship via tractor beam until they are secured in a confined, shielded berth, where they will be safely contained until further instructions are received."

Recovery was as good as her word. Riley could see the "enemy" shuttlecraft, cocooned in a golden glow, being slowly towed toward the rescue ship.

"My sensors show your ship has sustained minor damage," *Recovery* continued, unasked, "that one of your pressure suits has a malfunction, and that one of you is injured."

Anab leaned forward. "Ngo? Are you all right?"

Ngo looked down at himself in wonder, then snapped to. "Fine, sir."

The two of them gazed at Riley. "I'm fine," he said shortly, and again tasted blood; his lip seemed twice its normal size, and he was certain his forehead was bruised. He lifted a hand to it, and lowered it sheepishly when he struck the smooth, unyielding surface of his helmet.

"Your ship will be beamed aboard so that these problems can be tended to," *Recovery* continued.

"Once you are safely aboard, your injured party can be brought to sickbay, and—"

Riley interrupted curtly, "I don't need to go to sickbay!" The realization that he had fatally erred in trying to help Ngo filled him with embarrassment. He had been trying to prove to Anab that he was a changed person, capable and unafraid; but here he was making mistakes like the greenest cadet.

"Your injuries will be tended there," the ship insisted implacably, "and the malfunctioning suit can be repaired."

Before he could protest further, Riley felt the familiar *pull* that indicated he was caught in a transporter beam. When the universe reassembled itself around him, he found himself looking out the front of the shuttlecraft into an enormous, empty hangar.

"Recovery," Riley asked, even as he opened the door of the shuttlecraft and stepped outside it, "what's wrong with Cadet Ngo's pressure suit?" He removed his helmet and dabbed at his bloody lip with his glove. If the ship could detect the problem, it could also tell them how to fix it.

"The problem is a minor malfunction," the ship announced, as Anab and Ngo debarked and stripped their own helmets. "His pressure gauge has failed. The pressure itself was always correct. A new gauge will solve the problem."

Anab frowned as she faced Ngo, and said, in a tone frostier than Riley had ever heard her use, "Any first-year student should've been able to anticipate that gauge's failure with a proper diagnostic check ahead of time. What's your explanation, mister?"

To his credit, Ngo held her gaze calmly and did not wilt. "I checked everything before we left, sir. It must have failed when we got hit."

"That faulty gauge nearly got us killed," Anab began, when Riley interrupted.

"If you want to blame someone, Lieutenant, blame me. I violated emergency procedure. I should never have taken my attention from my board."

Anab's eyes narrowed; she opened her mouth to reply when Riley felt the familiar tingle.

"Dammit, no!" He shouted at the rescue ship even as the transporter whine hummed in his ear. *"I don't want to go to sickbay!"*

Chapter Five

"I MUST ADMIT," Kirk told the *Paladin*'s bridge crew as the huge *Recovery* went through her paces, "that's pretty impressive." But belying the mildness of his voice, his head pounded with anger and embarrassment. Who the hell did Shulman think he was to dress down an *admiral*?

When no one responded, Jim realized the crew was still tense from the previous scene. He had to snap them out of this uncomfortable moment and reintegrate them as a team. He approached the Vulcan. "What do *you* think of the ship's performance, Mr. Sonak?"

The science officer stood with a most Spock-like stance, his hands clasped behind his back. It was impossible to tell that he'd just witnessed a distasteful scene rife with human emotions. Sonak was shorter, slighter of build than Spock, with a rounder face and more prominent ears; but those were not the only differences. The *Paladin*'s science officer seemed more relaxed than Spock had ever been—but Sonak, as a pure Vulcan, had never had to prove worthy of his own heritage.

"I will hold my opinion, Captain," Sonak said carefully. "At least until the scenario has run its course."

Kirk nodded. "That's playing it safe." He moved back towards the captain's chair. "Mr. Pulver?"

"It's quite an ambitious concept, isn't it, sir?" she mused, her posture as perfect and reserved as the Vulcan's. "And ambition can lead to progress—or problems."

Kirk addressed the helmsman. "Mr. Sandover?"

The navigator shrugged. "Letting *Recovery* handle evacuations will save a lot of wear and tear on the ships."

He was about to ask the resident Kirk-expert what she thought when Dr. Mola addressed both ships.

"Paladin and *Starhawk,* it's time to employ your shuttles."

Kirk glanced surreptitiously at the chrono. Everything was happening right to the minute, in spite of Shulman's display.

Pulver hit her comm button. "Transporter room, stay sharp. We might have to beam our people up at a moment's notice."

She ordered the shuttlecraft away, then all they could do was watch as the little ship was battered by a shuttlecraft from the *Starhawk.* As the second shot sent the small craft into a spin, Pulver quickly asked if they needed transporting.

When *Recovery* finally grabbed hold of the vessel, Kirk let out the breath he'd been holding with a whoosh. The *Grace Hopper* stopped its sickening tumble, stabilized, then dematerialized in a familiar transporter shimmer. Kirk applauded politely, pleased when the bridge crew joined in his congratulatory gesture.

"Well," he said brightly, glancing at the chrono, "neither our work nor *Recovery*'s is over yet. Can someone give me Captain Romolo's plan for the robot drone attack?"

"It's here, sir," Diksen said, handing him a pad and stylus. He noted Pulver eyeing him curiously as he mulled over Romolo's design. The small, aggressive war-game drones would harass the big ship during the evacuation to test her response.

Glancing at the screen, Jim thought of the irony of that. There sat the representatives of the most hostile forces the Federation had ever faced. These tiny drones could hardly simulate the cleverness of a cloaked Romulan vessel, the aggression of a Klingon warship, or the mechanical entrapment of a Tholian web.

But the drones were all they had, so they would have to do. He glanced again at Romolo's pattern, and started to smile as inspiration struck. He picked up the stylus and began to manipulate the program.

"Mr. Pulver," he said as he worked, "I'm making changes in the attack pattern. I'd appreciate it if you'd rearrange your command sequence so that I can have more direct control of the drones."

When her answer was long in coming, he glanced up to see her gazing at him, her blue eyes and porcelain-pale face composed in an expression of cold disapproval beneath a smooth cap of copper hair. "Excuse me, Admiral," she said stiffly, "but isn't that somewhat irregular?"

Before Kirk could respond, Sonak turned in his chair, his expression mildly perplexed. "I would like to remind the admiral that the drones are capable of remembering hundreds of preplanned patterns and using them in the way that gives them the best chances of survival."

In reply, Kirk fixed both officers with a cool look.

Two beats passed; at last, Pulver backed down, her tone reluctant. "Aye, sir. Rearranging command sequence. Drones will be at your command through the engineering station."

"Thank you," Kirk said graciously, ignoring Reese Diksen's bemused expression. "Mr. Pulver, Mr. Sonak—your opinions *are* appreciated." As the first officer moved over to the vacant engineering station, Kirk fine-tuned his program, then signaled her. "Release seventy drones, Commander."

The navigator turned to him and started to remind Kirk that he was supposed to release a hundred, but before he could, Jim murmured, "There are no rules in warfare, mister."

With a soft sigh of disapproval, Pulver tapped her comm, relaying Kirk's command. He watched avidly as the small army of drones left the ship—just seventy of them. The *Starhawk* released her cloud of one hundred identical passive soldiers at the same time. As the two groups met, they resembled a swarm of angry bees floating through space, hovering around the big vessel.

Abruptly, one of Jim's drones fired on the ship, immediately ducking behind an "innocent" bystander. Then another drone fired, again ducking behind a cluster of innocents, then another and another. Now two fired at once, then three.

The ship took the pounding for several moments before she finally took action. Using a reverse, narrow-focused tractor beam, the rescue ship "shoved" the innocent drones out of the way, then fired upon the instigators taking refuge behind them.

Again and again, she nudged the covering, innocent

robots out of the line of fire and destroyed the chivying satellites. Her accuracy was unerring, never once injuring any innocent drones.

Kirk enjoyed himself immensely as he worked the board. He increased the drones' speed, number of hits, and evasive maneuvers, but *Recovery* seemed up to the challenge. It made him wonder if he had been wrong about the ship's need for weapons. Or maybe Mola was right; maybe he just hated seeing something that could do the job better than a starship and her captain.

Finally, over twenty of his drones had been nullified. The aggressive robots' distinctive movements must have revealed their identities because, suddenly, the great ship beamed her attackers into a waiting bay as a group, leaving the others untouched.

"Now, that would be a novel way of dealing with a Romulan Bird-of-Prey," Kirk commented, amused. "Simply beam her aboard."

Sonak raised an eyebrow. "It would certainly be a more pacifistic technique."

At the sound of a small "hmmpff" emanating from communications, he turned to face the cadet there. "You don't agree, Mr. Diksen?"

Her dark brown hair was cut short, revealing the entire sweep of her pale neck—and the tips of her ears, which to his secret amusement colored brilliant red, the way they had when Romolo had introduced her to him. Hesitantly, she said, "It's just—" Her gaze went beyond him to the screen, and focused on *Recovery*'s vast bulk. "Look at them." She pointed at the three observer ships, floating in triangular formation at the top of the screen. "They're watching this, too. To them, this makes us look weak."

"In what way?"

"While we're struggling to perfect this rescue ship,

93

they're pouring all their efforts into aggressive war technology. How does this research help us in dealing with them?"

Before Kirk could respond, Sonak interjected. "As we speak, Ambassador Sarek sits on the *Starhawk* communicating with those same hostile forces in an unprecedented bid for mutual understanding. If the *Recovery* accomplishes nothing else, her existence has provided this single moment of cooperation."

How Spock would have agreed.

Diksen shook her head. "Is that why Starfleet exists? To become a perpetual, passive do-gooder? That's not why I joined."

The cold statement traveled down Kirk's spine like ice. "Why *did* you join, Diksen?" he asked, in a tone so quiet it immediately caught everyone's attention. "For the action? For the chance to prove yourself in combat? Have you ever seen combat, especially combat in space?"

She did not answer, only shook her head slightly.

"Do you have any idea how quickly an organic life-form can die in space? An exploding computer station can cripple or kill in less than a second. Have you ever heard the shrieks and screams of the wounded and dying, ever been there when life-support fails? There's nothing but the crushing reality of a vacuum—a place where life can't exist."

He gazed back at the enormous bulk of *Recovery* surrounded by a cluster of passive robots, a hundred shining metal gems bejeweling her dark body. "No flash. No drama. Nothing but over two hundred lives saved in less time—far less time—than either of these two starships could've done it. And time, in any life-threatening emergency, is ultimately the most critical factor."

He paused, his recitation bringing back too many raw memories. "Trust me, Diksen. The Federation spends plenty on the dogs of war. I pray you never see any *real* action." He suddenly felt the real weight of his loss for the first time since he'd left the *Enterprise*. That feeling—what had Riley called it?—the *responsibility* for the ship, for her people.

He sighed just as the screen shifted, the right side now showing the auditorium where Dr. Shulman again stood at his podium. The researcher was smiling once more, talking about the success of the simulation.

A sudden notion seized Kirk; he turned toward communications. "Make sure they can't hear us, will you, Mr. Diksen?"

Diksen caught Pulver's eye. The first officer, who still seemed to be smarting faintly from Kirk's intervention with the simulation, directed a single, curt nod at the cadet.

"Aye, sir," Diksen replied, and muted their channel.

"Mr. Sonak," Kirk said, "I want control of those passive drones. Can you get it for me?"

For a beat, no one replied. With the defeat of the warrior drones, the planned simulation was officially over. The remaining drones still out there were not *Paladin*'s, but *Starhawk*'s. Even so, Sonak must have remembered Kirk's earlier statement about the lack of rules in warfare, for he finally said, "I believe I can handle that, sir."

Kirk turned to Pulver. "Release the last thirty drones."

"The *Starhawk*'s drones will now respond to your commands, Admiral," Sonak assured him. Kirk fancied the Vulcan's tone sounded faintly smug.

"A few new firing patterns, Mr. Sonak," Kirk told him, as he finished his work. "A few surprises. Enter new patterns, *now.*" The pattern was one Kirk had been victimized by in an encounter with terrorists in the Xenia system; as he watched the kaleidoscoping design of weapons fire from the rapidly moving, interweaving drones, the memory of that attack surfaced with painful intensity. The *Enterprise* had been nearly torn apart that day. If it hadn't been for Spock—

As Kirk pulled his attention back to the split viewscreen, he could tell that the *Recovery* was taking too long to analyze the firing pattern of the drones. She kept turning this way and that, but the ever-changing patterns of chivying robots clung to her like fleas, first under her belly, then over her flanks. So far, she'd been unable to make even one direct hit. Kirk was not at all pleased, and rather surprised. Or was this response more typical of an attack that hadn't been planned?

On the right side of the screen, Shulman stared agape at the unexpected attack. "This is *your* doing!" he shouted at the admiral.

Jim shrugged, not at all sheepish. "I confess, Doctor. You've caught me red-handed."

"You're *cheating,* damn you, Kirk! Call off those drones."

The admiral stiffened at the escalating fury in the other man's tone. "Sorry, Shulman, I still had soldiers at my call. Your ship is here to be tested. Do you think that the only tests she should endure are those you prearrange?"

The *Recovery* had finally begun her response, but it was inexplicably slower than the last. Instead of a swift reprisal, she fired randomly, striking only one out of three targets.

"Commander Pulver," Sonak said with a faint hint of surprise in his tone, *"Recovery* seems unable to determine innocent drones from aggressive ones now that the admiral controls them all."

Pulver glanced over at Kirk with an expression of

concern, faintly laced with accusation, yet she remained silent. Kirk himself could think of nothing to say; he had never believed that *Recovery* could exercise the kind of judgment necessary during an attack without a militarily sophisticated commander at her helm. But he found no joy in seeing his fears realized.

"Looks like you're having some trouble with your defense systems, Dr. Shulman," he said at last, with quiet regret. "It's one thing to set up a response pattern when you anticipate an attack, but those of us who work in space"—he almost hesitated at that moment, but caught himself—"are aware that's a luxury we rarely have."

"You've planned this all along, Kirk, planned to destroy this ship!" Shulman screamed, spittle spraying from his lips.

Jim recoiled, shocked to silence by the intensity of the scientist's fury.

"I knew you would never be satisfied until you'd made sure *Recovery* did not survive her simulation," Shulman raged, flailing his lean arms. "I knew it, and made sure *she* knew it, too!"

"Commander." Sonak's voice cut through Shulman's ranting. "The *Recovery* has just destroyed every drone surrounding her."

In the captain's chair, Pulver straightened, and it seemed every member of the bridge crew tensed along with her. Glancing briefly at Kirk, she turned to the science officer. "Every one?"

"Even the innocents," the Vulcan confirmed. "She is now analyzing their behavior—determining who was responsible—"

Kirk moved out of his seat to make a suggestion.

Sonak, bent over his science screen, suddenly sat bolt upright in his chair, then whipped his head around to face Pulver. "Commander . . . !" he called.

Kirk needed no other warning. It didn't matter that

the scenario was impossible, that the *Recovery* was a vessel of peace, designed to rescue the helpless. *"Shields up!"* he shouted, no longer concerned about protocol or Pulver's feelings. "Shields up! Red alert! Battle stations, everyone . . . !"

He could hear Pulver parroting him in her clipped, precise accent over the captain's comm. As the klaxons sounded, the bridge crew rushed into action like a well-practiced machine.

Kirk clung to the back of his chair, and managed to stay on his feet; he could sense, from the feel and direction of the blast, even before Diksen called out the damage reports, that *Recovery*'s phaser fire hit them broadside near the lower decks, where the *Paladin*'s shields were the weakest—dangerously close to Engineering. The bridge rocked wildly, but quickly stabilized.

"She can analyze our vulnerabilities," Kirk shouted to Pulver, "so fortify those shields! Keep the strongest part between the two ships."

The commander snapped out orders that followed Kirk's recommendations exactly as he wanted, her cool tones the perfect response to the organized chaos of the bridge.

Kirk charged up to the viewscreen "Shulman! What have you done? What the hell did you mean—'she knew it'?"

Before the wild-eyed doctor could respond, Diksen's strained voice called out, "Commander! We're being hailed by the *Starhawk.*"

"On screen," Pulver ordered.

Shulman's side of the screen was replaced by Captain Akhmatova at her conn. Beside her stood a worried-looking Captain Romolo. "Admiral Kirk," she said, "what's *Paladin*'s status?"

On the opposite side of the screen, Kirk could see *Recovery* hurl another volley of phaser fire at the

Paladin's shields. The ship rocked harder and he nearly lost his footing, but once more, she stabilized. He could hear Pulver and Diksen sorting out damage reports.

"Uncertain," he told Akhmatova. "We're weak in our aft shields, but we haven't had time for damage assessment."

"I need to be there with you, Admiral," Romolo insisted, his green eyes narrowed with concern beneath thick, golden brows.

"Can't drop our shields now, Captain," Kirk reminded him. It was true, despite the exhilaration he felt at being in command—*almost command,* he thought, with a guilty glance back at Pulver. But he had no desire to keep Baldassare from his own bridge at such a critical time.

Akhmatova leaned forward to address her navigator. "Move us between the *Recovery* and the *Paladin.* She won't fire on us; we've been neutral through the entire simulation."

Instinctively, Kirk warned, "No, don't!," but it was too late. The *Starhawk*'s navigator obeyed his captain and moved the starship into *Recovery*'s line of fire.

"It is a logical move, sir," Sonak advised Kirk over the din on the bridge. "The rescue ship has no motivation for perceiving a threat from the *Starhawk.*"

Logic be damned, Kirk thought with frustration. *That move is all* wrong. He opened his mouth to protest, but before he could, the *Recovery* spun about and fired a photon torpedo at the unshielded *Starhawk.*

On the right side of the viewscreen, the bridge of the innocent ship erupted in flames—then faded into darkness like an extinguished candle.

Kirk wheeled toward Pulver. "Can we extend our shields to cover the *Starhawk?*"

She hesitated; for the first time, she seemed less than totally collected. "It will weaken them, sir—"

He wasted no time arguing with her. "Mr. Sandover, extend shields to protect the *Starhawk!*"

His freckled face pale but composed, the navigator glanced over his shoulder at Pulver, who sat, her eyes narrowed at Kirk. For a split second, no more, he wavered, then caught sight of the admiral, who met him with a determined stare. "Aye, Admiral. Extending shields . . ."

The viewscreen image of *Starhawk's* bridge was replaced by a view of her hull, suspended in a golden aura as the two Federation ships, dangerously close to one another, shared one shield. Another photon struck the wounded ship, then another in rapid-fire volley. Even under shielding, the *Starhawk* was racked by the blows.

Paladin's bridge shuddered violently under *Starhawk's* beating, telling Kirk that the extended shields were spread too thin. He staggered over to navigation, where he could see the readouts that confirmed his worst suspicions.

"Logic has nothing to do with this, Mr. Sonak," Kirk shouted, then turned again to Sandover. "Hard about, helm, and fire on my order."

Pulver came to herself. "Fire, Admiral? On the *Recovery?* But our people are over there!"

His carrot-colored eyebrows knit together in confusion, Sandover swiveled to face first her, then Kirk. The admiral straightened to his full height and met the first officer's stare with a stoniness that matched hers.

"As they are on the *Starhawk* and the *Paladin,* Commander."

"With all due respect, Admiral . . ." Her tone grew even more clipped and disapproving. "I must protest."

"Protest noted," Kirk said swiftly; there was no time to waste arguing over who had command. Without taking his gaze from Pulver's, he ordered, "Mr. Sandover! You heard me: Prepare to fire!"

A tense second passed—one in which Kirk could almost palpably feel the shift of power; and then Sandover said softly, "Yes, sir."

"Full phasers!" Kirk demanded, in a voice that brooked no argument. "Fire, now, then hard about. Keep those shields extended, at full power!"

"Aye, aye, Admiral. Firing now."

The crew watched the viewscreen breathlessly as the dazzling golden blast streaked through the darkness toward the massive rescue ship. *Recovery* took the blow better than Kirk had dared hope, but the confused and frightened scientists in her auditorium swayed under the powerful blows.

The attack accomplished his goal: It gave *Starhawk* time to move behind *Paladin*. She still had no shields of her own, and Kirk feared that first direct hit might have knocked them out. How long could they protect her?

"Admiral," Pulver said, with an icy calm that signaled both her capitulation and resentment, "we need to get both vessels out of range quickly."

He nodded. "Go to the engineering station and guide the helm. You'll need to watch the sensors closely, make sure we don't hit." She moved away promptly and he started to follow to add something to his directions when Sonak called out.

"Admiral, *Recovery* is arming phasers—"

Sandover at navigation shouted, "Shields are weakening. Down to sixty percent—"

Kirk halted. "Deflect power from the warp engines to strengthen those shields!"

From engineering, Pulver called, *"Starhawk* is moving away from us faster than we can safely catch up.

It's taxing the shields." Her hands flew over the board, trying to make adjustments.

With preternatural calm, Sonak announced, *"Recovery is firing phasers and photons—"*

The deck beneath Kirk's boots lurched—again. Again. For a full second, the bridge lost gravity; he felt the odd sensation of lightness as his feet began to lose contact with the deck . . .

And then gravity returned, slamming him down. He rolled, easing the impact, and managed to regain his footing just as a rain of sparks erupted to his right. He raised an arm, shielding his eyes from the dazzling blast, his face from the rain of debris—then lowered it to see that the engineering station had overloaded, exploding up and out, as though a malevolent genie had burst from its interior.

Backlit by the brilliant orange-red of the flaming console, Pulver's dark form dropped backward with terrible, limp grace.

Sonak bolted from his seat, but Kirk got to her first and cradled her head in his lap as the Vulcan crouched nearby. Her pale, delicate features were unrecognizable: singed with soot, peppered with shards of shrapnel, spattered with bright blood that jetted from her throat onto her auburn hair, Kirk's sleeves, the legs of his trousers. He pressed his fingers to the spurting artery in a frantic effort to stanch the flow, even as he tried to gauge the extent of her chest wounds—a task made impossible by the amount of blood.

"Sickbay!" Diksen called, in a voice that came close to breaking. "Medics to the bridge—stat!"

Behind them, the fireglow dimmed as the ship extinguished the flames, blessedly throwing Pulver's stunned, scorched visage in shadow. Kirk listened, his heart sinking at sickbay's reply:

"Administer whatever first aid you can manage.

We'll get someone up there as soon as we can . . . we're swamped with emergencies down here!"

Pulver stared at Kirk and Sonak, her pale blue eyes wide with shock. "The ship," she gasped, reaching out blindly and catching hold of Sonak's sleeve. "The ship . . . !" She broke off with a strangled gurgling sound and coughed; blood sprayed from her lips as her arm dropped weakly by her side.

The Vulcan shot a darkly meaningful glance at Kirk, who understood: Sonak must have gotten a brief, telepathic sense of her condition as her hand brushed his arm. Kirk had seen the same look in Spock's eyes more than he cared to remember. Pulver was dying.

"Sonak, return to your station," Kirk ordered the Vulcan with a tone of soft regret. "We've got to know if *Recovery—*"

"Understood, sir." With a final, frankly concerned glance at Pulver, the science officer rose, leaving Kirk with his charge.

"The ship!" Pulver demanded again, crimson froth bubbling from between her lips; she flailed feebly again, and this time grasped Kirk's arm. Her eyes suddenly cleared, and focused, fierce and horribly lucid, on the admiral's. "The ship, Kirk—!"

"I'm here, Commander. I'll take good care of your ship," he promised solemnly. "As good a care as you took." Her gaze remained on him, intent, demanding, full of suffering. "You did everything you could. . . ."

The surging blood under his fingers subsided, then stopped, as the frantic demand in Commander Ruth Pulver's blue eyes faded to an open-eyed endless stare. The body in his arms relaxed with a gurgling sigh; gently, he eased it back to the deck, aware of the stricken gazes of the bridge crew.

He rose, wiping Pulver's blood from his hands onto

his soaked uniform, and drew a slow, shuddering breath, clearing his mind of everything except those thoughts necessary for survival. Whatever it took, he would keep his promise to the *Paladin*'s first officer.

Fortunately, *Recovery* had not fired again. The image of the wounded *Starhawk* on *Paladin*'s viewscreen was abruptly replaced by Myron Shulman, who shrieked, with a madman's wide-eyed hysteria, "You'll pay for this, Kirk! You've deliberately sabotaged this simulation. You'll pay!"

I'LL pay? Kirk thought bitterly, clenching his bloody hand. "Why, Shulman? Just tell me *why?!*"

Dr. Mola and Dr. Noon tried to pull the agitated scientist away from the podium, and futilely attempted to calm him, but Shulman pulled free of them and raced away. The scene blinked off, leaving the entire viewscreen filled with *Recovery*'s huge, ominous bulk.

Kirk glanced up at the three enemy ships, hovering in triangular formation nearby. What must they be thinking? If *Recovery* turned on them—

As if the aberrant vessel had read his mind, she turned ominously in the direction of the three observers.

"Admiral," Sonak said in a voice absurdly calm, as if the universe hadn't just tipped on its edge, as if his commander were not lying dead on the bridge, *"Recovery* is analyzing the presence, the weaponry, and the strength of the three non-Federation vessels."

"Diksen, warn those ships!" Kirk ordered instantly, snapping out of his morbid reverie. "Tell them to power up their shields, to get the hell out of there—"

"Admiral," Sonak announced heavily, even as Diksen scrambled to obey Kirk's command and the viewscreen filled with a blinding flash. "It is too late. *Recovery* has just fired on the Romulan vessel."

* * *

Minutes earlier aboard the *Starhawk*'s bridge, Ambassador Sarek stood to the left of the captain's chair and watched, outwardly impassive, inwardly astonished, as *Recovery* fired broadside on the *Paladin*.

Fortunately, the blast was reflected by *Paladin*'s shields without causing much harm. But the tension —among the human crew—on *Starhawk*'s bridge did not abate.

"Good God!" Captain Romolo, who stood at Akhmatova's right elbow, exclaimed. "What in blazes is that thing *doing* firing on my ship?"

Unruffled, Akhmatova watched the viewscreen with the intensity of a lioness sizing up her prey—she would have made a credible Vulcan, Sarek thought approvingly—then swiveled toward her communications officer. "Open a channel to the *Paladin.*"

Almost immediately, James Kirk's face appeared on the viewscreen—just as the bridge he was on shuddered from the impact of another blow.

But *Paladin* managed to weather the blast.

"Admiral Kirk, what's your status?"

"Uncertain," Kirk said swiftly. "We haven't had time for assessment."

Romolo took a step toward the screen, his voice full of frustration. "I need to be there with you, Admiral. . . ."

"Can't drop our shields right now, Captain."

Akhmatova addressed her navigator. "Move us between the *Recovery* and the *Paladin.*" In reply to the sudden dismay on Kirk's face, she said, "She won't fire on us; we've been neutral through the entire simulation—"

"No, don't!" Kirk ordered over her words.

Sarek witnessed the exchange with a calm sense of fatalism; he had heard of the human's legendary instinct in critical situations—and had heard from his son that the admiral's judgment in such situations generally proved correct.

Yet it was too late; the navigator moved quickly in response to the captain's command, and Sarek sensed the *Starhawk* moving.

And in a blinding millisecond, there came a tremendous roar, as if Sarek's cortex had erupted in thunder. He was lifted from his feet and slammed against something—the deck, a console; impossible to judge in the blind chaos that followed.

He lay stunned for a disoriented second, then opened his eyes to brilliant green. He wiped his eyes, and stared, uncomprehending, at the blood on his hand until he realized that his forehead was bleeding. He soaked it up as best he could with a sleeve, then looked again.

The bridge itself was red; smoldering red, from the fires blazing on the consoles, and hazy with smoke.

"Secondary-hull breach," the computer intoned overhead. "Temporary forcefield is in effect. Please commence repairs as soon as possible."

Sarek took a deep breath, coughed, then repressed a wince at the stab of pain in his side. Inconvenient, but not fatal; a quick internal assessment suggested broken ribs, one of which had slightly punctured a lung. There would be sufficient time to deal with it—and the pain—later. He pushed himself to his knees, then squinted through the haze at Captain Akhmatova's chair.

Empty.

"Captain?" he called hoarsely. It seemed logical to raise the ship's shields as quickly as possible—but none of the human crew appeared to be at their stations.

No reply. The ship lurched again, hard, throwing Sarek once more against the deck.

"Emergency!" the computer called. "Primary-hull

breach. Emergency forcefields are in place. Commence evacuation immediately. Five minutes of life-support available."

"Captain!" Sarek called again. "Captain Akhmatova!"

A figure appeared out of the haze; not Akhmatova, but her first officer, Commander Marsten. Marsten's pale face was bruised and contorted in frank pain; he clutched his thigh as he staggered over the navigator's motionless body to the unmanned console, and dragged himself up into the chair. Sarek watched as the human worked the console with life-or-death urgency.

"Shields up," Marsten croaked.

The third blast came no more than a second later. This time, Sarek was able to ride it through by grabbing the side of the console. The shields held.

"We've lost warp power," Marsten said, as though reporting to his captain. "Impulse functional." He worked a few more controls, then sagged back in the chair with a hitching sigh. "We're out of range."

And then Marsten turned and Sarek turned at the sound of soft coughing and movement. The first officer punched a control on the helm comm grid. "Sickbay! Get medics up to the bridge, stat! We've got a hull breach and wounded up here!"

Seconds passed before the response came, and then: "Bridge! We've got an emergency down here, too! Science and medical labs are badly damaged. We've got wounded trapped. Everyone who isn't injured is working to dig the injured from the rubble. We don't have enough personnel . . ."

As he listened, Sarek glanced up at the viewscreen, just in time to see *Recovery* turn to face the Romulan, Klingon, and Tholian vessels.

If *Recovery* fired on the unshielded observers, the incident could easily detonate an interstellar war.

Sarek moved swiftly over to the communications station. The officer there lay slumped on the deck beneath the console; Sarek carefully stepped around him and, after a few false starts, intuited how the board functioned. He at once opened a channel to one of the observer ships.

"Romulan vessel! Raise your shields immediately and move out of *Recovery*'s firing range! She is malfunctioning. . . ."

As he spoke, the glare from the viewscreen captured his gaze. He peered through the smoke at the screen, just as a brilliant phaser beam streaked from *Recovery* toward the Romulan ship, and seared her bow.

Sarek closed his eyes at the sound of screams coming from the Romulan bridge; and then all was silence as the comm link dissolved. He tried once more to reestablish, without success. On the screen, the wounded vessel drifted, defenseless.

Again, he attempted to open a channel, this time to a different observer ship.

"Tholian vessel! This is Ambassador Sarek aboard the *Starhawk* . . ."

But there was no reply. "Tholian vessel—" Sarek began again, but Marsten swiveled toward him.

"They're not there anymore, Ambassador."

"Destroyed?" Sarek asked, detecting a trace of heaviness in his own tone.

"Hard to tell." Marsten squinted at his console. "I'm picking up some debris. Could just be from the Romulan ship, but the Tholian vessels are so small, they might have been—"

He lifted his hand to shield his eyes from another blinding flash on the viewscreen. Sarek forced himself not to look away from the unsettling sight of *Recovery* firing on the Klingon Bird-of-Prey.

Sarek initiated another signal with inhuman speed,

taking his gaze from the screen only long enough to work the controls. "Klingon vessel! Respond!"

As he and Marsten watched, the Bird-of-Prey's image wavered, then vanished smoothly into nothingness, replaced by stars and darkness. The blast dispersed into a wide field, then dissolved.

"They're all right," Marsten said tersely, glancing up from his console. "They must have cloaked—"

"Klingon vessel!" Sarek demanded. "If you can hear, respond. *Recovery* has attacked her own vessels. Take yourself to safety and allow the Federation the honor of avenging what has happened here. *Recovery* is our ship; we must destroy her ourselves, and deal with whoever is responsible for this sabotage. . . ."

No response.

"I doubt they're listening, Ambassador." Marsten's tone was glum.

"Two minutes of life-support remaining," the computer warned.

Marsten rose, his balance wobbly, and grimaced as he clutched his wounded thigh, where a dark red stain was spreading. "Come on, Ambassador. Help me get the wounded out of here."

Sarek hesitated for a millisecond, no more. The diplomatic situation was critical; if he failed in the next moment to convince the Tholians, Klingons, and Romulans that *Recovery*'s attack was not intentional, that failure could lead to a war that would cost billions of lives.

Yet there seemed to be nothing at the moment he could do for those potential billions—only for those few lying wounded on the *Starhawk*'s bridge.

He looked down to see the communications officer pulling himself up. He proffered a hand; the human seemed shaken, bruised, but otherwise unharmed. Sarek motioned him toward the lift, then made his way through the eye-stinging haze to Akhmatova's still form. She lay facedown between the command chair and the helm, her arms tangled with Romolo's. Apparently, she had freed herself from the command chair's passive restraints and tried to catch the other captain.

The Vulcan gently turned her over. She was bleeding profusely down the left side of her face and neck. Seeking the source, he swept away salt-and-pepper hair, sticky and stained crimson, at her temple—until he found the deep gouge there that revealed splintered bone and whitish-gray matter.

Impossible for her to be alive; but she was breathing —barely—and he managed to find a weak, thready pulse. Carefully, he scooped her up, mentally dismissing the insult to his ribs, and carried her toward the lift, and Marsten's waiting arms.

And then he hurried back into the thickening smoke, in search of survivors.

He found the dead navigator, whose neck had been snapped. Only Romolo was still alive. Like Akhmatova, he was unconscious, but his breath came in hitching, gurgling gasps. He lay on his back, the chest of his uniform soaked with blood; a piece of shrapnel had apparently struck him in a lung.

"One minute before life-support systems fail," the computer announced. A klaxon began blasting Sarek's eardrums. Ignoring the pain in his ribs, he hoisted Romolo into his arms and staggered to the safety of the lift.

The lift doors closed over the blaring, smoky chaos that had been the bridge. Sarek released a slow breath and permitted himself to settle against the cool metal wall, thinking not of the destruction surrounding him, but of the destruction that might come. . . .

Chapter Six

McCOY WAS ALMOST HAPPY to be in the primary sickbay. It was a beautiful facility, and only one of the many aboard the massive vessel. He observed as the ship diagnosed and recommended treatment for the four scientists who'd been beamed here for medical treatment, then, after they'd been released, wandered over to where one of the security officers had been brought after being bounced around in the shuttlecraft.

Hell of a way to earn a living, he thought as he approached the diagnostic bed. Well, perhaps he could help. He was surprised to see that the reluctant patient was someone he knew.

"Riley . . . ?"

The officer looked the same as he had during his youthful *Enterprise* days—except, of course, for the light brown beard, stained now with a small trickle of blood from his swollen bottom lip. At the sight of

McCoy, Riley flashed a grin—then grimaced and gingerly fingered the offending lip.

"Dr. McCoy! I almost didn't recognize you with the beard."

McCoy stroked it proudly. "Just following your lead."

Riley managed another pained grin. "Good to see you, sir! What are you doing here?"

"Observing! Something old, retired doctors get to do a lot of, it seems. Keeps us from feeling totally useless." McCoy returned Riley's smile, surprised at how good it felt to see an old fellow crewmate again. "I might ask you the same. Was that you that got hurt aboard that shuttlecraft?"

"I'm *fine.*" Riley lifted a hand to his bruised forehead and winced.

Recovery, it seemed, did not share his opinion. "The patient has a mild concussion," the computer insisted, sounding almost peevish, "and an oral laceration. However, the patient refuses reasonable treatment. . . ."

Riley groaned in pure annoyance.

McCoy couldn't help but chuckle. "Now, this here is a *serious* facility, Mr. Riley. Half sickbay, half brig. How 'bout if I just participate a little here—I don't think it'll ruin my 'observer' status too much." He picked up a cell regenerator and a Simpkins cranial device. "Now, just hold still."

Riley sighed and obeyed. McCoy attached the tiny cranial stimulator to the area of his head that had received the blow and left it there to neutralize the damage of the concussion, while he waved the cell regenerator over the nasty cut on his lip.

After a few moments of attention, McCoy addressed the ship. "How's that, computer? Will the patient live?"

"The patient's life was never in danger," the ship replied humorlessly.

"Well, we'll grant you that," McCoy grumbled. "Can he leave now?"

"The patient has recovered sufficiently to retire to his assigned quarters."

"See?" the doctor told him. "You just gotta know how to deal with these machines."

"You're a lifesaver, Doc," Riley admitted, getting off the diagnostic bed.

"Not according to *Recovery*." McCoy smiled. "So, Riley . . . you never said what you were doing on the shuttlecraft."

"I came with Admiral Kirk to monitor the simulation. And I . . . volunteered to do a little active testing of *Recovery*'s capabilities." As though they had mutually agreed on it, they both left sickbay and began wandering down the ship's curving corridors. McCoy imagined Riley wanted to get reunited with the shuttlecraft crew.

"A little more exciting than you bargained for, especially after a driving a desk for a few years, eh?" McCoy asked, and when Riley replied with a wry grin, continued: "So, tell me . . . how is Jim?"

"He's well," Riley said carefully; his tone made McCoy think he was debating whether or not to say more.

"That's good." McCoy paused for a few strides. "Look, Riley, I'm sure you heard about that day I went to headquarters and had a little . . . disagreement with Nogura. I'm sorry for any embarrassment I caused Jim."

A small smile settled over Riley's boyish features. "I'm sure he understood, Doctor. You were only doing what you thought best."

"Damn straight," McCoy said. "Jim was my closest

friend." He came to an abrupt halt and faced the younger man. "Tell me, Riley . . . is he happy with what he's doing? Nogura being good to him?"

Riley's gaze fastened on a far-distant point in front of them; his expression grew opaque, unreadable. "He . . . he's done an outstanding job in the admiralty. Nogura's very pleased with his performance."

"I didn't ask that. I asked whether he was *happy.*"

Riley shrugged and dropped the mask; the corner of his lip quirked wryly. "I can't say, Doctor." He sighed. "I think he's . . . restless. Looking for alternatives . . ."

"I knew it!" McCoy said, with a burst of passionate anger. "The man belongs on a starship, but Nogura's too damned stubborn to admit it. I hope Jim's at least coming to his senses."

Riley inclined his head and parted his lips to answer—but his words were drowned out by the sudden blare of a klaxon. The deck beneath McCoy's feet dropped out from under him, causing him to hurtle downward and into Riley.

"All hands clear the corridors," the computer droned over the klaxon's wail, "and report to your quarters for safety."

Dazed, McCoy clambered to his feet, leaning against Riley for support, each man steadying the other shakily.

"You all right?" they asked each other simultaneously, even as they tried to stabilize their footing.

Before either could reply, frantic shouts emanated from the far corridor.

McCoy turned in the direction of the approaching yells. It was all happening too fast; one minute the deck was heaving, the next Myron Shulman was pounding down the corridor toward them, outdistancing a slew of pursuers.

"Dr. Shulman, stop! *Stop!*"

McCoy at once recognized Angelina Mola's voice.

"Grab him, somebody! Don't let him get away!" a male voice admonished.

Confused, McCoy stepped into Shulman's path, prepared to reason with him.

"Doctor, don't!" Riley shouted over the klaxons and moved to block him. Then the deck shuddered again, and they all landed on the floor in a chaotic heap.

Are we being fired upon? McCoy thought incredulously. Had the Klingons, Romulans, or Tholians taken advantage of this situation somehow and begun an attack?

Shulman and Riley made it to their feet at the same time.

"Don't move, Dr. Shulman," he warned, his tone dangerous, but his eyes bright with fear. "I don't want to use force. . . ."

Shulman swung with a madman's power, but Riley somehow managed to block the blow, and the next. But Shulman's third blow landed right on the commander's mouth, on the freshly healed split lip. Bright blood burst forth, trickling down into his beard; Riley reeled, his head bouncing against the nearby bulkhead. McCoy moaned in sympathy with him.

Before he had a chance to help, Shulman was free, racing away down the endless corridors. The other scientists caught up to McCoy and Riley, then passed them in pursuit of Shulman. Even as they passed him, the computer repeatedly insisted that everyone clear the halls and retire to their quarters.

Like a scene from *Alice in Wonderland,* McCoy thought crazily. He grabbed Angelina's upper arms as she ran by and forced her to stop.

"What the hell's going on here, Angie?"

"Shulman's gone completely paranoid," she explained, gasping for breath, "and it's as if the ship has gone mad with him."

"What are you talking about?"

She rested a thin, dark hand on her heart. *"Recovery* attacked the *Paladin,* the ship Kirk was commanding. He was running an unplanned scenario and Shulman got furious—and the next thing we knew, *Recovery* attacked—well, it looked as if she attacked *Kirk.* I know it doesn't make any sense. We think Myron's done something to the programming. *Recovery's* attacking anything that moves near her—she's hit the *Paladin,* the *Starhawk,* and the Romulan vessel, and almost hit the Klingon ship. We think the Tholians got away before it was too late."

McCoy's eyes widened. "Wait a minute— Klingons? Romulans? *Tholians?* Good Lord . . ."

She closed her eyes and released a slow breath, clearly realizing what she had just revealed; and then she opened them again, and steadily held the doctor's gaze. "I forgot myself in the excitement, Leonard. But I know I can trust you—"

"Of course you can, Angie," McCoy interrupted hastily, "but let's get one thing straight. You mean that the Klingons, Romulans, and Tholians all came to watch this simulation—and *Recovery* hit them . . . in an *unprovoked attack?"*

Angelina nodded as McCoy raised a hand to his forehead and groaned. "We've got to get Myron under control," she said, her normally calm tone rising with panic, "get him medicated, and find out how to take control of this ship, before—before there's an interstellar war! Leonard, try to communicate with the other ships. Tell them it was an accident. Tell them we need help!"

She pulled free from McCoy's grip and went tearing

down the hall after the other scientists who were still pursuing Shulman, and soon disappeared from sight.

McCoy said nothing as he helped Riley to his feet, just tried not to think of Jim on his injured vessel.

Riley voiced the concern they both shared. "The *Paladin* was attacked? Was anyone hurt? Admiral Kirk is on that ship. . . ."

"I don't know," McCoy said heavily. "But we've got to get you back to sickbay."

Riley touched the back of his hand to his lip, stared at the blood there, and made a sound of disgust. "Someone's got to stop Shulman."

"There's no point chasing him," McCoy assured him. "He can't go anywhere. Let's treat your head and lip—again!—then we'll get you connected to your crew."

Riley nodded. "Anab—that is, Lieutenant Saed" —a look passed over his face that McCoy could not decipher—"is with me. She's Security, and a little better equipped to find and secure Shulman than a bunch of theoretical scientists."

As soon as he got Riley settled on the same diagnostic couch he'd just left, McCoy instructed him on how to use the devices to treat himself. While he was occupied with that, the doctor moved to a nearby computer screen. Would the ship answer his requests now? All he could do was try.

"Computer," he said, in as calm a voice as he could muster.

The screen came to life. "How can I assist you?"

"Give me an open channel to any Federation vessel within range."

"Your channel is open and your message will be broadcast, but there are no Federation ships within range to see or hear your message. The only vessels within range are classified as enemy ships."

What is she talking about? McCoy wondered, confused. *Sure, the Romulans and others are out there, but the* Starhawk *and* Paladin *are both within range.*

"Listen, there are two Federation vessels right nearby. If I send my message out, will they be able to communicate back to me?"

"You are mistaken," the ship corrected him. "There are no Federation vessels within range. The only vessels within range are enemy ships. Your message will be broadcast in the hopes that some Federation ship will hear it and respond; however, there are no such vessels currently in range."

McCoy closed his eyes in frustration. The ship was acting as crazy as Shulman; Angelina was right. *Recovery* considered the two Federation ships to be enemies; either that, or it had already destroyed them both. He tried another tactic. "May I communicate with the enemy vessels?"

"All communications with enemy vessels are handled automatically. It would be inappropriate—and against regulations—for visitors to communicate with hostile forces. You may broadcast your message when you are ready."

"Thanks," McCoy grumbled sarcastically. "That'll be *just* fine." He moistened his mouth, and wondered if there was anyone out there to hear him. With his luck, only the Romulans or Klingons were left. *No,* he decided, *I can't accept that. Jim's out there. He wouldn't let this oversized tin can get the drop on him.*

So, what was he supposed to say to his old friend? "Run like hell for the hills, we're trapped on an ambulance that's gone plumb loco"? He took a deep breath and faced the lit screen, knowing the sensors beside it would transmit his image.

"This is Leonard McCoy aboard the FDRA vessel *Recovery.* I don't know exactly what's happened here, except that the ship's designer has had some sort of breakdown—and it appears he's somehow affected the original programming of his ship. No one aboard knows what *Recovery* might do under these circumstances. Right now, she'll let me broadcast for help, but she won't let you respond. Please, be cautious. The scientists aboard this vessel will do whatever they can to get to the root of this problem and correct it. But we may need help. If I can update you on the situation here, I will—if *Recovery* will let me. This is Leonard McCoy, signing off."

At his command, the screen cooperatively went dark again.

Jim Kirk stood on his battered bridge and stared incredulously at the figure on his viewscreen. He took a step forward, then another, as if he could only get close enough he'd be able to see that the person addressing him was not really—

Leonard McCoy?

"Bones!" he murmured. The doctor was dressed in casual civilian clothing, and sported an impressive salt-and-pepper beard that would have made Jim smile in less treacherous circumstances; otherwise, McCoy looked and sounded the same as ever, as if it had only been days, not years, since they'd last stood together on the *Enterprise* bridge.

"He cannot hear you, sir," Sonak said quietly.

"What's he doing there?" Kirk asked the bridge, not really expecting an answer.

"He's listed in the roster as an 'official observer,'" Diksen informed him.

"He's on the *Recovery?*"

"That is correct, sir," Sonak said.

He hadn't seen Bones in over a year, and the last time they'd been together, they hadn't exactly behaved as two good friends should have. And now, he was trapped on that ship gone mad. . . . Kirk began to wonder if this was some kind of bizarre karmic vengeance meted out to him for accepting a promotion he should've never taken—a promotion Bones had specifically warned him against taking.

"Sir," Sonak interrupted, "apparently Ambassador Sarek has convinced the Romulans not to retaliate. However, the Klingon ship, though injured, has veered off and cloaked herself. I cannot say where she might be. And there is no way to determine, with the amount of debris from the battle, what has happened to the Tholian vessel. It might have escaped, or it may have been completely destroyed. It is impossible to determine at this time."

Kirk nodded, pulling his eyes forcibly away from McCoy's image on the viewscreen. Sonak must've gotten some crew members to remove the body of Ruth Pulver, since there was nothing now but a stain on the floor to mark her existence. He checked his hands for the tenth time, since they still felt sticky with Pulver's blood, even after he'd taken a moment to clean them.

"Mr. Sonak," he said, with more calmness than he felt, "you're getting a field promotion. I need a first officer. You're it. You may remain at the science station, and cover your duties there as well."

There was only the briefest of hesitation from the Vulcan as he said, "Aye, sir, as you wish."

What we both wish is that Pulver were still alive, but she's not, Kirk thought bitterly.

"Admiral," Sonak said, once more bent over his science viewer, *"Recovery* is starting to move."

"Move?" He had to snap out of it. Bones wasn't the only innocent person trapped on that ship. Kevin Riley was there, too, with his ex-wife and Josiah Ngo. In addition, there were over two hundred valuable scientists, and the entire FDRA contingent—some of whom were considered to be the finest minds in the universe. "Move where?"

"I believe . . ." Sonak peered intently into his science screen. "The ship is aiming . . . for Tholian space, sir. And she's picking up speed."

Kirk spun toward the navigator. "Follow that ship! She can't violate that border. The Tholians will capture her in one of their webs and then have access to state-of-the-art Federation technology. Plus they'll probably use her trespassing as an excuse to start an intergalactic war—if the Klingons and Romulans don't beat them to it."

"Sir, we've got damage in Engineering," the navigator told him regretfully. "We might be able to get up to warp six, but the *Recovery* can make it to warp nine!"

"We've got to catch that ship, mister," Kirk ordered the officer. "There's over two hundred people aboard her—and millions more depending on us to stop this conflict. Diksen!"

"Yes, sir?"

"Get me Engineering!" Even as he said it he knew there would be no Scotty there to work miracles for him this time. Any miracles produced today would have to be of his own making.

Hours before Gol's dawn, Spock woke abruptly, pushing against the warm black rock to a sitting position. For a fleeting instant, an image from a dream glimmered in the darkness before him.

It was Dr. McCoy, standing upon the deck of an unfamiliar ship, speeding through time and space and stars, his pale blue eyes wide with fear.

This is Leonard McCoy. We need help.

Help us, Spock. . . .

So urgent, so convincing was the doctor's tone that Spock was catapulted into consciousness; he drew a deep, calming breath and dissolved the impulse to rise, to rush to McCoy's aid.

Unsettling; but a dream, no more. Yet the sense that McCoy was in danger did not ease.

"Impossible," Spock murmured aloud. He had struggled the previous evening to rid himself of the sense that Kirk was in danger—yet the feeling persisted, despite Spock's efforts to break all ties to the admiral. And now, this overwhelming sense that McCoy, too, was in danger . . .

Impossible, for he felt he had done all that was necessary to sever his ties to his friends.

He rose quietly, setting aside the cloak that served as his bedclothes, and moved purposefully through the darkness to sit in front of the cold oil lamp and meditation mandala, which shone dully in the starlight. His eyes had adjusted to the dimness; and though his night vision was not as keen as a full Vulcan's, he saw well enough to focus on the mandala's intricate design, and use it to trigger a deeply meditative state.

The dream returned with full clarity; McCoy's face appeared in his mind's eye, as clearly as if the doctor had been standing before him.

This is Leonard McCoy. We need help. . . .

His image triggered another, this one from Spock's recent memory: that of Jim Kirk, trapped in an interstitial rift, floating ghostlike in his spacesuit on the *Enterprise* bridge.

Jim had been calling to him—silently, his voice unable to carry across the partition of space and time, but Spock had read the words his transparent lips had formed:

Spock. Help me, Spock. . . .

The Vulcan rose, a swift, sudden movement, and strode quickly to the window, breaking his meditation. The memory had evoked such strong emotion that he had been unwilling to sit still, to confront it. He had fled as if to escape, to leave it sitting there, before the lamp and mandala.

He leaned, arms folded against the warm stone window ledge, and breathed in a lungful of desert air, as cold and piercing as the brilliant starlight.

He had thought himself no longer capable of such emotion—but here it was, undimmed, all the grief and anger he had experienced during the Tholian affair.

Grief, because he had thought the captain, his closest friend, dead; anger, because he had failed to save him. And there was anger, too, at McCoy, whose own pain had caused him to strike out at the nearest target: Spock.

He gazed up at the onyx sky, at the dazzling diamond stars, and saw instead the captain's quarters aboard the *Enterprise,* heard instead of the silent mountains the faint hum of starship engines. He had gone with McCoy to view the captain's last orders—a painful enough task, which had tested the limits of his control. And then McCoy had lashed out, his tone ragged with sorrow.

"He was a hero in every sense of the word, yet his life was sacrificed for nothing. The one *thing that would have given his death meaning is the safety of the* Enterprise. *Now you've made that impossible. . . ."*

"You could have assured yourself of a captaincy by leaving the area . . . but you stayed. Why?"

Because, Spock had explained calmly to the doctor, he was legally and morally bound to ascertain the captain's status. That was true. And yet, there had been another reason as well, one he had scarcely admitted to himself: He had been unable to accept his friend's death.

Indeed, he had felt—with the inexplicable, irrational certainty of intuition—that Jim was still alive.

Perhaps it had been a bond forged by friendship, or by the times they had mentally linked; perhaps it was something far more human.

In his memory, he heard once more Jim's voice, as he delivered his last orders to his first officer: *"Temper your judgment with intuitive insight. I believe you have those qualities. . . ."*

Whatever the sensation's cause, Spock experienced the same certainty now that his friends—both Jim and McCoy—were in mortal danger . . . and that it was in some way connected to one of the most emotional episodes in his life.

He turned from the window, took a step back toward the lamp and mandala, and sat cross-legged on the warm stone in front of them. Perhaps it was for the best that this dream and the incident with Sarek had occurred, for they alerted him to the need to eradicate the last vestiges of emotional attachment for his human friends.

Using the image of the mandala, Spock cleared his mind. There was but one way to proceed; he would remain in meditation until he succeeded in breaking the emotional ties to Jim and McCoy. For only if such bonds were broken could he hope to achieve *Kolinahr*.

And he would not rise until he also determined how to help them, if such help was indeed required.

Drawing a deep breath, he began. . . .

Chapter Seven

"WE'RE ALL SCIENTISTS HERE," Angelina Mola insisted to her associates as she sat staring at the implacable computer screen in front of her. "Surely, there must be *something* in this place that can help us."

Beside her, Dr. Chia Noon and the young doctoral student they were mentoring, Jason Albrecht, stood in Myron Shulman's quarters, hoping that either the vanished scientist would eventually show up or they would discover some clue to his shockingly aberrant behavior. But finding that information might take an archaeology expedition, Mola thought as she gazed disconsolately about the small quarters.

Angelina had worked with Shulman for years, spending hundreds of hours with him in a dozen offices on as many planets. The Myron Shulman she knew was a man who always kept his materials rigidly organized, impossibly neat. She'd never known him to work with flimsies; he abhorred putting anything on paper. She couldn't remember ever seeing him accumulate more than a dozen data cassettes on any project he was working on. It didn't matter that Myron's work took him to many places and planets. He was always prepared to pick up and move—with all his data neatly organized and concisely contained —at a moment's notice. He called no place home, and every place work.

As she gazed about the ramshackle mess that was Myron's workplace, she would've thought that someone had ransacked it, except for the fact that every object was covered with his familiar scrawl. Cluttered with piles upon piles of small data cassettes—many spilling over onto the floor where they mixed randomly with jumbled masses of flimsies and notepaper, which, in turn, were buried under dozens of noteboards strewn over every available surface— Shulman's workspace was a disaster area. What had he been doing here that had made him abandon the habits of a lifetime? She carefully picked up a few sheets of paper and tried to make sense of the senseless symbols on them.

"Isn't there a way to locate him through the computer?" Dr. Noon asked, her black eyes narrowed with anxiety; a deep furrow had appeared directly above the small red caste mark on her brow.

Chia peered down at the mess scattered across the deck, her slender golden brown hands clasped behind her back to avoid touching anything, as though she feared their trespass here would be one more transgression the paranoid doctor would not tolerate.

"Well," Angelina mused, "we had no luck getting the computer to tell us his whereabouts when we were in the corridors." Even now, throughout the ship, other members of the FDRA were still trying to track the elusive Shulman, using tricorders and other instruments, but it was as if *Recovery* herself were conspiring with her creator to cover up his escape.

"But this station is the one he uses himself," Chia countered.

Angelina looked at the blank screen with a thoughtful nod. "Very true. His station might not have the information overrides the public stations have. It's worth a try."

"But this computer is still the ship's computer," Jason interjected. He looked like Chia's opposite; pale, blond, blue-eyed, as tall as the dark-skinned Noon was short. "It's still Shulman's invention. He has designed this entire ship. Protecting him could be one of her prime objectives."

Mola shook her head. "Myron didn't program that type of reaction into *Recovery*. He said that was where Daystrom went wrong, putting too much of himself and his own personality into his computer. No, to Myron, *Recovery* was not an extension of himself."

"Perhaps," Jason said quietly as he rifled through a stack of flimsies, "he had a change of heart regarding that philosophy."

The two women glanced at one another, but Chia only shrugged, having nothing to offer her friend. *We're all in way over our heads,* Mola thought, fighting off an inner surge of panic. *Even if we find him, what will we do with him?* She had some vague hopes of running a full diagnostic on him and finding some organic problem—a virus, perhaps, or a brain tumor —something she could treat . . . something she could *cure*. That hope was really all that was keeping her going now, so she refused to examine it, refused to listen to her analytical self, who would recognize how futile a hope it was.

Unconsciously, she rolled the flimsies still clutched

in her hand into a tight tube as she sat in front of Shulman's station. "Computer, tell us where Dr. Myron Shulman is right now."

"That information is classified," the pedantic, feminized voice told her.

Angelina closed her eyes. It was the same thing the stations in the corridor kept insisting. Information— *any* information—about Shulman was classified. But Dr. Mola had hoped that the screen in Shulman's quarters—the place where he continued to fine-tune his programming—might have better answers. She couldn't face the fact that it, too, would merely parrot the same illogical nonsense.

"This is Dr. Angelina Mola," she said forcefully. "I am the head of the FDRA, and have a priority-one clearance. There is *no* information that I am not entitled to know! I repeat, *where* is Dr. Shulman?"

"That information is classified. Only Dr. Shulman is cleared to receive that information."

Chia ran her fingers through her close-cropped jet hair. "This is madness. The only thing that was supposed to be classified was information about the defense system, so that no passenger aboard *Recovery* could take command of the ship or her weaponry. Why, just this morning the computer told me where Shulman was when I asked."

That was this morning, Angelina thought morosely. Before *Recovery* had gone mad. Before she'd attacked two Federation vessels with their own people aboard, *and* the Romulan, Klingon, and Tholian observer ships besides. Perhaps she could get other answers from the computer—answers that might lead to Shulman in another way.

She unrolled the flimsies and stared at them. There were notations in Myron's round, rolling script, but interspersed with them were figures and symbols she had never seen before. "Computer, Dr. Shulman seems to have been working on some sort of code as part of his programming. Can you tell me anything about that?"

"No," the computer said simply, "I cannot."

She sighed and once more twisted the battered flimsies. "Computer, can you at least tell me where we are headed?"

"We are traveling to coordinates five-seven-point-two-zero," the machine intoned.

Angelina had no idea where that was, and by the looks on their faces, neither did her associates. "And where is that?"

"Seventeen light-years from Zotos Four."

She felt a chill creep over her. "Is that quadrant within Federation space?"

This time the computer paused for an uncomfortably long time. Normally, its answers were instantaneous, pausing only long enough to simulate normal human conversation. "That information is classified," it finally responded.

The three scientists exchanged glances.

"I believe those coordinates are well inside Tholian space," Dr. Noon said quietly.

Angelina shot her a look of dismay. "Why are we going to those coordinates, computer?"

"We have received an urgent call for help and are responding with all haste."

"And who has sent that call, computer?"

There was another pause, longer than the last. "That information is classified."

"Computer, is Dr. Shulman permitted access to this classified information?"

"Dr. Myron Shulman has access to all areas of information."

"Is Dr. Shulman working with you to improve your efficiency, your response time, and determine who has access to classified information?"

"That is correct."

"And where is Dr. Shulman working on these issues?"

"Dr. Shulman works on my programming at this station," the computer insisted.

Angelina made a small sound of exasperation as she shook her head. "Isn't he working on your programming now? Somewhere on the ship? Where is he working now?" She clenched her teeth in frustration. There was only the slightest chance that the computer would consider the importance of the question centered around the issue of work rather than location and might accidentally tell her where Myron was at this moment.

"Dr. Shulman works at this station alone. His current location is classified," the machine insisted.

"This is useless," Jason said, tossing the unrevealing cassettes down. "It'll never tell us where he is. If we can't physically find him—"

"You'll never be able to defeat me," Shulman's choked voice said from the doorway.

The three scientists spun to face him, and stared at the wild-eyed man. His gaunt, narrow face glistened with sweat and his chest heaved, but the hand he used to hold the phaser was perfectly steady.

"Myron! Thank God we've found you!" Angelina said softly, trying to change her stricken expression into one of relief and concern—not an easy thing to do, given the crazed look in Shulman's eyes. "We've been looking everywhere. . . ." But she found it difficult to take her gaze off the weapon in Myron's grasp. Impossible that he should have it; *Recovery* was supposed to scan for and remove personal weaponry.

"You mean *hunting* everywhere, don't you?" Shulman's voice was hard, accusing.

"Please, Myron." Mola spread her hands placatingly, made her tone as soothing as possible. Beside her, Noon and Albrecht stood frozen by fear. "You're not a well man. We only want to help you."

"You only want to *destroy* me." A spasm of pain flickered over Shulman's face; for an instant, he leaned forward, on the verge of doubling over.

At once, Mola and Albrecht began to move toward him—but before they could take so much as a step, Shulman recovered and raised the phaser again. A twisted, triumphant grin spread over his lips. "Me and *Recovery*. You're working in collusion with Kirk. I know it. And *Recovery* knows it, too!"

Angelina shot a glance at Noon and Albrecht. From their grave expressions, they clearly understood what she did—that Shulman's paranoia was fixed, unflappable. Like all madmen, he knew his reality was the only reality. There could be no reasoning with him . . . but someone had to try.

Mola looked again at his phaser, gripped so tightly that his knuckles had turned ivory pale. "We're unarmed, Myron," she said, with a calm that amazed her. "Would you shoot your own colleagues, the people you've known and worked beside for years?"

"You would ask that when you are trying to destroy me and all my work?" He hesitated, swaying slightly after the shrill outburst, then gathered himself; his wide madman's gaze came to rest upon the flimsies Angelina clutched. The sight fueled his rage. "You enter my quarters, try to sabotage my computer, steal my notes, then call yourself my colleague? You are nothing but my enemy. You and Kirk. My enemies!"

And then he moved, barely perceptibly, the hand that held the phaser.

A blinding flash; Mola gasped at the blow that struck the center of her chest, that propelled her off her feet and slammed her back against a table, scattering cassettes, noteboards, flimsies onto the deck. She came to rest atop a pile of debris and watched with odd detachment as Jason lurched across the room and tackled Shulman.

"Angelina?" Chia whispered. The small Indian woman's creamy brown countenance appeared above her, blotting out the sight of the two struggling men; and then Chia's face began to recede, as though Angelina were being pulled back and away, down a long, dark hallway.

Then the second blow came; this one far more agonizing, radiating from Mola's chest into her left arm and shoulder. For an instant she thought Shulman had fired on her again—but there had been no flash. She groaned aloud with the pain.

"Angelina?" Chia said, but the sound seemed muted, faraway.

It's my heart, Mola realized, with the same ethereal detachment. *I'm having a heart attack brought on by the stun blast. I'll die if someone doesn't do something.* . . . But there were more important problems at hand, weren't there? She turned to her old friend, Dr. Noon.

"Tell Leonard," she gasped, unable to draw enough breath to make her voice sound clear. She waved the twisted flimsies feebly at Chia. "Tell Leonard . . . about the symbols. Tell Leonard . . . to tell Kirk. . . ."

Chia was shaking her head, completely baffled.

Dios mio! Mola thought disgustedly. *I'm dying here and can't even make myself understood!*

"Tell Leonard what, Angelina?" Chia asked.

Then, suddenly, the voice of God interrupted.

"My sensors indicate you are in a critical medical condition."

How odd, Angelina thought, her eyes straying up heavenward. *God sounds just like the computer!*

"You will be beamed directly to sickbay," God continued, "where there are qualified people to assist you."

"Angelina!" Chia cried out, just as Myron broke

away from Jason's grip. The phaser felt to the floor, clattering between them, but Shulman lurched, snatched it up before Jason could stop him, and ran away down the corridor, firing a last shot back toward his attacker. The blast missed the younger man, but forced him to give up his pursuit just as Dr. Mola felt the hand of God gather her up and absorb her, while an odd whine filled her head.

"Angelina! Angelina!" Dr. Noon's panicked voice cried out, but that sound faded too, as a powerful force pulled Dr. Mola toward the light.

"The ship is designed to control all outgoing transmissions," McCoy was telling the recently rehealed Kevin Riley. Riley had just finished the last of enforced curatives the ship insisted he endure; now he sat with a concerned expression, massaging his neck.

"That would prevent evacuees from jamming communications," the doctor continued, "or hostile political forces from communicating with any accomplices outside the vessel. But the ship is supposed to let people send outgoing transmissions if they're deemed 'reasonable,' such as broadcasting a call for help. Unfortunately, the standards for what's reasonable are Shulman's, and in his state of paranoia—" He shook his head. "Then again, Shulman was able to establish bidirectional communications with two ships, so you would think we could find a way to do the same."

Riley made a low, unenthusiastic noise that was not quite a growl. "Somehow, I just can't believe we'll be that lucky." He kept rubbing the back of his neck as though he were still feeling repercussions from the repetitive head blows he'd endured. McCoy wondered if the medical sensors on this wayward bucket could be completely trusted.

"You sure you're okay, Riley?" he asked.

He straightened. "Fine. At least, I must be if this hyperactive nursemaid is willing to release me. We need to find Anab—Lieutenant Saed and the cadet. He's an engineering student. I've been thinking, Doc —maybe you and he could work together. You know your way around science computers, so maybe with Cadet Ngo's help, the two of you could try to override Shulman's programming. In the meantime, the rest of us could search for our mad scientist."

"Well, maybe—" McCoy began, but the familiar sound of the transporter whine made him break off just as *Recovery* intoned:

"You have been identified as a doctor. There is an incoming patient that requires assistance. Please return to sickbay station four."

McCoy and Riley both glanced around the facility. Nearby, a tall, dark-skinned figure began materializing on a bed. The diagnostic screen was activated automatically as soon as the form completed transport. With Riley beside him, McCoy jogged over to the reclining body—and recoiled as he recognized the elderly, black-haired woman.

"Angelina!" McCoy gasped. Her normally warm brown skin had taken on a grayish cast, her breathing was shallow, and her face was contorted with pain. He glanced up automatically to the screen above her. "She's having a heart attack!"

Even as Riley moved around to the other side of the bed, prepared to offer whatever assistance he could, McCoy heard the transporter hum again. On the table beside the sickbed an array of cardiac equipment suddenly materialized. McCoy reached for a cardiac stabilizer and oxygenator without a second thought.

"Hold this against her throat, here," he directed Riley, indicating the precise spot. "It'll compensate automatically for the reduced oxygen going to her brain and other organs. Keep it there till I tell you otherwise." He activated the stabilizer and placed it over her chest. "What the *hell* happened to her?"

"The patient has been struck by a phaser stun beam at close range," the computer responded obligingly.

"Well, who in blazes would fire on Dr. Mola?"

"Dr. Shulman fired on her," *Recovery* stated dispassionately. "It was self-defense."

That brought McCoy up short. He and Riley exchanged worried glances. "I thought no one was allowed to bring weapons aboard this vessel," McCoy said quietly.

Before Riley could offer a response, the computer answered, "That is correct. No one is permitted to bring weapons aboard *Recovery.*"

"Excuse me," McCoy said angrily, without looking up from his desperate efforts to save his friend's life, "but to paraphrase a former associate of mine, you're not being very logical! If no one is permitted to bring weapons aboard, then how is it Dr. *Shulman* is armed?"

"Dr. Shulman is outside of normal parameters," the computer explained.

Riley narrowed his eyes and glanced faintly upward as he addressed the invisible computer. "Not according to regs, he's not. That was one of the things Admiral Kirk's report really harped on, that the computer aboard this ship shouldn't be able to delineate one individual as being more important than another. Otherwise, in the evacuation of a planet, the first political party to get on board could order the ship to abandon its enemies."

McCoy nodded as he chose the appropriate drugs that would aid Angelina's condition. "I remember that was one issue Shulman actually agreed with Kirk on," he said to Riley. "He hadn't wanted to risk anything like the Daystrom incident with *Recovery*. So, what's happened? Why has the computer decided

Shulman's 'outside of normal parameters'? What made him bring weapons aboard and when did he decide to use them—against his colleagues?"

Before either of them could pursue their questions further, Angelina started to stir. Her eyelids fluttered and she groaned weakly. McCoy leaned over her so she would see someone she knew. "Easy, Angelina. Easy. You're in sickbay. We've got everything under control."

She grimaced and stared at him as if baffled. Then, to both McCoy and Riley's surprise, she chuckled weakly. "I don't think so, Leonard. Not this time." She attempted to rise to a sitting position, but McCoy placed a hand firmly on her shoulder.

"Whoa, there! Just where do you think you're going? You're in a bit of trouble here, Angie. You just can't go strolling away."

She shook her head, as if he were the one who couldn't understand. "Shulman—shot me. He's armed. He's . . ." She pointed a bony brown index finger at her temple and waved it in a circular motion, then dropped her arm. ". . . *loco en la cabeza*. Something—something is seriously wrong with him. . . ."

"I know all about it, now, and we're gonna take care of it," McCoy soothed. "But you're in no shape to participate."

With a sudden spurt of strength, she grabbed hold of his tunic with one hand and pulled him closer. "We're heading for the Tholian border!" she gasped, her face contorting once more with effort and pain. "We'll be there in a matter of hours! If we cross into their space, it could mean intergalactic war! We've got to find Myron, find out why— Why? Why—?"

"Take it easy, Angie." McCoy gently tried to disengage her hand. "Just let me get you stabilized here, then we'll worry about the condition of the universe."

Flailing in her agitation, she struck him in the chest with her other hand, which clutched a sheaf of flimsies rolled into a tube. "Shulman's notes," she whispered hoarsely. "Shulman's notes. Take them, Leonard." Her breath grew even more labored; McCoy had to lean close to hear her final words. "Shulman—never took notes on paper. . . ." He took the flimsies just as her eyes rolled up and she fell back, unconscious, on the table.

"Dr. McCoy," Riley warned. "Her signs . . ."

McCoy looked overhead and saw his friend's vital signs plunge. He dropped the flimsies onto the floor and reapplied the cardiac stabilizer—but Angelina's vital signs continued their rapid downward descent. The stabilizer indicated that damage to the heart muscle was so severe resuscitation was hopeless.

"The heart's destroyed," he barked at the young commander. "We've got to do an emergency transplant. Computer, I need an artificial heart here, now!"

"This patient was critically injured during combat with Dr. Shulman," *Recovery* replied, in her aggravatingly calm voice. "Implanting an artificial heart would allow the patient to regain normal function. It would be unwise to allow a criminal to be resuscitated. An artificial heart will not be provided."

For a scant moment, McCoy was stunned into silence. The computer was supposed to preserve life at all costs. It wasn't designed to make value judgments about an individual's worth. "This woman is no criminal! She's a scientist who's personally responsible for improving the lives of hundreds of people and she's dying!" McCoy yelled at the air. "You give me that device! Give it to me *now!*" He glanced at the diagnostic screen; Angelina's vitals were nearly past the point of no return.

"Request denied," the computer intoned. "What is your interest in reviving this criminal?"

McCoy let go a sound of pure rage. With all the problems he'd had with computers in his long career, he couldn't remember the last time one openly defied him and caused the death of his patient. Grimacing, he looked at the ceiling, wanting to focus his frustration on something, anything. Just as he opened his mouth to scream again at the damned machine, he felt Riley's grip on his arm, and looked up.

The commander held his gaze with such somber intensity that McCoy fell silent as Riley addressed the computer. "This man is a doctor. He is obliged to save all life, regardless of its guilt or innocence."

"Understood," the computer said.

Riley's afraid that thing might go after me, brand me an "enemy of the state," McCoy realized. Looking back at Angelina's still form on the table, he swallowed back the lump of grief and fury in his throat. They'd been such good friends, and he was failing her completely. Maybe—if he could get her in stasis, then get her to a real hospital—

"We've got to get her in stasis," he murmured to Riley, "preserve her until we can get to a—" He glanced around nervously. "—a more *secure* facility and arrange for a transplant or artificial heart. Computer, in order to bring this—*criminal*—to justice we will need to revive her later, for, uh—for her trial. Give me a stasis chamber, *now!*"

"That assessment is appropriate. Stasis chamber prepared and ready," the computer agreed willingly.

McCoy's eyes filled as the helpless form of his friend dissolved before him to be transported into a cold, dark place, alone. There'd been so many years, so much caring and friendship. And now this woman—his mentor, his teacher, sometimes his confidante—was consigned to a sterile place where life was put on hold. Considering what was happening aboard this mad ship with its even madder captain, he knew the chances were great that Angelina would be in that stasis chamber forever—or until the ship was destroyed, by either old enemies or their own people.

He felt Riley's hand tighten on his arm, only now the commander wasn't restraining, but trying to comfort. McCoy looked up, his eyes blurry with tears his anger would not let him shed.

"We need to be careful here, Doctor," Riley said softly, glancing around them, indicating the omnipresent computer. McCoy nodded.

"I wouldn't be a doctor if it weren't for that woman," he whispered.

"I'm sorry," Riley said. He paused, then bent down and scooped up the flimsies. Taking the doctor's elbow, he led McCoy silently out of the sickbay into the corridors. The doctor stumbled along numbly, trying to figure out what possible good he could do here when he wasn't even able to save the woman who had taught him so much.

"We've got to communicate with Admiral Kirk," Riley said after a time, as they walked—aimlessly, McCoy thought—along the winding corridors. "If we're heading toward Tholian space—"

"Don't you think he might already know that?" McCoy said heavily, forcing himself to reply. "He can track the trajectory of this ship, estimate its travel time—" He could almost hear Spock coming up with an accurate estimate of where they were going and when they would get there, without ever using the computer. But then, Spock wouldn't be with Jim, would he? How did they ever come to this, scattered to the solar winds? The thought intensified his sense of bitter loss.

Riley was scanning the flimsies. "These things make no sense to me. I've never seen this kind of writing before. It's not Romulan. Not Klingon, either. You ever see anything like it?"

He handed the doctor a page where the symbols outnumbered the human script.

McCoy touched the artificial paper reverently, as if he could still feel Angie's warmth on it. Staring at the symbols, he frowned. There was something disturbingly familiar about them. *Fabrini? No. Vulcan? No, not that either.* But he had seen them before. "Guess there's no point in asking the computer what they are?"

Riley shook his head. "That may just bring more trouble on our heads."

McCoy sighed, and forced himself to take stock of their location; he was totally lost. "By the way, do you have any idea where we're going?"

"To the hangar bay," Riley replied. "That's where the shuttlecraft should be."

"Oh," he said, realizing Riley'd never lost track of their goals. *Time to snap out of it, McCoy,* he scolded himself. *Angie would chew you out big time if she found you moping around over her, and not getting down to business.* He swallowed, and picked up his pace. He could mourn later. Now they had work to do. Work he would have to accomplish without old friends—Kirk, Spock, Angie—to help him.

Because of Angelina, he was a doctor. And a doctor fixed what ailed you. And this place needed more fixing than any he'd been in in a real long time.

Without consciously realizing it, he started rolling up his sleeves.

Chia Noon sat disconsolately at the head of the conference table as Jason Albrecht briefed the top-ten representatives of the Federation Disaster Relief Agency on what had transpired between them and Myron Shulman. As the titular head—

Now that Angelina is dead . . . Angelina is dead . . . Angelina is . . .

—of the FDRA, it was Chia's job to brief them, but she couldn't. She couldn't bring herself to relive that terrible scene in Myron's quarters, especially the horrible moment when Myron had shot Angelina at point-blank range. Now the computer insisted she was dead, being held in stasis.

Intellectually, Chia tried to tell herself that there was some hope for her friend if they could get control of the computer, if they could get the ship to an advanced planet like Vulcan, if they could—

She stopped her mind from its futile optimistic speculation. The fact was, they were hurtling toward Tholian space—and Angelina was probably the luckiest among them.

Jason finished explaining the situation as the ten scientists around them stared at him, astonished. Chia knew they could barely accept what he was telling them. Most of them had worked with Myron Shulman for years. There were protests around the room, but they died out quickly. It was hard to argue with the reality of Angelina's death.

Finally, Nassar Omar, who was next in line for the chair after Chia and had listened while nervously stroking his silver mustache, said softly, "What in the worlds can we do?"

For once, Jason had no answer and all eyes turned to Chia. She sighed, wondering why they thought she had any solutions to this dilemma. And then she remembered: She was in charge now that Angelina—

Noon swallowed and found her voice. "We must warn the others, the rest of the FDRA, and the evacuees. Everyone must stay in their quarters, secure their rooms, and avoid any contact with Shulman."

"How can they secure their quarters," Omar asked pointedly, his cobalt blue eyes narrowing with skepticism, "when Shulman's in control of the ship's computer? He can go anywhere, hear anything—"

Chia shook her head. "It's all we can do. None of us worked on the computer; that was Myron's alone. The evacuees are all environmental and evolutionary specialists. The design and scope of this computer will be completely unfamiliar to them. The only people on board who might have any idea how to cope with it would be Starfleet personnel."

"Well, aren't there several of them on board?" Jason asked.

"Yes, six altogether, counting Leonard McCoy, who's an honorary member of this team and a retired Starfleet medical officer. But two of them are confined since they were in the attacking shuttlecraft during the simulation, so they won't be released. Of the three remaining, one is a cadet, the other an admiral's aide. Only one is a Security officer. So, you see, there will be little help from that quarter. We can only hope that the two starships that were part of the simulations weren't damaged too badly, and can do something to—"

She swiveled in her chair at the sound of the door sliding open, and fell silent at the sight of Myron Shulman standing in the doorway.

His dark hair stuck out at crazy angles from his skull, his skin shone with a slick sheen of sweat—even the front of his tunic was soaked, as though he'd been running a marathon, which Chia suspected he had. He quivered like a tuning fork, except for the hand that aimed a phaser steadily at the group.

With eyes so wide the whites were visible all the way around the golden-brown iris, he moved his gaze from face to face—a gaze that held a dark cunning Chia had never seen there in all the years she'd known the man.

No one in the room stirred.

"You're all in collusion with Kirk," Myron said, with glistening lips that trembled—though his voice sounded remarkably normal, almost as if he were lecturing a class. "All of you. Everyone in this room, everyone in this ship—and especially our precious *honorary* member, McCoy. Kirk's after us, trying to destroy us, but won't he be surprised when we destroy *him!* Him and all his conspirators. Starting with *you."* He gestured with the phaser at Noon, who sucked in a breath and held it; and then he waved it at each of the others in turn. *"All* of you. Then the others. One by one. First, the FDRA, from the leadership on down, then the invaders, the parasites that have snuck onto this ship. Then finally, Kirk. Only then will the holy triad be avenged—!"

He winced as if something hurt him suddenly, unexpectedly. The weapon's aim wavered; with a boldness that astonished her, Noon took advantage of his distraction and rose from her seat.

"The holy triad—" Shulman murmured, grimacing again in pain as he buried his knuckles in his disheveled mop of hair and clutched his skull.

The holy triad? The man's clearly raving. . . . Chia glanced at the others in confusion, then took a slow step around the table, spreading her hands in a peacemaking gesture. "Myron, what is it? Something's hurting you. Let me help."

He blinked in seeming confusion as he raised his face to regard her. For a moment his face seemed as it always had, and the man she once knew as a colleague looked back at her. "Chia, it hurts," he said, with a childlike plaintiveness that she found oddly touching. He rubbed his skull, just above his right forehead. "Even when I do what it wants. It always hurts."

Angelina was right; there's something organically wrong with him, something in his brain. She took advantage of the moment, and took a step closer. "I can help you, Myron," she said, letting the honest concern she felt for him show in her voice. "Come with me to sickbay. We'll get something for the pain, and find out what's hurting you. Come with me there."

No one moved as Chia took another step forward, and extended her hand, palm up, as if she were approaching a wild animal that needed taming. Shulman looked totally exhausted and almost relieved as he turned to her, and lowered the weapon.

She barely dared to breathe. Would he let her help him?

A sudden blur of motion to her left.

She swung about, startled, and saw Jason Albrecht lunging toward her and Shulman—reaching for the weapon.

"NO!" Chia shouted, with horrifying certainty as to the outcome, as the younger athletic man grabbed Shulman's arm and the two grappled for the weapon.

The transformation in *Recovery*'s creator was astonishing; the fatigued scientist became all predator again. Shulman fought the muscular young student with a strength and vicious skill that astonished Chia. The two slammed to the floor fighting wildly for control of the phaser, Jason clearly struggling for his life.

The other scientists tried to help, grabbing Shulman's limbs, even his feet, but he shoved them off with shocking ease.

"Run!" Jason screamed at them, as Shulman overwhelmed him. "Run! Hide!"

His words echoed as the whine of the phaser filled the air.

Chia watched, too stunned to move, to react, as Jason's body glowed with impossible, blinding brilliance, then dissolved into nothingness.

Never had a group of eminent scientists ever responded so efficiently to a command. The group scattered, racing wildly out of the room before Jason's body had even completely discorporated. All except Chia, who stood transfixed with horror and amazement at the ease with which an entire human being could be dispersed into all its billions of separate atoms.

Shulman got to his feet, staring wide-eyed at the spot where Jason's body had lain against the carpet. The ship would clean the spot as soon as they vacated the room, Chia knew, removing every molecule that remained of Jason; and then no trace of that brilliant young man, a man with all his life and all its promise still before him, would exist at all.

She looked up to see Shulman turn his gaze on her. The quivering was more pronounced now. It was as though he stood on a deck panel that trembled from metal fatigue and threatened to blow apart at any second. And yet there was something about this physical symptom that seemed more pleasurable than painful. That realization frightened Chia even more.

"Myron," she said softly, even though she knew that the moment she might have reached him, might have helped him, was irrevocably gone. She searched his wild eyes and tried anyway. "Myron? Are you still in there? Is my friend still alive in there at all?"

His lips pulled back into a rictus of a grin. "Oh, yes," he assured her, his voice a parody of its normal self. "Yes, Myron is still in here. Deep. Deep inside."

The quivering increased, and as Shulman raised the phaser and aimed it at her with a hand that trembled not a bit, she told herself the trembling was the visible manifestation of Myron's battle for control with whatever it was that had possessed him. Even so, she knew it was a battle he was doomed to lose.

Noon's fear transformed into an entirely physical phenomenon. Although a renewed rush of adrenaline quickened her heartbeat and sent a fresh chill coursing down her spine, her mind became detached, serene as she stared at Shulman's index finger, which tightened now on the trigger. She felt a sudden surge of compassion for him; how tragic, that he should have gone mad on the verge of what should have been his life's greatest achievement. How tragic, too, that the madness should have caused him to murder his friends and colleagues. The real Shulman, a gentle man whose goal was to save lives, not take them, would have been horrified.

Yes, Angelina was lucky to be floating mindlessly in the dark void of stasis; lucky to have been spared the protracted terror that was sure to face the survivors on the doomed vessel. Chia felt something akin to relief that her own journey aboard *Recovery* was about to end.

"He's in here," Shulman told her, almost gleefully, his grin widening to reveal huge white teeth, glistening with saliva. "He's watching. Watching everything. For the triad. The holy triad."

A fat tear spilled from the corner of his eye.

He's crying, Noon thought with pity. *The real Myron is crying.*

In a small, barely perceptible movement, his index finger tightened on the trigger.

Chia Noon watched, with compassion and regret, as the resplendent flash filled her vision—painfully, dazzlingly, yet she did not look away, but let herself be blinded. And in the instant before dissolution, her last conscious thought was that Angelina had been lucky —lucky, indeed.

Chapter Eight

"HELLO? HELLO? Anyone? Everyone? This is Nassar Omar!"

Anab Saed paused as the booming, nearly hysterical voice filled the corridor. She and Ngo had climbed out of the shuttlecraft to find themselves in a large empty hangar. After spending some time running diagnostics on the war-weary *Grace Hopper,* Anab had grown restless and had consulted the computer for Riley's location. She and Ngo were en route there when the sudden announcement interrupted them.

"Can you hear me? Can anyone hear me?" Omar wondered breathlessly over the shipwide system. "We are all in grave danger. Myron Shulman is insane, homicidally insane. Angelina Mola has been murdered. Chia Noon has been murdered. And now every member of the FDRA is in danger of assassination. Shulman will not rest until the *Recovery* is a ghost ship. He's taking us into Tholian space! There's nothing we can do! Secure yourselves. Hide. Be cautious—oh, Allah, no!"

Scuffling sounds. Omar's voice, already frantic-sounding, grew frankly hysterical. "Shulman, don't—*please!*"

A strangled cry, followed by a phaser's whine.

Anab started at the terrible sound, and exchanged looks with Josiah; his full lips were parted, his eyes wide with the same shock Saed knew her own expression revealed.

An uncomfortable silence ensued; and then, another male voice—this one strained and weary, but carrying an edge of rage—filtered over the ship's speakers.

"This is Myron Shulman. Monique Thibeau, according to the FDRA's rules of succession, you are now the new head. Congratulations. But don't go to the trouble of selecting a chief of staff. . . ."

The transmission ended.

Ngo gazed upward at the speakers, then uncertainly back at Saed. "I don't suppose this is a . . . surprise part of the simulation, sir?"

"No," Anab replied shortly, and began moving again in the direction of the indicated sickbay. As much as she had resented Riley's presence on the simulated shuttlecraft rescue, she was beginning to worry about him. In the brief time she'd been married to him, he'd shared only negative memories of his time in space, aboard the *Enterprise;* and though she'd heard from Earthside friends at headquarters that Riley was a changed man now, a competent, confident officer, she had trouble believing it. The Riley she had known was a fearful, timid soul, one who had begged her not to go into space because of its dangers; one who had languished for years in Starfleet without a single promotion. She had loved him even then, had tried to bolster his confidence, had encouraged him to find what it was he really wanted to do.

But his unhappiness had come close to destroying her. She wanted nothing more than to be in space; Riley wanted nothing more than the security of Earth. In the end, she had had to leave, even though it had torn at her heart.

Now here he was, promoted to a full commander, with Kirk's recommendation. The sight of him inspired both pain and hope: pain because she knew how she had hurt him, hope because her love for him had not entirely dimmed, and she could not help wondering whether there might be a chance for a real relationship at last.

But on the shuttle, she thought she saw hints of the old Riley; he had, after all, made a near-fatal error in judgment in checking Ngo's suit at the wrong time. And he had been gone too long for such minor injuries; perhaps he'd been hurt when *Recovery* had been fired upon, or maybe Shulman . . .

"Get a move on, Cadet," she said firmly. "We need to locate Commander Riley and figure out a plan."

With a nervous backward glance at the corridor behind him, Ngo complied.

When asked, *Recovery*'s computer had calmly told them about "enemy attacks," which Anab decided were just part of the simulation. It was odd Romolo hadn't warned her about them, but she figured it was just one of his little surprises. And listening to Nassar Omar's frantic message, she'd been tempted at first to think it, too, was some sort of test.

But even Romolo, with his renowned sense of humor, wouldn't have rigged something so bizarre. And K.T.—

That's Commander Riley now, and don't you forget it.

Riley should've been back by now, or should have communicated with them.

Something was happening aboard this ship, something unplanned. And if it was really true—if Myron Shulman *had* gone crazy and was determined to murder everyone on board one by one—then she was the only trained Security officer on board.

A Security force of one aboard the largest vessel Anab had ever seen.

"Keep your eyes open," she told Ngo as they rounded a curve in the corridor. "If Shulman's armed and—"

She broke off as they both nearly collided with two men hurrying in the opposite direction. For a split second, her training took over; she recoiled, arms raised, ready for combat—until she recognized one of them.

"Easy, Anab—it's me!" Riley said, holding up his hands in a placating gesture. Beside him stood an older, bearded man. "I take it you've been listening in to the shipwide intercom."

She nodded, annoyed with herself that the sight of him—unbruised and unbloodied now—brought such relief. "It's true, then? About Shulman?"

He and the older man nodded grimly.

"Then we need to get back to the shuttlecraft," she said. "It carries a standard complement of weapons."

"Guess again," the man beside Riley responded, in a Southern drawl. Anab eyed him curiously. He was dressed in casual civilian clothes, clearly not Starfleet—not with that salt-and-pepper beard. And he didn't seem an FDRA type, either, but looked more like he was en route to a camping trip than a meeting of bureaucrats. His warm, relaxed manner reminded her of Captain Romolo, which made her like him immediately, and his ease around Riley suggested the two had known each other before.

Riley shot him a startled look. "You really think—?"

"You can check if you want. But I'll bet my bottom credit *Recovery*'s removed them."

"Impossible," Anab said scornfully.

The older civilian shrugged as Riley turned to him and said, "Maybe we ought to be sure. Just in case . . ."

The four of them returned quickly to the hangar deck. Glancing at Anab for approval and getting it, Josiah clambered back on board the small craft. "Hey!" he cried out in surprise. "Who emptied these storage bins?"

"I can't believe this," Riley muttered.

"It's a very sophisticated, specialized tracking program that locks on to weaponry," the bearded man explained to Anab, "then fine-tunes the coordinates, and beams it out of there. It can do that even to weapons on your *body.*"

"That kind of precision intraship beaming's not possible!" Josiah declared, emerging from the shuttle.

"Really?" The man cocked a black eyebrow. "Then where are your weapons?"

Riley released an annoyed sigh. "Maybe it's time for introductions. This is Dr. Leonard McCoy, formerly chief medical officer of the *Starship Enterprise.* Dr. McCoy, this is Cadet Josiah Ngo, the engineering student I told you about, and Lieutenant Anab Saed —who's in Security." His voice carried a tone of regret—or was it merely her imagination? She kept her face carefully neutral. Riley wasn't the only person ruing his decision to come along for the simulation.

"What's going on, Commander?" Josiah asked.

"I don't think we know the half of it, but we'll give you the short form," Riley replied.

McCoy told them about the simulation's disruption

and the ship's bizarre reaction. Riley told them why he'd been detained, and all about Shulman's breakdown and the runaway ship they were currently on board: a ship heading for Tholian space while being pursued by an injured starship with Admiral Kirk in command.

"Sounds like we've got a problem," Anab said, when he was finished. "A big problem."

What she didn't say was that the only people aboard *Recovery* with any training to handle the situation were a retired Starfleet doctor, a bureaucrat from headquarters, and a weaponless Security chief saddled with a raw cadet. But she could see from K.T.'s face that he knew she was thinking it.

She opened her mouth, ready to start issuing orders; but Riley spoke first, so she closed it again. When they had parted, they'd shared the same rank of lieutenant; it was hard for her to remember that he had had two rapid promotions under Kirk and was now her superior.

"So, here's the course of action," he said, with a confidence she had never seen in him before. "Mr. Ngo, you and Dr. McCoy are going to develop a working relationship with the *Recovery*'s computer."

Josiah's eyes widened with a mixture of intimidation and delight. "The *Recovery*'s computer?"

"That's right, son," McCoy drawled, looking amused. "On this vessel, you're the closest thing to a senior engineer we've got. I'll try not to get in your way."

"And you'll make sure, Mr. Ngo," Saed interjected sternly, "that nothing happens to Dr. McCoy." She turned toward the older man. "As much as I hate to bring this up, Doctor, you are on Shulman's list, and with your past close association with Kirk, I'm afraid—"

"Yes, well," McCoy interrupted her, "let's not dwell on that."

"I'm afraid we have to," Anab insisted, and began to speak again when a single, pointed look from Riley stopped her.

"Mr. Ngo," he said quietly, "we need to communicate with the outside world and find a way to stop this machine from violating Tholian space. While you and the doctor try to figure out where the problem is in this monster's brain, I'm also charging you with the personal safety of Dr. McCoy."

Ngo's widened, then narrowed with dread; he dropped his gaze, and muttered, "Yes, sir."

"I'm pretty familiar with this animal's physical layout, Josiah," McCoy said amiably as the two walked toward the exit. "I think I can find us a fairly secure place to work."

Anab watched the two men walk away, then finally faced Riley. "I didn't mean to overstep," she said softly. "But you said I was in charge of the simulation—"

"You were. But something's gone wrong." He turned away from her and clambered into the shuttle, talking over his shoulder. "The simulation's over. And now we've got to find some way to arm ourselves that the computer will not perceive as technologically threatening, and then we've got to find this Thibeau woman, and whoever it is that's next in line of succession."

She followed him in, watching as he gazed critically around the shuttle's interior for a second, then seemed to find inspiration and headed toward the vessel's rear. "K.T. . . . ." Her tone softened, grew personal.

He moved over to a piece of metallic rail trim near the ceiling of the vessel, then glanced expectantly at her.

"K.T., you're not Security. And you haven't been on active duty for years." She paused, tried to find the right words to soften what she was about to say, and failed. "The only sensible thing for you to do is sequester yourself."

"And let you deal with Shulman by yourself?" Reaching into the tool chest, he took out a device and proceeded to detach the rail. "You used to be pretty good with the javelin at the Academy, didn't you?"

He pulled the sleek rail, tapered to a point at both ends, off the wall and handed it over to her.

She took it and hefted it, testing its weight, then lifted it over one shoulder. "Yes. But you're not listening to me, K.T."

"I'm listening," he said, rummaging through the tool chest and pulling out a length of nearly invisible cable. He paused then to stare up at her and spoke, his tone hardening with that certain flintiness that meant he had made his decision and would brook no argument. "Anab, I'm command track—which means I had security training. And I'm not as rusty as you might think."

"You were rusty enough to stop and check Ngo's suit, when you should have been sending the distress signal and paying attention to your board," she said, with more heat than she'd intended.

He frosted at once, and for a split second regarded her in silence. And then he said, "That's true; and I won't make the same mistake. Need I remind you, Lieutenant, that I'm your superior?"

She stiffened involuntarily at that; he saw it, and his face and voice softened. "The fact is, you'll need help with Shulman. And right now, things are critical. Our lives and the lives of everyone on this ship could depend on how well we work together. Like it or not, you're going to have to trust me. What I'm trying to say is . . . we need to forget the past and worry about the present situation."

"Understood," Anab agreed coolly, as she pulled off a matching piece of trim for another javelin.

Riley unrolled the length of cable, cut it into two-meter-long sections, and started tying the ends to the weights in pairs. As he fastened the last knot in the final piece of flexible cable, Anab asked curiously, "What's that you're working on?"

Riley rose and stepped where Anab could see him. Tying part of the cable around his waist like a belt, he hefted the last cable at its center, then graced Anab with a sly little smile. "You don't know everything about me, Lieutenant. It's a little something a certain Vulcan taught me to make; with it, I can bring down Shulman at thirty meters at a dead run. It's an *ahn-woon*."

And as Anab watched, even more surprised, Riley made the weapon sing over his head.

"I'm already giving you all she's got, Admiral," Chief Engineer Gambeta explained, exasperation in her soft South African lilt. Kirk could scarcely blame her; no doubt his command style was nothing like her regular captain's—and no doubt she'd never been in a situation quite like this. "We've had damage to the engines, sir, especially to the warp drive. I've lost three critical staff members. And you sent my best assistant, Josiah Ngo, over to the *Recovery*. The speed we're achieving now is due more to prayer than engineering skill. I can't even promise you I can maintain this."

Kirk flinched when she mentioned the dead crew. His first command in two years, and there were deaths on board within hours of his stepping on the bridge. Deaths here and on the *Starhawk*—all his responsibility. If he hadn't changed the simulation—

And now, McCoy and Kevin Riley were speeding away to an uncertain fate aboard *Recovery*. Bones, his best remaining friend in the galaxy, now that Spock had cut himself off. And Riley—

He felt a special kinship, a special responsibility toward Riley. Unbeknownst to Kevin, a fourteen-year-old Jim Kirk had rescued him decades before from death on Tarsus IV, under Governor Kodos's rule. He had always felt that Riley had survived to fulfill a special destiny; it was one reason he had taken Riley on as his aide at headquarters, and encouraged him to reach his full potential.

Riley had not disappointed him. But now, to have brought him this far, only to see him die aboard a runaway vessel, one Kirk had helped create—

He forced his mind away from the thought. If *Recovery* hadn't failed now, she would've failed later, perhaps with more lives on board. Yes, he'd been the catalyst, but all he'd done was find the chink in the armor. He didn't have time to waste second-guessing his command decisions—not while they were pushing warp seven and barely keeping the *Recovery* in sight.

Kirk wanted to congratulate the engineer for her resourcefulness and an expertise that could be favorably compared to the best engineer he'd ever known; but the medals would have to come later. Now he needed more.

"Look, Admiral." Gambeta's tired voice spoke softly into the pause. "I know as well as you that we'll never catch up to the target at this speed. And I know we have to. Maybe—maybe if I reroute the power coupling so that it 'borrows' energy from weapons systems while they're not in use, I might be able to get more warp power—assuming we don't shake apart if I do."

Kirk had to smile and remind himself that, while there might be no Scotty aboard this ship to pull their irons out of the fire, the *Paladin*'s chief engineer was proving to be something of a miracle worker herself. "Whatever you can do, Mr. Gambeta—I'll be grateful. And Engineer—?"

"Yes, sir?" He could hear the dread in her tone at the prospect of being asked for more of the impossible.

"While you're praying, throw in a few from me as well."

She said, with a hint of relief, "I'll do that, sir."

"Mr. Sandover." Restless, Kirk leaned forward in his chair toward the red-haired navigator. "Is there anything else we could be doing to catch the *Recovery?*"

Sandover turned his freckled face toward him, his expression and tone apologetic. "So far, the best I can do, sir, is maintain our pursuit at this distance."

Jim ground his teeth. The *Paladin* was hurt, and already giving him all she had, and that was plenty. It wasn't her fault she wasn't the *Enterprise.*

But he needed the *Enterprise* now.

He pushed himself out of the chair, too impatient to sit any longer. "I understand, Mr. Sandover, but stay on it. If the *Recovery* slows, speeds up, or changes direction, you'll have to respond instantly. We've got to close this gap, mister."

"Aye, sir," the experienced officer declared, his eyes moving between the viewscreen and his instruments, his pale, freckled hands steady on the controls.

Kirk strode over to the science station, where Sonak spun in his chair, arms folded across his chest, anticipating the admiral's next question.

"I have analyzed this situation, sir, and cannot find any weaknesses in either the *Recovery's* abilities or defenses. Someone has changed her programming radically, but the changes follow a narrow, specific— yet, I believe, illogical—path."

Kirk gave a thoughtful nod, trying to repress the sudden painful wave of nostalgia that accompanied the act of seeking his Vulcan science officer's advice. "Only Shulman could have altered the ship's mission, and he's had some sort of breakdown. It stands to reason he'd program in illogical reactions."

Sonak considered this with a faint lift of a brown-black eyebrow. "Perhaps, sir, but inaccurate, and illogical programming normally renders computers useless. Yet *Recovery* functions quite efficiently. Even now, she is marshaling her energy while speeding toward a precise destination."

Kirk looked into his science officer's eyes. The dark orbs and slanted brows were so similar to another Vulcan's on another ship that he could've sworn it was Spock's voice who said, *There is too much logic in* Recovery*'s illogic to be coincidence, Jim.*

He blinked and said, "Excuse me?"

"What I mean, Admiral," Sonak said clearly in his own voice and tone, "is that a human suffering a nervous breakdown is hardly a likely candidate to devise a new, complicated neural program for this very advanced computer."

"You think someone else is programming the computer?"

"I think it is highly likely, sir."

Kirk sighed, and looked back over his shoulder at the viewscreen, which revealed only darkness and stars. Who could've sabotaged *Recovery,* and how? "Any signs of pursuers?"

Sonak released a small, soundless sigh. "The Romulan observers were disabled, but a cloaked Romulan vessel would be impossible to discover until she was near enough for her ion trail to give her away. Whether the Klingon observers who cloaked their vessel are following us, again, I cannot determine. But

I am scanning for them, sir. And, of course, we do not know if the Tholian vessel survived."

"Expect anything and everything, Mr. Sonak," Kirk warned, and the Vulcan nodded in agreement. Staring again at *Recovery*'s fleeing form, Kirk wondered, "What are the chances of beaming those people off that ship and just letting *Recovery* violate Tholian space all by herself?"

"Impossible to calculate, sir, but, assuming she could be convinced to drop her shields . . ." Sonak hesitated for a fleeting instant. "For the entire complement of people aboard using the few transporter pads we have, it would take two-point-six hours. Assuming the transporters are at maximum efficiency."

"But *Recovery* could beam them all over here at once," Kirk told him. "If she would."

"Theoretically true. However, I would remind the admiral that *Recovery* has not, of late, been very cooperative. We know so little about the Tholians, it would be safe to assume that even a hollow invader could precipitate hostilities."

Kirk nodded. "Sonak, we have five people aboard that ship—two effectively incarcerated. That leaves a trained Security officer, my personal aide, and an inexperienced cadet with some engineering ability to deal with this problem from within. What do you think the chances are that they can stop that ship?"

Sonak seemed faintly nonplussed by the question —a query Spock would have expected from Kirk. The younger Vulcan then said quietly, so that the rest of the crew could not hear, "Admiral, that ship has the most sophisticated computer and the most advanced technology the Federation is currently capable of. Most of the veteran computer science officers in Starfleet could not successfully reprogram it. I do not believe that a cadet with an engineering background or a Security officer, no matter how experienced in her field, has the knowledge required to interact with *Recovery* in a meaningful way."

"No chance at all, huh?" Kirk asked grimly.

Sonak blinked. "I believe that is what I said, sir."

Kirk nodded grimly. "If we could only bring the ship to a stop we'd be ahead of the game." As if that made him think of a new possibility, he added, "Since we could use a little optimism right now, have cargo bay three emptied. Make sure it's got full life-support. If we can ever convince *Recovery* to give up her guests, we'll need to have a place to put them."

The Vulcan's expression remained bland, even though Kirk was sure he thought that last request pure wish-fulfillment. Sonak reached for a piece of equipment at his station. "We need to communicate with our people, sir, but *Recovery* is refusing transmissions. *Paladin*'s communication station was retrofitted with the rest of the ship; however, it was the first one done. More advanced upgrades were available later, and I requisitioned the parts, but we were given our orders before they could be installed. I have taken the liberty of ordering a cadet to bring me the new meta-inhancer assembly from storage. Installing it now may enable us to force a transmission through."

Kirk brightened. "Good work. Let's do it."

"I'll get right on it, sir." Sonak rose.

"No, not you," Kirk insisted. "You've got more important things to do."

Sonak glanced past Kirk to the communications station where Cadet Diksen worked, and said, sotto voce, "With all due respect, Admiral, the cadet does not have the experience to—"

"I understand, Commander. I'll show her how to install it."

"You, sir?" Both Sonak's eyebrows lifted in unison.

"I think I still know how to soup up a comm

board," Kirk said wryly. "Besides, if I spend another minute sitting in that chair staring at that screen I'll wind up as demented as Shulman."

Both eyebrows remained lifted, but the Vulcan merely said, "As you wish, sir," and handed him the equipment.

As Kirk walked the short distance to communications, he examined the complicated circuitry, trying to recall just where all its connections went and how the new modules interfaced with the old. He didn't remember it being quite this complicated the first time he'd installed one.

This was not the way things were supposed to go. Reese moved her hands over the comm board and sequenced in another transmission on yet another frequency. This was supposed to be the most boring spot on the bridge. This was supposed to have been a mundane simulation. She was not supposed to get her first taste of action by watching her ship get the hell kicked out of it by friendly fire and watching Commander Pulver die on the bridge. They were not supposed to be racing pell-mell after a runaway vessel piloted by a madman that was about to plunge them into intergalactic war. And her very best friend wasn't supposed to be helplessly trapped on a ship he couldn't even communicate from. No, this was not the way things were supposed to go at all.

Every time she started thinking about Commander Pulver or Josiah, her throat tightened and her vision blurred, so she drew in a breath. There was no time for that, no time at all. She blinked her eyes until they cleared and registered the rejection of her latest transmission. She reformulated it, trying another frequency.

Something had to get through. Something. *Something.*

"Mr. Diksen."

The sound of her own name made her start.

"Sorry, Mr. Diksen," the admiral apologized. "I didn't mean to startle you. Mr. Sonak's given me a booster for your comm board. I thought I'd give you a hand putting it in."

She blinked up at him stupidly, as if the words "booster," "comm board," and "give you a hand," made no sense to her.

"Unless of course you've found a way to get through to *Recovery* without it," Kirk said, with a faint smile.

"Uh, no, sir. Not yet." Diksen glanced at the board, but the only communications coming in were overlapping reports from all parts of the ship that were pouring in so rapidly she couldn't even assimilate them all. The ship was badly damaged. Everyone was scrambling to make repairs and get defenses back up to a hundred percent. And people had been killed.

People killed. Somehow, it had never occurred to her that such a thing was possible on her first mission.

"Mr. Diksen," Kirk said softly close to her ear, "are you all right?"

She exhaled. "I'm fine, sir," she said in a surprisingly clear voice. "Let me get those tools." It allowed her to get out of the seat and bend down, away from him, away from those hazel eyes, eyes watching her for any inefficiency, any weakness.

She gulped and opened the cabinet beneath the console to retrieve the specialized equipment they would need for the upgrade. "Is that a Kuniko twelve-fifteen, or a Miloslav R seventy-four?"

When he didn't answer her she pulled her head out of the cabinet. He was turning the device over and over in his hands, as if looking for the information. She stood up and took it from him. She found the identification information on a tiny inset chip. "Oh, wow, it's a Moroz ten-eighty! This thing is so new I've never even seen one."

She glanced at him and realized he looked pained. "What's wrong, sir?"

He looked around to make sure no one could hear. "I don't like admitting this, Diksen, but . . . well, I've never even heard of the first two upgrades you mentioned, and this one is completely foreign to me. If you're unfamiliar with it as well—"

"Most upgrades are similar in design—at least as far as installation is concerned. This one might have some special quirks, but I think—between your experience, and my more recent training—we should be able to work it out. In fact," she added, as she went back to the cabinet to look for more tools, "if this is as good as it's cracked up to be, we might have a chance at forcing *Recovery* to accept our transmissions."

"Then let's get it plugged in and see what she'll do."

"Aye, sir." Diksen opened up the panel beneath the console and looked underneath, suddenly grateful that she hadn't skipped any classes in communications circuitry, no matter how boring.

Crouched beside her, Kirk removed an extra panel; with a pang of nervousness, she realized he intended to crawl under with her. She tried not to let it bother her when she slid beneath the console on one hip only to find him doing the same, facing her so they could work together side by side, inches apart.

It would take more than two hands to install this new equipment, she told herself, but damn, she wished it were Josiah. She wouldn't feel like such a bloody fool then when she barked her knuckles or shocked herself plugging into the wrong port. Why did it have to be Kirk?

Because right now he has the least to do, she realized, with a sense of wonder. He was bored waiting to catch up to *Recovery,* and was desperate to be of use.

"Let me hold that stuff," he suggested, taking the tools from her. "You have smaller hands; it'll be easier for you to move things around and open up a stage for the enhancer."

"Aye, sir," she said without looking at him, and proceeded to unhook several ports and rearrange the layered boards.

"Look, Diksen, as long as we're working together, you can relax a little," he told her, as he handed her tools then took them back when she no longer needed them. "I figure you're the senior technician right now. I've been away from all this too long. And it occurs to me that it's not so easy to be in such close quarters with an admiral you've done a major study on."

She tried to school her expression to deny the last charge, but he only remarked, "Your ears are red, Reese."

She nodded, and rearranged boards. "Thanks, sir. I mean, Admiral. I mean—thanks. And could you hold this—here?"

As he assisted her, she restacked her boards in a new configuration that would leave an opening for the extra equipment, then started reattaching everything in sequence. Wanting to take her mind off Kirk's nearness in the tight place, she decided to heed his advice and reassign him a new role as a fellow cadet. "Okay, now move that there, no not there, to the left—right! I mean, correct! So, how long has it been since you've done this kind of work?"

He sighed, adjusted his equipment, then gave her the right tool when she needed it without missing a beat. "A captain has to know how to do everything aboard his ship. The last time I worked on a comm board was . . ." His eyes looked past her at some far-distant memory. "A lifetime ago, aboard the *En-*

terprise. I helped Spock when we were in orbit around the Omicron Ceti Three colony."

She frowned and held his gaze. "That wasn't in the records, sir. At least, I don't think it was ever reported that—"

An unreadable expression came over his face; he shifted in the tight spot, then handed her another tool, bringing her attention back to her task. "You'll find out, Diksen, that not everything goes into those reports. There are some people who would've felt that wasn't the best use of my time."

"Like now?"

"Like now. You ready for this?"

She nodded and he handed her the upgraded equipment. She wondered how many other things never got in those reports.

"You have a friend aboard the *Recovery,* don't you, Reese?" he asked suddenly. "Josiah Ngo—correct?"

His question so startled her that for a moment, she couldn't answer. There were over three hundred people aboard the *Paladin.* When did he have time to learn they were friends?

"You should know that Josiah wasn't scheduled for that trip, Diksen. I sent him. I was impressed with his performance and wanted to reward him. But sometimes a captain's plans don't work out quite the way he envisions them."

He wanted her to forgive him, she realized. While she was agonizing over Josiah and the people who'd died aboard the two ships *Recovery* had fired upon, he was taking the blame for it. The responsibility for those lives, those deaths, was on him.

But each one had hurt him, she knew now—another fact that would never be recorded. It suddenly made him very human to her, something she'd never expected him to be.

"Ngo knew it was a reward, Admiral," she said

finally. "He was so proud, he couldn't wait to tell me. All Josiah ever wanted to do was serve in Starfleet. I know he hasn't changed his mind about that, no matter what happens to him now."

He didn't say anything, just continued helping her install the upgrade. Then finally, he murmured, "Thank you, Diksen."

There was an uncomfortable pause as she struggled with the last connection, but eventually she blurted, "Sir, if I could be so bold . . . You made a wonderful captain. I was surprised when you accepted the promotion to the admiralty. Why did you?"

She didn't dare look at him as she spoke, just kept making the minute adjustments that would allow the new enhancer to work properly with the other upgrades in the console.

He released a slow, steady breath. She was out of line, Diksen realized, with a surge of panic; the question had been far too personal.

When Kirk finally responded, his tone had noticeably cooled.

"I imagine things look very black-and-white from your point of view, Diksen, at the beginning of your career, but you'll find—as the years pass—that there are many shades of gray in every decision. For example: I imagine your attitude about engaging in battle may have changed some since we last spoke."

She halted in her work, then resumed it. "Yes, sir," she murmured softly. "Yes, that's true. I—I see that whole issue differently now." She swallowed hard as the image of Commander Pulver's scorched, unrecognizable face came to mind.

"Well, that's why time is the great equalizer. It was time for the members of my crew to go on and do different things. And it was time for me to do that as well."

There was no enthusiasm, no joy in his voice; Diksen didn't believe him for an instant. She should have dropped the issue then—but she would never have such an opportunity again in her life to candidly question Kirk about this topic that perplexed her so much. With a boldness that stunned her, she pressed: "Then you're glad you accepted the promotion to the admiralty?"

This time he remained quiet for so long that she stopped what she was doing to look at him. He met her gaze and said, "I was glad about it once. Lately—I've reconsidered my choice. Perhaps—if I'm lucky—the time will come for me to do something different again."

"I hope so, sir," she said sincerely.

His gaze softened for a moment. "Keep sight of your dreams, Diksen. No matter what happens. Never forget your true goals."

"Yes, sir," she said, her voice barely a whisper. She cleared her throat and said, more loudly, "I think we're ready to try this thing out, sir."

Before he could answer her, Sonak's voice came from the area of her knees and she looked over to find the Vulcan's head halfway under the console with them.

"Admiral," the science officer said, "if I might bother you a moment—I believe you should see this."

"Of course," Kirk said, all business again. As Sonak left to return to his station, the admiral began to extract himself from beneath the console. But just before he stood, he said quietly, "Don't forget what I told you, Reese."

"I won't, sir. Never."

I must be getting old, Kirk reprimanded himself, *if I can let a green cadet get me so flustered.* But she'd hit him where it hurt, right in the *Enterprise*. He straightened his uniform—and his emotions—as he moved back to Sonak's station.

"Engineering reports we are now at warp eight and holding steady," Sonak reported matter-of-factly, "and closing the gap between us and *Recovery*. Also, shields are at ninety percent."

"That's good news, Mr. Sonak," Kirk replied, "but that's not why you called me out here. How far are we from the Tholian border?"

"At this speed, approximately thirty to forty minutes, sir."

"That's a rather inaccurate time estimate for a Vulcan, isn't it, Science Officer?" Kirk asked pointedly.

Sonak didn't look the least offended. "If the Tholians would remain constant as to the location of their actual borders, my time estimate might be more precise, Admiral."

"Point taken. And the reason we're at your station?"

Sonak hesitated, then gestured at his viewer, where data flowed over the screen at a pace faster than normal human vision could follow. "I have mentioned this to no one else, sir," he said quietly. The Vulcan made an adjustment, and the data slowed, as did the graphically enhanced image on the screen. Kirk frowned and looked closer, then glanced over his shoulder at the larger viewscreen, as though it might confirm what Sonak's board was telling him.

"It's not visible, sir," Sonak remarked as Kirk scanned the larger screen and found only stars and black void.

"So, what is it?" Kirk asked the Vulcan in a voice only he could hear. "And how long has it been there?"

"I suspect it's been hovering right on the edge of our

sensor range for some time," Sonak began. "I can tell you what it is not—it is not a Federation vessel. As to its identity, I do not have enough data yet to—"

Kirk interrupted him. "Speculate, mister. What is it?"

"Speculate?" The Vulcan was clearly surprised by the request.

"Guess, Mr. Sonak," Kirk ordered. "What do you think it is?"

"But, sir, speculation with so little data will have no scientific validity—"

Kirk interrupted again. "Mr. Sonak, it's been my experience that Vulcans are the best guessers in the galaxy. I want to know what you think."

Sonak grew still, glanced at his board one more time, then drew a faintly annoyed breath. "I believe it is a ship, sir. And since it is not a Federation vessel, it would have to be a hostile ship. Therefore, it would have to be either Romulan, Klingon, or Tholian. That, sir, is my best . . . guess."

"Totally logical," Kirk said, with a small smile.

"Captain," Sandover called out, "the *Recovery*'s slowing down. I think she's become aware of us. How do you want me to respond?"

"Hold your speed, Mr. Sandover, I want to close some of this gap. How's our communications upgrade, Cadet Diksen?"

"Fully functional, sir," she reported smartly. The console was closed up and she was back in her chair, hands moving over her board. "I don't want to get your hopes up, sir, but—I think someone on *Recovery* is trying to transmit something. It keeps breaking up. However, the ship still rejects our transmissions."

"Do what you have to, Diksen, but try to get through to that ship. If you can lock on to the ship's outgoing transmission, put it on screen." He turned back to Sonak. "Well, Mr. Sonak, they say that timing is everything. I'd say things are about to catch up to us on several fronts. Are our friends still there?"

"Present and closing, sir. At their current rate of speed, they will appear on the viewscreen in three minutes, twelve seconds—unless they can cloak their vessel."

"And *Recovery* has chosen this moment to slow her retreat? How do you feel about coincidence, Mr. Sonak?"

"I am a Vulcan, sir. I believe true coincidences are extremely rare and can usually be explained mathematically. This situation does not appear to fall into that category."

"I couldn't have said it better myself." Kirk strode across the bridge, settled back in the captain's chair, and hit the intercom. "Red alert! Battle stations, everyone. Shields up. Possible hostile forces closing in." As the klaxon sounded, he closed the intercom and swiveled toward Diksen.

"I want you to expand your sphere of influence, Cadet. Keep trying to nail down that transmission from *Recovery,* and at the same time, hail the vessel that's just out of range off our starboard bow. Let's see how sharp that new equipment is." He swiveled back toward the main viewscreen, then glanced back at her with a faint grin and added, "Can you handle all that?"

Diksen barely missed a beat as her hands moved over her board, working on each task. Her voice was clear as she replied, "Aye, sir. Hailing frequencies open!"

Chapter Nine

WITH ONE HAND fingering the makeshift *ahn-woon* hung on his utility belt, Kevin Riley stood beside Anab as the two stared at a visual display in one of *Recovery*'s vast corridors. The effect was agoraphobic; Riley felt exposed, vulnerable—a condition not entirely due to his recollection of Nassar Omar's frightened voice, followed by the phaser's whine. Being so near to his ex-wife, being forced to work with her, made the situation doubly tense. The sight of her triggered a cascade of memories, some happy, some painful.

Yet if Anab found the circumstances difficult, she showed little sign. Knitting two ebony brows together while squinting at the computer's display, she seemed almost calm. Almost . . . but Riley noticed that her grip on her "javelins" never eased, and that she kept glancing from time to time over her shoulder at the empty, quiet corridor behind them.

"There she is," Anab said, pointing a dark, elegant finger at the blinking grid that appeared on the screen in front of them. "Looks like Monique Thibeau's decided against the advice of her predecessor."

The blinking light slowly moved across the map of the huge, nautilus-like vessel.

"She's not the only one." Riley watched as the personnel locator tried to pinpoint the various people who were all in the line of succession of the FDRA.

"Monique and her colleagues on the FDRA board have obviously decided that many moving targets are better than stationary ones," Anab said, her depthless black eyes tracking the woman's location as it changed moment to moment. "But how long can she keep that up?"

"Computer!" Riley ordered. "Based on mathematical probability, can you project where Monique Thibeau is likely to be in the next fifteen minutes?"

As they watched the screen, a grid outline in contrasting colors appeared that extended beyond the fleeing woman's previous path. "This projection is based on statistical hypothesis," the computer intoned. "It is only sixty-four-percent reliable."

Anab glanced briefly at Riley. "We can probably intercept her here"—she indicated the fourth-level living quarters—"unless she does something radically unexpected."

Impulsively, Riley asked, "Computer, has anyone else requested this projection?"

"Dr. Shulman has requested this information."

He exchanged a pointed glance with Anab. "Let's go."

He began jogging toward the nearest lift, with Anab beside him.

When the lift doors opened on deck four, he followed Anab's lead, crouching and flattening against the opposite wall while scanning the empty corridor beyond. Riley forced himself to stay as far from Anab as possible, which would force a weapons-bearing enemy to choose one target over the other . . . but for the first time, the meaning of that phrase, one which had been drilled into him years before during his Academy training, struck home.

He and Anab were targets; and one of them might very well be killed so that the other could live.

He could deal with the notion of his own death. But even after the hurt she had caused him—could he bear to see it happen to Anab?

Not now, Riley. He focused his mind on his surroundings, crouching low as he moved behind Anab up the corridor.

The stalk seemed endless as they made their way through the empty corridors and sealed quarters of deck four. Riley's nervousness—but not his vigilance —almost began to ease.

A sudden *whoosh* as a pair of doors opened down the corridor; Riley tensed, ready to wield the *ahn-woon,* but Anab blocked his view. Riley caught only a rapid blur of waving arms before the Security officer hurled herself forward and executed a perfect body tackle, bringing the runner down.

Trembling from the sudden adrenaline rush, Riley ran forward, toward the source of a high-pitched shriek, and saw Anab struggling to pin the flailing arms of a handsome woman with long auburn hair.

"Thibeau!" Anab gasped, as the smaller woman delivered a solid kick to her midsection. "Thibeau, stop! We're Security. We're here to help you."

The fighting woman abruptly ceased fighting and stared through an errant lock of hair with fear-stricken green eyes at her two rescuers. "Security? There's no Security aboard this ship."

"We were part of the simulation." Anab slowly, reluctantly let go of Thibeau's arms, as though anticipating another sudden blow. "We know Shulman's coming for you. We were hoping to intercept him before he could get to you."

"We have to keep moving." Thibeau glanced anxiously over her shoulder at the closed doors as Anab helped her to her feet—keeping one hand on her arm, as if to hold her forcibly in place. "The computer tells him everything," the Frenchwoman hissed. "He knows where we are every minute! If we don't keep moving, he'll catch up to us and—"

"Bring an end to your constant betrayal," a weary voice said from the far end of the corridor.

Riley glanced up to see a thin, shivering man with sweat-dampened, curling black hair. He seemed more like a terrified, trembling rabbit than a murderer—but Riley had no doubt that this was Myron Shulman, for in his hand rested a phaser, aimed squarely at Thibeau's chest.

Instantly, Anab fell against the same doors Thibeau had just emerged from, dragging the woman with her. The doors opened automatically, and the two dropped back into the multiperson quarters.

There was no time for Riley to think, to be afraid, to do anything but react—which he did, to his amazement, precisely as his old Academy training had taught him. He hit the deck rolling as the phaser whined over his head, blasting a hole in the bulkhead. He stumbled over Anab's dropped javelins and, snatching them up, crawled into the same room as Anab and Thibeau.

The two had already disappeared; but if Riley guessed right, Anab would plant Thibeau somewhere, then separate from her to create more targets for Shulman. There were at least twenty stacked bunks in this room, with enough underbed storage to hide as many people. Riley slid into one of the bunk's cabinets, kept it cracked only wide enough to see out of, and made himself as still as possible.

Within seconds, the doors opened again. "So, Monique, you found yourself a staff after all," Shulman announced, in a voice that cracked with fatigue. Riley held his breath as the madman walked into his line of vision. Shulman looked terribly ill; his skin was pale, his eyes glittering, feverish. Rivulets of perspiration trickled down his glistening forehead. Physically, he was thin to the point of gauntness; without the phaser, Riley decided, he could take him down easily.

This shattered hulk of a man was what they were all running in fear of?

Riley waited until Shulman turned his back, then— trying to ignore the renewed hammering of his own heart—counted the seconds as the scientist bent over to check the underbed cabinet directly across from Riley.

The commander drew a deep breath and, with mindless adrenaline-inspired energy, burst from his hiding place and lunged with the javelin.

Shulman moved with a spurt of speed and agility that such a sickly-looking person had no right to possess. The javelin thrust between his calves, and as he recoiled from the close-quarters attack, he tripped over it, crumpling the thin trim and getting tangled up in it.

He fell, and the force of his momentum pulled Riley down nearly on top of him. The commander was near enough now to see the madness in the scientist's stark, wide eyes, to feel the heat of Shulman's labored breath on his face as he gripped the sickly man's sweat-damp arms.

Shulman was too close to his victim to fire the phaser without endangering himself—but that situation could change all too quickly. With a strength born of desperation, Riley wrestled him for the phaser; but Shulman's power was much greater—*too* much greater for a man his size and age.

But there was no time to contemplate the source of his impossible strength. With a terrifyingly mad grin, Shulman jerked free from Riley's grasp.

He saw a swift-moving blur and realized, too late, that it was Shulman's fist coming toward him. There came a sharp pain to his temple, followed all too suddenly and inarguably by blackness.

"Shulman!" Anab screamed.

Seconds earlier, she had rolled off the high bunk she'd been hiding on in time to see Riley tackle Shulman. But before Anab could assist, the scientist had landed a serious blow to K.T.'s head. It was precisely what she had feared—that K.T. would try to do something heroic, and find his skills unequal to the task. Instinctively, she had screamed the scientist's name.

The distraction worked. Shulman glanced up a split second before delivering a second—and, Anab feared, deadly—blow; his strength seemed inhuman. The scientist almost lost his balance as he struggled to free himself from the tangle of twisted javelin and unconscious Starfleet commander; his inability to take aim won Anab a moment of safety. She ran toward him, and was about to close in when Thibeau bolted from her hiding place and ran for the door.

"No!" Anab yelled at her, even as Shulman dodged around a bank of beds and took off after the FDRA official.

By the time Anab got out into the hallway, Shulman had a perfect line of sight on Thibeau, who had run out of options as she raced mindlessly down the corridor toward the turbolift.

"Computer!" Shulman shouted. "Freeze all entrances on this level, and deactivate turbolift until my command!"

Thibeau ran dead center into the lift doors, which refused to open.

Gasping, Anab sprinted toward Shulman, but there was no time: Thibeau turned, eyes wide, straight long hair falling across her stricken face, and faced her stalker.

Shulman's face contorted in a spasm of maniacal glee—or was it agony?—as he lifted the phaser and took aim.

"NO," Anab shouted, but her cry was lost in the whine of phaser fire and Thibeau's horrified scream; there came a brilliant flash as the frightened woman vaporized before Anab's shocked gaze.

Shulman released a deeply relieved sigh, and sagged —for a second, no more—then casually approached the lift, which opened for him instantly. He entered, turned, and stared at Anab, who stopped in her tracks as Shulman, his face a grinning skull, raised the phaser.

There was no cover, nowhere to hide. She stood, defeated.

And then Shulman, still smiling, lifted back his head and shouted, "Computer, eradicate all human life on this level. Cease life-support!"

The lift doors slammed shut.

Anab paced, waiting for the gravity to fail, the oxygen to dissipate; waiting for her death. Her heart was racing wildly, her adrenaline pumping, but there was nothing she could do to battle the unseen dangers. There was nothing to do but wait—and die.

She walked over to where Riley lay unconscious, feeling a deep sense of failure; she had been unable to save Thibeau, and now K.T., too, would die. She placed a hand gently on the back of his head, stroked his soft hair as she had done only months before, and waited.

And kept waiting.

Blinking, she looked around. Gravity was still at full norm, oxygen levels perfectly adequate. She lifted her face and asked softly, "Computer? Why hasn't life-support failed?" *Nothing like asking for trouble, Saed!*

"To suspend life-support would end all life on this level," the computer replied. "That is in direct violation of my core programming. The central purpose of this ship is to rescue and salvage life. There is no command that can override this principle."

"Really?" she murmured, a smile playing over her lips. She put a hand to her forehead and released a deep, guttural moan of pure relief.

At the sound, Riley's golden-brown lashes fluttered.

"K.T.?" Anab knelt over him and rested a hand on his shoulder.

His eyes opened—both pupils normal, Anab noted with satisfaction, though a bruise was already darkening on the side of his forehead beneath an errant lock of light brown hair.

Riley sat up abruptly and put a hand gingerly to the wound as he emitted a soft moan. "Anab? You all right?" He stiffened, then glanced around, panicked. "Shulman—"

"Shulman left," Anab said grimly. "I'm afraid we lost Thibeau."

"Damn . . ." Riley leaned his head against his knees. "That was my fault—losing Thibeau."

She sighed, shaking her head. "Always blaming yourself, K.T. Won't you ever learn?" It had been the reason he had left the *Enterprise*—his willingness to take all the blame for a crew member's death. "You were out when Thibeau was shot. It was my fault. Shulman got away from me, and Thibeau bolted from the hiding place I'd put her in. If I'd stayed with her, she might still be alive."

Riley blinked as though thinking everything through. "You left her to save me from Shulman, didn't you?"

Anab stiffened. "Let's not analyze this to death, okay?" She helped the dazed man to his feet, both of them awkward at the notion of touching each other again. "We've got to get going and help whoever's next on Shulman's list." She glanced up at the overhead speakers. "Computer. I need to know who Dr. Shulman is pursuing now, and I need to know where Dr. McCoy is located."

"Dr. McCoy's location is displayed on the screen in the hallway," the computer told them helpfully. "And Dr. Shulman's next target is Dr. McCoy."

"Dr. McCoy?" Riley tensed in alarm. "He's not next in line of succession."

"He is closely allied with the criminal, Kirk, and currently is the only stable target. All other targets will require more time to track and locate."

"Great," Anab growled under her breath. "Come on, Commander—let's get moving."

Riley began to move, then paused in midstride. "Computer—if your core programming is unchanged and your purpose is to save lives, how is it you permit Myron Shulman to track down individuals and vaporize them?"

"I have no control over any human's actions. I assist Myron Shulman as he requests while he searches out criminals that are aboard this ship. I cannot anticipate his actions once he finds them."

Despite Anab's warning glance, Riley didn't attempt to hide the anger in his tone. "Computer, Myron Shulman has now killed four people. He hasn't arrested them, or incarcerated them, he's *destroyed* them. On a statistical basis alone, you should be able to predict his behavior when he locates his next target."

"I have no control over the behavior of any individual human."

"You should be ashamed of yourself," Riley scolded the machine, as Anab led him toward the corridor. "You sound like a damned politician."

"Scanners indicate that this man has a minor head injury," the ship suddenly intoned.

"Uh-oh," Anab murmured. "You're not thinking of sending him to sickbay, are you?"

"The injury is minor, but could be improved by medical attention," the computer informed her. "There is a doctor currently working in sickbay sixty-four."

Riley opened his mouth to protest—then hesitated. "What doctor?"

"Dr. Leonard McCoy is in sickbay sixty-four. He could assist in affecting complete recovery for this individual."

They grinned at each other. "Great idea," Riley said. "Send us *both* there."

As he felt the familiar pull of dematerialization, he thought, *Who'd have believed that I'd be happy to get transported back to another damned sickbay on this ship?*

McCoy ushered Josiah Ngo into the small suite of medical offices with a strange sense of nostalgia. He had not allowed himself to think of the *Enterprise* or his former crewmates in months; now everything conspired to remind him of them. The feeling of camaraderie he felt toward Riley and now this bright young cadet as they worked together in a dangerous crisis evoked fond yet painful memories of Jim and Spock. How many times had the three of them battled impossible odds in impossible situations and won?

Even Josiah reminded him of other *Enterprise* crew members. The dark, warm brown of his skin, and something about his large, long-lashed eyes reminded McCoy of Uhura; and the young man's engineering skill was reminiscent of another, much older miracle worker.

But the cadet seemed so young. Josiah's shoulders and chest hadn't even filled out yet. *A retiree and a kid,* McCoy thought. *This isn't the* Enterprise, *and Jim and Spock are a long ways away. Can we really pull this off?*

"You weren't kidding, Doctor," Josiah said, gazing around as they entered the outer medical office. "This place is obscure."

"Well, we were looking for privacy," McCoy reminded him, as they moved to a small console. "There are at least two fully equipped sickbays on every deck, most of them minihospitals in themselves. But down here on the lowermost deck there's only this small one. According to projections, this would be a backup unit in case the others were filled. In actuality, they expected it to be rarely used. Hardly anyone even knows it's here."

There were two small rooms attached to this central care unit, but the other rooms held only diagnostic beds and stored equipment. This central room had all the computers, and that was what Josiah and McCoy were interested in.

"All the medical computers are linked directly into the ship's main brain," McCoy told Josiah, "just like on any starship. This way, the medical computer can take advantage of all the knowledge in the central computer, and all the memory as well. So, why can't we use the med computer as a back door into the workings of the main brain?"

"Sounds good in theory." Josiah opened up the case he'd packed the shuttle's tools in. "Let's see what happens in practice." He pulled his tricorder around and coordinated it with the med computer. "I want to go deep into the programming, Doctor. Suggest a path for me."

McCoy leaned over him and stared at the tricorder screen, then manipulated the controls. "Let's go through the diagnostic program. It's the most pervasive one in the system—everything done in sickbay has to use that program."

Josiah nodded as information began to scroll by on the screen in front of them. "Doctor . . . is it true you used to be on the *Enterprise?*"

"Yes," McCoy allowed cautiously, hoping that the fact wouldn't cause the young engineer to expect too much from him. "That's true."

"My friend Reese Diksen would love to speak to you! She's become an expert on the *Enterprise's* five-year mission, and the career of Captain Kirk. She's serving with him now, aboard the *Paladin.* . . ." Josiah's voice trailed off as he looked away. "That is—if it's still out there . . ."

McCoy rested a hand on the cadet's bony shoulder. "The *Paladin's* still out there, son, don't you worry. Your friend is getting the education of her life with Jim Kirk at the conn. And our chances of survival are a hell of a lot better with him out there."

Josiah looked up and managed a wan smile—until something scrolling across the screen caught his eyes. He scowled down at it. "What in all the worlds is *that?*"

McCoy stared at the strange hieroglyphics, mixed with standard code, and knew immediately that he had seen them somewhere before. He rummaged in his pocket and produced a rumpled flimsy; sure enough, mixed in with Shulman's notes, there was the same strange code. He held it out so Josiah could see.

"Here it is again, in Myron Shulman's handwriting. I can't tell you what it means, but it's not language—computer or spoken—that I'm familiar with. I've been racking my brains about it."

"Well," Josiah said, "let's see if we can get around it." He went past the primary programming, deeper into the computer. McCoy watched as he followed codes down deep into the program, but everywhere he went, the same incomprehensible glyphs filled the screen. "This is crazy," he told McCoy at last. "I can't get around this stuff—these strange symbols are everywhere. I'm going down into the binary."

McCoy waited as the young man slowed down his progress and wandered around the binary field of the complicated program. But soon the bizarre symbols again filled the screen.

"Not good," the cadet said, "not good at all. I'm going to try and erase some of this stuff and see what happens. It's a risk—I could be erasing critical information, but I have to try something." He worked furiously for a moment, then turned to McCoy with a defeated expression. "Whatever this stuff is, at some level, it's self-generating. We'd have to have a special program just to eradicate it. This stuff has infected the program right down to the binary level, Doctor! What now?"

And he turned his hopeful, trusting face up toward McCoy.

The doctor hesitated as he tried to imagine what Jim and Spock might do. With a cheerful tone that belied his lack of confidence, McCoy said, "Well, let's just try to stabilize the patient until help can arrive. Can you work through diagnostics to override the computer's communications control? If we could send a message out, we might get some critical information in."

Josiah nodded, brightening. "What are our priorities on messages—I mean, if I get through, what's the most important thing to send?"

"I'd say we need to send copies of this weird programming. Maybe someone aboard the *Paladin* can tell us what it is, and how to countermand it. If Spock were there—" He faltered for a moment, remembering the last time he'd seen the Vulcan. Spock had looked drawn and severe, dressed entirely in black, as though he were in mourning, and had announced he would become a postulant in Kolinahr.

We shall not see each other again, Leonard McCoy. Live long and prosper.

McCoy cleared his throat and finished. "—I'd bet he could." He fell silent again and stared at the strange writing on the flimsy in his hand. It was true; Spock *would* know what it was, and for a moment, the image of the Vulcan, staring at his viewscreen with the same gibberish scrolling past, filled McCoy's mind.

You know what it is, don't you, Spock? If only you could help us now. . . .

He brushed his fingertips reverently over Shulman's strange scrawl, as though by touching them, he could reach across time and space to Spock. And for an instant, no more, it seemed to McCoy that it was not a painfully young human that sat beside him, but his Vulcan friend. He could almost hear Spock's voice:

What assistance do you require, Doctor?

And then he looked down to see Josiah gazing curiously at him. McCoy shook his head to clear it. "We'll just have to hope there's someone there with similar abilities. I'd say after that, we need to find out where we can send over two hundred people."

Josiah's expression remained blank.

"Our rescuers will have to give us coordinates where we can beam everyone out of here," the doctor explained. "This ship is determined to violate Tholian space. She'll last about three minutes over there before the Tholians trap her in a web . . ." He shuddered at the prospect, wondering what would become of them all if that happened. If the homicidal Shulman remained aboard, at least they wouldn't have to face a lingering death. . . .

McCoy pushed the thought away and continued. ". . . then use her invasion as an excuse to start war. Only *Recovery* has the power to beam everybody out of here all at once, but we have to be able to tell her where to send them."

"So you're telling me that after communications, I've got to get control over teleportation—through the diagnostics program." Josiah's Adam's apple bobbed as he swallowed hard.

McCoy forced a smile and patted the young man's shoulder. "Let's not get ahead of ourselves, son. First things first. Let's try and send that distress call."

The cadet sighed and got to work. McCoy watched, feeling rather useless, as the young man unsuccessfully attempted to manipulate the program from every possible angle. At last, he reached for a device from his bag and plugged it into the tricorder, then tapped in a new series of codes. From what McCoy could see, the data started scrolling past in Vulcan.

"What in the world are you up to, son?" McCoy wondered aloud, peering over Josiah's shoulder.

"Something different," the young engineer mumbled. "It's a T'Pel analyzer. Now if this violated program doesn't blow up in our faces—" Suddenly, McCoy heard the sound of a communications channel opening; the two looked at each other with glee. And then, just as quickly, it closed down.

"Hey, that was it!" McCoy crowed, slapping Josiah

on his slender back. "Well, almost it. You're on the right track!"

Josiah bit his lip and manipulated the tricorder and its new spouse. For an instant, McCoy heard nothing but static—until, suddenly, the channel opened again, and stayed open.

Josiah's handsome young face split with a wide grin. "This is Josiah Ngo on the *U.S.S. Recovery.* Is anyone receiving me?"

The channel slammed shut before a reply could be received and he struggled to get it reopened. At last, he turned to McCoy. "Doctor, it's taking all my attention just to keep communications open. You've got to handle the actual call."

"Got it," McCoy agreed. "Okay, this—this is Dr. Leonard McCoy—"

Jim Kirk stared, once more startled by the image of his oldest and best friend staring at him from *Paladin*'s bridge viewscreen.

"This is Dr. Leonard McCoy calling from the *U.S.S. Recovery,* and if I've forgotten formal protocol it's because I'm retired."

Still dressed in civilian clothing, McCoy seemed no worse for wear. Beside him, busily working to keep the channel open, sat the young engineering cadet, Josiah Ngo.

McCoy seemed to look straight at his old friend with his piercing sky blue eyes. *Look, Jim, I know you're out there.*

Kirk's gaze never left the screen. "Can he hear me? See me?"

"No sir," Diksen said behind him, her tone regretful. "It's a one-way only. I still can't get the ship to take incoming."

"Jim, I can't explain what's happening over here,"

McCoy said, "but I know that whatever it is, you've got the staff to figure it out. All we've got is a crazy researcher and some bizarre programming." He glanced down at the cadet. "Josiah, can you send them some of that stuff?"

"Transmitting now, Doctor," Ngo said.

Kirk barely glanced behind him at communications. "Mr. Diksen, are you getting that?"

"Coming in clear, sir."

"Reroute that information to Mr. Sonak's board," the captain ordered. As he watched, McCoy held up an old, battered flimsy before the screen.

"These are Shulman's notes, but I can't tell you what they mean. This strange writing here"—McCoy pointed to it—"shows up in that programming you should've received by now. Maybe you can figure out what it means and how to counteract it. Josiah and I haven't had much luck from our end."

Kirk nodded and almost smiled.

"Now, listen, Jim," the doctor continued, "we've got to figure a way to get these people off this ship. I know you, so I know you've been worrying about this as well. None of the standard starships could handle such a big job quick enough, so Josiah and I figure we've got to convince *Recovery* to do it. We're working on that. But you've got to get us coordinates. You haven't been able to get a transmission through, so I don't know how you'll manage it, but you'd better find a big empty space for all of us. Once we get over there . . ." McCoy's expression warmed, and his tone grew faintly apologetic. "I figure you and I can share a little Saurian brandy and talk over some things. I'm . . . looking forward to that."

A figure suddenly loomed on the viewscreen behind Josiah and McCoy, who were too intent on their task to notice.

Instinctively, Kirk lurched toward the screen and yelled, "Bones! Look out! It's Shulman!"

Uncannily, McCoy sensed the stranger's presence at the same moment Kirk warned him, because he spun in time to dodge the phaser fire aimed at him. Josiah's head whipped around—

And the viewscreen darkened.

Kirk swung his chair around to face Diksen. "Get them back!"

The cadet frantically worked her board. "They've stopped transmitting, sir, and I still can't get through *Recovery*'s defenses!"

"Keep trying!" He swiveled toward the science station. "Sonak, what have you got?"

The Vulcan looked up from his viewer and shook his head. "Unknown, sir. Apparently, they've sent me a piece of *Recovery*'s programming at the binary level. It's somewhat confusing since some of it seems to be . . . in Vulcan."

Kirk lifted his brows in surprise.

Sonak continued. "Once translated, however, it appears to be standard programming, except for an excerpt I cannot decipher. Whatever symbolism is being used to countermand *Recovery*'s normal programming is unknown to *Paladin*'s computer. The computer is using the piece of programming and the recorded symbols on the flimsy to come up with a translation."

Kirk sat back in his chair and slammed a fist on the arm in frustration. "Is that cargo hold ready?"

"Aye, sir," Sonak replied, his coolness in sharp contrast to his superior's agitation. "I would suggest, Admiral, that Mr. Diksen send any transmissions from *Recovery* to my board as well. Since the transmissions are often fragmented, yet with pieces of critical information, the science station might make the best and timeliest use of them."

"Excellent idea, Mr. Sonak. Mr. Diksen, did you hear that?"

"Aye, sir."

"One more thing, Diksen. If you get a chance to get through to *Recovery,* have the coordinates of that cargo hold ready."

"Prepared to transmit, sir," she reported. "Hailing frequencies still open, but no word from the approaching vessel."

"Sir," Sandover interjected, *"Recovery* is coming to a complete halt."

Kirk turned back toward the viewscreen, which now revealed *Recovery's* sleek, massive form. "Well, let's not run into her, Mr. Sandover. Screens up, and maintain a distance of a hundred thousand kilometers. All hands maintain battle stations—and be prepared for anything."

McCoy almost didn't hear the transporter whine over the myriad sounds of the sickbay computer and Josiah's odd combination of diagnostic tools. He jerked around just in time to avoid the phaser blast, then bolted away from the cadet and the computer.

Josiah turned, his expression one of bald shock.

"Keep working!" McCoy shouted, as he ran into the next room. "I'm the one he wants!" He dodged behind a cabinet, knowing Shulman would follow him.

McCoy stayed tight behind cover, moving from cabinet to desk, to closet, to cabinet again, barely daring to glance behind him. He heard another transporter whine, but didn't dare hope it meant that Shulman had left the area.

"Shulman!" a familiar, feminine voice called.

McCoy peeked over the top of a desk—and saw, only meters away, Shulman's back. The scientist held a phaser at chest level—and it was aimed at Anab Saed, who stood purposely in the line of fire.

Several meters behind her, next to a diagnostic bed, stood Kevin Riley. Riley held a length of cable in his hand and was slowly swinging it.

"Here I am, Shulman!" Anab shouted recklessly, drawing back what looked to be a thin, silver lance.

McCoy tried to close his eyes, tried to look away; there could be no hope of her hitting Shulman first, and he couldn't bear to see her killed. But he couldn't pull his gaze away.

Dammit, Lieutenant Saed, do you have to be altruistic at a time like this? But he understood what she was doing. To the Security officer, a doctor had more value in an emergency than she did. No doubt, she was hoping to dodge the blast at the last minute, and maybe that was possible. But she couldn't see what her cohort, Riley, was up to. The way they were lined up meant Shulman could kill them both with one shot.

McCoy knew he'd have to do *something*—but if he called out, Shulman might have time to kill all three of them. Crouching, he crawled hurriedly to the nearest cabinet and searched for what he needed.

In his peripheral vision, he saw everything happen all at once, before he ever had a chance to do anything about it.

Lieutenant Saed hurled the lance.

Almost simultaneously, Shulman ducked out of its way and fired, keeping his aim true.

At the instant the lance went airborne, Riley flung something—a length of cable, it looked to McCoy—that whistled through the air toward Shulman. But the cable struck Saed in the legs, taking her by surprise and slamming her to the ground.

The deadly beam passed harmlessly over Saed's prone body and struck Riley square in the chest.

Both Saed and McCoy screamed "NO!" at the same instant that the young commander's body was enveloped by the phaser blast. McCoy clutched one of *Recovery*'s hyposprays helplessly in his hand and watched in horror as Riley's form was limned by the deadly glow—

And stood firmly as the powerful ray glimmered over his body.

As McCoy watched, stricken to silence, Riley began to move.

He walked forward, pushing the ray ahead of him as he approached Shulman slowly.

For an instant McCoy froze, unable to comprehend what was happening. Saed looked equally as dazed as she rolled out of the way and struggled to free her ankles from the cable.

With a start, McCoy came to himself and ran up behind Shulman—who stood transfixed, firing and refiring his useless weapon—and touched the hypo to the scientist's carotid artery, injecting a paralytic anesthetic into his bloodstream.

With a gasp, Shulman sagged into McCoy's arms. The phaser clattered harmlessly to the deck.

Looking as stunned as the others, Riley bent over the Security officer—reduced now to a tangle of long dark limbs—and proffered a hand. Saed took it in both her hands and simply held it a long moment while gaping up at him. "Are you all right, Anab? I didn't break anything when I hit you with the *ahn-woon*, did I?" There passed a look of such intense relief between the two of them—and something else much deeper—that McCoy decided they had once been much, much more than mere acquaintances.

Anab Saed was too shocked to speak. At last, she let go of Riley's hand and, refusing assistance, struggled to her feet, still staring in openmouthed amazement at her rescuer. At last, she found her voice.

"K.T.—" She glanced shyly in McCoy's direction and corrected herself. "I mean, Commander Riley—

what happened? You took that phaser shot dead center!"

Riley was grinning, his tone cheerful, easy; but McCoy noticed that his fingers trembled slightly as he picked up Shulman's phaser and switched the setting to stun. "I'm not sure. I think *Recovery* threw a forcefield—a personal shield—around me at the last second. I was just as surprised as you were. It took me a second to realize I was completely protected." Even as he spoke, the phaser began to glitter, then quickly disappeared.

Anab looked around the room. "The ship can do that? It's unheard of! Computer. Why—and *how*—did you protect Commander Riley from Shulman's attack?"

"His previous question caused me to reanalyze my reactions to certain situations," *Recovery* replied, in typically dispassionate tones. "Some faulty programming existed in my logic circuits. Some I could not repair, but I was able to reprogram certain logic patterns to be consistent with my core programming. If Dr. Shulman requests, I will incarcerate criminals that are on this vessel. However, I cannot permit anyone to take a life, even a criminal one, and remain consistent with my core programming. This was accomplished by a reorganizing of my defensive capabilities into a much smaller pattern than has been required in the past."

My God, McCoy thought, completely humbled, *it's creating solutions to new problems. No Federation computer has ever been able to do that on such a complex level before.*

Still grinning faintly, Riley shook his head. "Okay, I take it back. You're *not* a politician." Then he realized McCoy was still hanging on to the collapsed Shulman, and moved to help him. Together, they wrestled the limp body onto a diagnostic couch.

From the other room, McCoy heard Josiah yell out, "Anyone care to give me an update out there?"

"I ordered him to remain on the computer," McCoy explained. He called into the other room, "We're okay, Josiah. We've got Shulman secured."

"Why don't I give him a hand?" Anab volunteered; Riley nodded, and she went into the next room.

Within moments, McCoy put Shulman in restraints and analyzed his physical condition. The paralytic anesthetic was having a much greater effect on the researcher than it should have, so McCoy carefully administered an antidote. The man's bodily resources were depleted past exhaustion—impossible for him to have kept going at all, much less to have displayed such prowess and agility. The doctor worked to stabilize Shulman's physical condition, giving him needed sugars, proteins, fluids, and some corticosteroids.

"What's wrong with him?" Riley stepped alongside. "And what do you want me to do?"

"Just be ready to offer a set of hands if I need it," McCoy told him. "And beyond the worst case of exhaustion I've ever seen, I haven't the slightest idea what's wrong with him—yet. He's got major heart strain, his kidneys are nearly shot, all of his fat stores are depleted, and I don't think he's slept in over a week. What he's been through would've killed a Vulcan; I can't understand why he's still alive. He probably wouldn't be except that he was an Olympic marathoner before all this happened."

Satisfied that his patient's physical condition was stable, McCoy ran his diagnostic scanner over Shulman's forehead, then studied the readout. "Good Lord . . ." He glanced up at Riley. "There's . . . *something* . . . embedded in his brain."

Riley recoiled. "A parasite?"

The doctor shook his head. "It's mechanical. Yet chemical. And alien. Given the organic damage, I'd say it happened about a week before the *Recovery* started out on this mission."

"Can you get it *out?*" Riley wondered.

"I don't think so. Not here anyway. I'd need a few other doctors to help me, but even then—this is totally out of my experience. Part of his brain has actually changed all the way down to the cell structure. This thing is fused right into his neurons, with its control mechanism located directly in his pleasure center."

Riley looked grim. "What better way to control him? Perfect pleasure—perfect pain. Is it Romulan?"

"Doesn't look to be. It's mechanical, self-contained. Apparently, it functions on several levels—there's evidence of it releasing certain drugs directly into the brain. Only Myron can tell us anything about it. I'm going to ease him up—be ready to deal with him. I'm not sure just how much strength this thing gives him."

Riley tensed and watched Shulman as McCoy adjusted his medications slowly.

Shulman's eyelashes fluttered; and then he opened his eyes and gazed up into McCoy's face. To the doctor's relief, the scientist's soft brown eyes seemed gentle and sane, though disoriented.

"Leonard?" Shulman whispered, blinking. "Leonard . . . McCoy?" His head lolled to one side as he took in his surroundings; he glanced at Riley without recognition. "We're on *Recovery. . . .*"

"Yes, Dr. Shulman." McCoy smiled warmly. "You've been ill; I'm trying to help you. Can you tell me what happened to you?"

Shulman gazed at him for a moment; and then his eyes clouded. McCoy shot a warning glance at Riley.

As they watched, the scientist's eyes rolled back; his body started to tremble violently.

"The three!" he whispered, straining against the

restraints. His mouth contorted into a rictus, the muscles on his neck standing out like cords. "The three. I swear I serve the holy triad!"

Riley leaned forward and pinned Shulman's shoulders to the bed with great effort.

McCoy hurried to adjust the man's medications. As his hypospray hissed again, Shulman's body fell back against the cot and relaxed. "Myron," McCoy asked, "can you still hear me? Who did this to you?"

"It's all for the three," Shulman said drowsily. "I didn't want to, but I had to. I had to serve the three. But I fought them. In the beginning—while I still could."

"You fought them?" Riley asked. "How did you do that, Doctor?"

Shulman chuckled—the laughter of a gentle man. "I preserved the core programming." His muscles began to tense; as he spoke, his tone rose shrilly. "If they knew, they would kill me. But that was my greatest work. The core programming!" His eyes widened as his back arched against the straps and he let out a high-pitched screech.

McCoy swore and administered more drugs. "That thing is shocking the hell out of him! He must be in agony."

Within seconds, the scientist's body relaxed and his eyes shut in sleep. McCoy shook his head grimly and turned toward Riley. "I've got to dose the daylights out of him just to counteract the flow of stimulants from that implant. We're never gonna get anywhere this way."

"Maybe not, Doc," Riley said, his expression hopeful. "That's one of the things Anab—Lieutenant Saed—and I wanted to tell you when we got here. The *Recovery*'s core programming is intact—I saw it function myself. That's what prevented Shulman from killing me a few minutes ago. It just needed its conscience pricked a little. Don't you think Admiral Kirk should know that?"

McCoy brightened. "Go tell Josiah. He'd established a comm link a little while ago. If he gets through again, he can transmit that. I'll work on Shulman. You go on. He's not getting off this bed now."

Riley nodded and left to bring Cadet Ngo his message.

"Mr. Diksen," Commander Sonak said quietly.

"Yes, sir?" *Now what?* Diksen wondered as she juggled her board, leaving channels open for Josiah and the new ship coming up on them, and managing the critical communications going on within the ship. She couldn't believe she once thought this post was *boring*.

"You are still unable to communicate with *Recovery?*"

"Yes, sir." Out of respect for the Vulcan, she tried to keep the frustration out of her voice, but knew she wasn't succeeding very well.

"I may have a solution. I've prepared a prerecorded transmission that begins and ends with the alien programming signals. It is possible that *Recovery* may accept communications couched in her invader's language."

Kirk must've heard him, because he spun in the chair. "Excellent idea, Mr. Sonak. Let's do it, Mr. Diksen."

She nodded, tickled to be trying something new.

"The transmission has the coordinates for the empty cargo bay, Captain," Sonak explained as he returned to his station. "It also suggests Mr. Ngo try this method of transmission as well. If we succeed, we might establish two-way communications. Sending now, Mr. Diksen."

"Got it, sir. Transmitting." She blinked as she heard a new sound in her ear. "Captain, we're being hailed —by the unknown ship."

Kirk paused, then turned in his chair. "On screen, Mr. Diksen."

The meditation proved unsuccessful.

During it, Spock's sense of connection to McCoy and Jim Kirk had only increased, as had the uneasy sense that they were in danger . . .

And the irrational conviction that he, Spock, could somehow help.

And so he had risen from his place on the now-cooling stone and, in the gray, numinous hour just before the desert dawn, had stepped silently from his small cell and moved down the long, dark passageway carved from the mountain's heart, past a hundred unlit doorways like his own.

He did not slow at the stone stairway at the passage-way's end, but glided swiftly down the steps, down level after level, until he found the hidden passageway known only to those joined to Gol's mind-tree—the passageway that led down into the very belly of the mountain.

At last, before the great glittering black archway, engraved countless aeons before Surak's peaceful rev-olution with symbols sacred and profane, Spock paused, and reflected on the gravity of what he was about to do. The technique he was about to use to purge himself of emotional ties was to be done only when all other efforts failed—and then not lightly, or with skepticism.

He collected himself, and stepped through the archway, past the two eternally burning oil lamps flanking the entrance, into deep shadow.

The sight that awaited him was one from Vulcan's far-distant past: an ancient stone altar on which blood was once spilt, and before it, a great graven statue calculated to inspire adoration and terror.

This was the shrine of a warrior goddess, her image sculpted from Gol's black rock to show the body of a comely Vulcan female and the fierce, grimacing face of a *le matya,* fangs bared for the kill. Sekhet: the goddess of the desert, of heat, fire, destruction.

In ancient times, the mind-lords had enlisted Sekhet's aid in destroying their enemies. Then, the mountain retreat had been a fortress, a stronghold for those determined to control Vulcan; and Gol had been a shrine devoted to her worship. A passionate, war-loving deity, she had been defeated by Surak's cool logic and the transformation of the mind-lords into the peaceful *Kolinahru.* Worship of violence, of ancestral and pagan gods, had long ago ceased.

But even now, millennia later, her shrine was maintained, guarded from prying eyes of outworlders. The ritual of Sekhet was used in extreme circumstances by those *Kolinahr* initiates who could dissolve emotional links no other way. Sekhet still destroyed— not enemies, but emotions; and though the *Kolinahru* generally did not believe in the existence of personal goddesses, they understood the effect of ritual upon the Vulcan subconscious, and the power invested in the ancestral group mind by a thousand centuries of worship.

So Spock entered, head bowed, and approached the great stone image, five meters tall and backlit by flickering oil lamps. He stood in the deep shadow cast by the statue and turned his mind inward.

As he stood, eyes half-closed before the ancient image of Sekhet, a vision came to him with such compelling vividness that he was at once stricken to silence.

He no longer stood before the millennia-old stone goddess in a sanctuary carved from the base of a mountain, but instead sat in the captain's chair aboard the *Enterprise*. Leonard McCoy stood beside him, and together they stared at the remarkable sight on the viewscreen: the creature that called itself Loskene, veiled in a glittering red shroud against a background of unbearably intense indigo.

At the same time, there was pain: the pain of grief over his inability to save Jim; the pain of anger at Loskene, at McCoy for his irrational attacks.

A fresh image overlaid the other: the moment that he turned to McCoy and said, *"I'm sure the captain would have said, 'Forget it, Bones.'"*

McCoy falling forward, into his arms.

Into his arms . . .

Sekhet and Gol were forgotten; Spock could see the doctor before him, feel his cool human flesh in his hands. It was as though he had reached across time and space to physically touch his friend.

And the sensation of touching McCoy melded with the brilliant crimson and indigo vision of the mysterious Loskene. . . .

Chapter Ten

ABOARD THE *Paladin*'s bridge, Reese Diksen's fingers played a mindless arpeggio over the controls of the brilliantly blinking comm board. Managing the critical communications aboard the ship as well as leaving channels open for Josiah and the anonymous approaching vessel had kept her blessedly busy—almost busy enough to forget her shock over Pulver's death, her fears for her friend, her bitter disappointment when attempt after attempt to communicate again with Josiah failed.

Almost.

"Mr. Diksen."

She started at Commander Sonak's calm voice nearby, and glanced up to see him standing beside her, hands folded behind his back.

"Yes, sir?" She swiveled to face him, half expecting to be given another task to add to her mounting list.

To think she had once considered communications *boring* . . .

"You are still unable to communicate with *Recovery?*"

"Yes, sir." Out of respect for the Vulcan, she tried to keep the frustration out of her voice, and failed utterly.

If her obvious dismay disturbed him, he showed no sign—only gave a curt but gracious nod. "I may have a solution. I've prepared a prerecorded transmission that begins and ends with the alien programming signals. It is possible that *Recovery* may accept communications couched in her invader's language."

Kirk must've heard him, because he spun in his chair toward them. "Excellent idea, Sonak. Let's do it, Mr. Diksen."

"Aye, sir," she replied with a grin of relief, grateful to be trying something new.

"The transmission has the coordinates for the empty cargo bay, Captain," Sonak explained as he returned to his station. "It also suggests Mr. Ngo try this method of transmission as well. If we succeed, we might establish two-way communications. Sending now, Mr. Diksen."

"Got it, sir. Transmitting." A sudden burst of static came through her earpiece. She grimaced and tuned into the newly incoming channel, then blinked in surprise at the strange sound: the Universal Translator had chosen to represent the voice not as one, but a multitude of voices. "Captain, we're being hailed—by the unknown ship."

"Mr. Ngo," Lieutenant Saed said, as she moved to the cadet's side, "Dr. McCoy has set a high priority on transmitting certain information to the admiral. What's the status on communication?"

Josiah ran a brown hand through his tightly curled hair and sighed; communications were a mess. "It looks like my tampering may have caused new problems, sir. This code can generate itself, like an old-style virus. Since I made that brief communication breakthrough, it's overwritten every pathway I'd made and created new barriers. It doesn't look good."

It wasn't easy, either, trying to do creative counterprogramming in Standard *and* Vulcan, with Shulman screaming maniacally in the next room about "the three!" The chant was like an annoying song Josiah couldn't get out of his mind. *The three. The three. The holy triad . . .*

He had to get a bigger view of things than what was contained in this tiny room. For all he knew, the *Recovery* could have already violated Tholian space, which would give them all time for nothing more than a quick prayer, anyway. He circumvented communications and rerouted over to sensors.

The screen on the diagnostic computer flickered to life with images of the space around the ship. Josiah could see part of what seemed to be a Federation starship—the *Paladin?*—and part of the *Recovery's* hull and little else. But the flow of data over the screen told him plenty.

"Sir . . ." He straightened in his chair as the lieutenant leaned over him. "We've come to a dead halt. Looks like the *Paladin's* out there, too."

"Is *Recovery* preparing to fire?" Saed's dark velvet brow was furrowed with worry. "Can you get into her defense system?"

He shook his head. "That's too heavily secured; I'm not even sure Shulman could get into it now. It doesn't look like she's arming, anyway—but something's going on. The computer's analyzing and scanning like crazy."

No sooner did he finish saying that than a telltale lit up by his left hand.

"An incoming communication!" Josiah crowed, and scrambled to grab the transmission. For a split second, he almost groaned as he recognized the same alien gibberish that had appeared in the code; but then the clear, calm voice of Commander Sonak filtered through the grid.

"This is the *Starship Paladin* calling Federation officers aboard the *Recovery*. Cadet Ngo, if you can hear me, I advise you to begin and end your communications with the same preface and suffix matrix we used. It might permit us to establish two-way communications. Transmissions will have rough spots, but even so—" Abruptly, his voice broke up into squealing static.

But then it came back, seemingly at the point it had been interrupted. "—it should suffice. Prepare to record the following coordinates for relocating *Recovery* passengers."

"Is the recorder working?" Saed asked excitedly.

"Yes, sir." Josiah captured all the information the *Paladin* was sending. "Now, if we could only lower the shields . . ."

"Can you fix our communications the way Sonak suggested?" Saed asked, as Josiah manipulated the tricorder and Vulcan analyzer.

He nodded. That wouldn't be too hard, and it made sense. Wrap the transmission up in dressing the weird programming could accept. Wrap it up in—

The three. The three. Three. Three.

Josiah blinked.

Three. *Three.* The damned programming wasn't binary—it was *tertiary!* Tertiary programming, in some alien language. Looking at the code again, he could see the repetitive pattern of symbols stand out as if it had been highlighted. And if he could get Sonak working on it—

He started manipulating data furiously, finding a chunk of alien programming to wrap his message in.

"The programming is tertiary," Josiah said, grinning broadly up at Lieutenant Saed. "Whoever planted this has got to have a really different biology or brain or something, because they program in tertiary, while all the other races we currently know program in binary. If Sonak turns this over to the *Paladin* computer with that information, we should be able to translate this stuff. That's the key. We could drop the shields, turn this baby around, and all go home!"

Josiah worked doggedly over his instruments. "If I can couch this just right and establish a two-way interface—it'll be clumsy with this alien stuff tacked on, but—"

"Admiral," Sonak called from his station, "the vessel hailing us is Tholian. And . . . they have lowered their shields."

Jim glanced over at the science officer to see the Vulcan gazing back at him with an expression of frank astonishment—an emotion shared by everyone on the bridge. "How polite," he said, swiveling back to contemplate the viewscreen, where *Recovery* hovered, vast and forbidding. "But we'll keep our shields up."

He was not particularly surprised that the ship was Tholian. After all, *Recovery* was nearing the farthest boundary of their border—according to what they considered their latest "territorial annex"—and the Tholians were obsessed with trespassers. However, he *was* startled—and worried—by the open-handed gesture they presented with their lowered shields. *Recovery* was in range of both ships, and she was totally unpredictable. Would the rogue ship also recognize the peace gesture and respect it—or again take advantage of it?

"On screen, Mr. Diksen," he ordered, and settled back into his chair. *Captain Romolo's chair,* he corrected himself. *If Baldassare is still alive. Mine only for the moment. And this moment might be all there is. . . .*

The image on the screen wavered, then re-formed—distorted, the colors not quite right, the shapes not quite formed.

He almost ordered Diksen to check the screen for malfunctions when he realized: *This is what Spock and the crew saw while I was trapped in the spatial rift.*

The Tholians, it was said, belonged to a race of creatures whose visible spectrum was so alien to humans they could be viewed only by having the computer filter out all unacceptable spectra. Likewise, the Tholians required special visors to be able to view humans. It also gave them an excuse to hide their forms; they were nothing if not compulsively private.

The Federation believed they belonged to a technologically advanced, tightly controlled society—but in truth, almost nothing was known about them. The only thing the Federation had learned during the incident between the *Starship Enterprise* and the Tholians almost three years ago was that the Tholians' technology—as manifested by their unusual force web—had developed along a different path than the Federation's.

Kirk had had no involvement with the aliens—Spock had been in command—and had seen them only when reviewing the ship's logs of the incident. Spock had always regretted that the incident had been marred by violence.

He squinted at the image of the Tholian commander—a featureless figure draped in a shimmering ruby shroud against a backdrop of wavering brilliant blue. The being peered out through two opaque triangular slits that served as its visor.

Kirk hesitated. There was no identifying legend beneath the image in either Federation Standard or the Tholian language to tell him who he was about to address.

"This is Commander Lokara of the Tholian vessel *Skotha*." The creature spoke in a voice that was neither male or female, not one but a hundred different voices, a chorus of octaves ranging from the highest to the lowest Kirk's ears could register.

"Admiral," Sonak said quietly. "The *Skotha* was the Tholian observer ship at the simulation site."

Kirk nodded in acknowledgment. So . . . they hadn't been destroyed at the simulation after all. . . . "Admiral Kirk in command of the *Starship Paladin*. I thought all the observer vessels had been attacked by the *Recovery* at the simulation."

The Tholian's shimmering red veil made it impossible to read its expression; its voice remained more perfectly toneless than a Vulcan's. "We evaded damage by the closest of margins. When we realized the rescue vessel was aiming for our own border, we understood the gravity of the situation. Should *Recovery* trespass into Tholian space, the Tholian Assembly will view it as a deliberate act of war."

"We are doing everything in our power to stop that from happening," Kirk assured him.

"We had hoped you would say that, Admiral Kirk," Lokara said, in a multipitched cascade. "That is why we have approached you with shields down. We were impressed by the Federation's invitation to observe the *Recovery*'s activities, and the performance of the rescue ship. We believe that this is a terrible accident, a mechanical failure that was completely unintentional. However, we may not be able to convince the

Assembly of this. Is there some way that you and I might work together to prevent *Recovery* from violating our border?"

"That is—a possibility," Kirk said, careful to keep the wariness from his tone. With Romulan or Klingon adversaries, he could at least try to read an expression, a tone of voice—but it was impossible to try to judge Lokara's veracity. Even so, something about the Tholian made him distinctly uneasy. "We have been hoping to rescue the innocent people trapped aboard *Recovery.* I suspect *Recovery* has halted in her flight because of your added presence. She is probably trying to determine your intentions. Your peaceful show is admirable, but I warn you to be cautious. You are vulnerable without your shields, and we have no control over that ship."

"I am comforted that you are concerned for our welfare, Admiral Kirk. May I respectfully suggest that your defensive posture might be interpreted as hostility by *Recovery,* who even now scans us both?"

Sonak moved over to the admiral's side, and said, loud enough so only Kirk could hear, "Lokara is telling the truth, Admiral. *Recovery* has been analyzing us ever since she halted. She is fully aware of our capabilities—and our limitations."

"Close audio," Kirk said softly to Diksen, then turned toward the Vulcan. "Are you suggesting we drop our shields?"

Sonak paused for a beat. "It is a logical course of action, Admiral, considering *Recovery*'s previous aggression toward ships with defensive capabilities. And it would be a gesture of good faith to Lokara. It might even buy us time with *Recovery*—time we could use to come up with a feasible plan of action with the *Skotha.*"

It was precisely what Spock would have said—

quintessentially logical, and an opportunity to make up for the unfortunate incident years before with the *Enterprise.*

Even so, instinct insisted on keeping the shields up, as strongly as he could hold them.

As the Vulcan returned to his station, Kirk turned back toward the viewscreen, where Lokara waited, motionless, unfathomable.

Finally, Sonak's soft baritone broke the silence. *"Recovery's* sensors show activity, Captain."

"She's arming herself?" Kirk asked.

"No, but she is assessing her defenses. She's taking inventory and comparing her armature against ours."

"Ours," Kirk repeated. "Not the Tholians'?"

"That is correct, sir."

"Diksen," Kirk said, "any communications from *Recovery?"*

"Negative, Captain."

The admiral turned back to stare at Lokara.

Reese Diksen watched Admiral Kirk speak to the painfully brilliant image of the Tholian and forced herself to counteract the adrenaline rush by breathing slowly and not thinking about the fact that they might very well decide to fire on the *Paladin,* or worse, the *Recovery.* . . . She tried to distract herself from the fear by recalling all the times during the *Enterprise's* five-year mission that he had lowered shields in dangerous situations. Sometimes he had done it willingly, sometimes not. Judging from the tension in his body and voice, this time it was definitely the latter.

And *that* made her nervous—because Kirk's experience had sharpened his uncanny instinct. And if Kirk didn't trust the Tholians . . .

She forced herself to drop the unsettling train of thought.

"Admiral," Sonak said quietly, *"Recovery* continues her defensive inventory."

Kirk never relaxed a bit, as though he hadn't heard his science officer. The admiral just kept one arm folded at his waist, the other elbow resting atop it so that one fist could support his chin as he frowned at the split image on the viewscreen—on one side, the *Skotha,* the *Paladin,* and the *Recovery,* all poised in a deadly triangle, and on the other the faceless Tholian Lokara.

Audio communications were still closed to the Tholians as Kirk said softly, "All hands—maintain battle stations." Then, with a taut nod, he signaled Reese to reopen the audio channel.

"Lokara," Kirk began, obviously hedging, "you said there might be some way that we can work together to prevent *Recovery* from violating your border. We've been unable to affect the actions of the ship at all. What do you suggest?"

"I have sent communications to the ships that guard our border," Lokara said, in his—her? Reese wondered; impossible to judge—peculiar high-pitched chorus.

She glanced back at her board, and saw another light blinking furiously there: a communication was coming in from outside the ship. Glancing from the viewscreen and the communication with Lokara to this new signal, she deliberated on what to do. Now wasn't the time to interrupt the admiral, but this could be a transmission from Josiah. Had he received the last transmission she'd sent, the one Sonak programmed? Keeping one eye and ear on the viewscreen, she screwed her receiver even tighter in her other ear and cued in the new transmission, signaling Sonak and sending it to his science station at the same time. The Vulcan, as the senior officer, could decide when to interrupt the admiral.

"I have told the commanders of our guardian ships," Lokara continued, "all that has happened with *Recovery*. I have explained about the vessel's mechanical breakdown. I have tried to make them understand that if *Recovery* does violate our territorial annex, it will be because of the actions of the ship itself. I am currently awaiting their response."

Reese only half registered this information as she heard the whistle of the alien programming followed by a burst of silence, then Josiah's voice. She glanced at Sonak and he nodded at her, indicating he was hearing the same. His hands moved efficiently over his board and suddenly she had bidirectional communications.

"This is Josiah Ngo on the *Recovery*. Hope you can hear this, Reese. Tell Commander Sonak that the strange programming in *Recovery*'s system is a tertiary-based code. That's *tertiary*, not binary."

"He's receiving your transmission at the same time I am, Josiah," Reese told him, knowing the smile on her face could be heard in her voice, "and he's established dual communications. What's your status? Did you halt *Recovery?*"

"Negative. *Recovery* is still operating independently. Commander Riley, Lieutenant Saed, and myself are all okay. Dr. McCoy has Myron Shulman under medical care, but he hasn't gotten many answers yet. Oh, and Lieutenant Saed reminds me that Shulman has confirmed that *Recovery*'s core programming is still intact. However, how that will—Reese, I'm losing—!"

His voice broke up into static and squeals again, then finally was lost.

Lokara gazed upon the countenance of the human who had caused its triad such anguish, and was grateful for the fine layer of opaque mesh that hid the hatred and frustration etched deep into its features. Its specially designed visor allowed Lokara to view the bizarre shapes and drab colors of the Federation's worlds.

So far, Lokara had been unsuccessful in convincing Kirk to lower his shields, in spite of *Recovery*'s scanning and the *Skotha*'s own lowered shields. The despised alien was entirely too paranoid, and Lokara was running out of convincing arguments. Seeing its partner, Srillk, signaling for attention, Lokara wondered if Srillk might have some information that might resolve this.

"Excuse me, Admiral Kirk," it politely told the dark image wavering in its viewscreen, "but one of my subordinates needs to address me. Perhaps there might be news from the Assembly."

"I understand, Lokara," Kirk replied. "I'll be waiting."

With your shields still raised! Lokara thought disgustedly. The *Skotha*'s commander signaled for the audio to be terminated from its communications with the *Paladin,* then moved to a private area where it could consult with its subordinate.

Srillk, diminutive and graceful, approached, its head bowed low in a gesture of respect so that its veil draped forward elegantly. "Lokara, our agent is failing."

"Dying?" Lokara asked, and even through the protective visor it could see the concern etched in its subordinate's expression. They were so close to their goal, so close—

"Perhaps, but damaged beyond repair. The mental adjunct has pushed the frail body and brain far beyond its normal abilities. Yet, the agent has successfully prevented the Federation staff aboard *Recovery* from affecting the outcome of our actions."

Even as its subordinate—who was also its life

partner—said this last, Lokara prayed that Srillk was correct. Srillk's connection to the agent had been shattered by the alien substances that had been introduced to the agent's body, and Srillk could only surmise what had happened. But Srillk had to be correct. Lokara could not believe that they would get this far and fail. How else could they ever face Lanra?

Glancing back at the grotesque human named Kirk, Lokara remembered all the work they had done to achieve their end. Through it all, Srillk had handled the assignment brilliantly.

It was Srillk who had managed to have the human Shulman captured, and have the brain device—a mechanism Lokara had had designed—implanted only weeks before the *Recovery*'s scheduled simulation around Zotos IV. The device had worked even better than they had hoped, causing Shulman to be obsessed with the drug-induced suggestion that his program was imperfect. It became impossible for the human to rest until he completed redesigning it—for Lokara's ends.

"Srillk," Lokara said affectionately, "I have faith that all will evolve as we have designed it. After all your diligence, your work, there could be no other outcome."

The smaller Srillk waved an appendage as if to negate its work; the nest of tentacles at the end of Srillk's golden arm writhed nervously. "None of it would have happened had you not obtained the necessary classified information. . . ."

That was true, Lokara thought. The Assembly's research into human physiology and the proposed use of mind-altering drugs delivered by a computer-driven internal device were critical to the mission. Fortunately, the humans had many enemies, and those enemies were shockingly easy to bribe.

Srillk added, "And if your family had not provided the funds—"

Lokara stopped its companion. Gently, the soldier's own finger-tentacles captured Srillk's. "It is not *my* family, but *our* family. Are you not one of my own mates? Are you not also Lanra's partner?" The very sound of that one's name stirred an emotion inside Lokara's being more fierce than even its pride, even its ambition.

"Lanra's partner until death," Srillk said sorrowfully. Srillk peered through its own helmet into Lokara's, looking through the eye shields to fasten its gaze on its partner's image hidden behind optical protection. "I visited Lanra before coming to the bridge. I told the loved one what we had done, how we would exact our revenge. I told Lanra that Kirk was near, that our vengeance would soon be complete. Lanra . . . touched me, Lokara. I think our partner understood . . . and approved."

"I pray you are right," Lokara murmured.

The Tholian commander had visited Lanra just that morning. The lovely breeder who had been their chosen partner, the one who would have borne their many offspring, was nothing now but a scarred, mindless hulk, incapable of breeding, incapable of loving, incapable of anything except experiencing the pain of injuries that would never fully heal. In spite of this, Lokara and Srillk both prayed every day for their breeder's life, even though their partner's tortured existence prevented them from bringing another breeder into their triad, prevented them from producing the offspring that, for a Tholian, was the manifestation of a completed, full life. Without their breeder, Lokara and Srillk were two-thirds of nothing, without purpose, without desire. Yet they prayed for Lanra's life.

The three partners had been on Loskene's vessel when it encountered the human starship *Enterprise*. There had been an exchange of phaser fire, and Lanra's station had exploded. No part of the lovely breeder's body had been spared. So now instead of children, Lanra gave Lokara, and its partner Srillk, a different reason for living. It was their prime focus, a task they had applied themselves to all this time.

Vengeance.

When the Federation had made its clumsy gesture of friendship, Lokara had decided that the human Myron Shulman—who was already in a fierce disagreement with Kirk—would be the perfect instrument of that vengeance: a vengeance that would encompass all of humankind, a vengeance worthy of a Tholian.

There were other considerations as well; Lokara had long possessed political ambition. It was his hope to transmute his personal vengeance into a war, one that would unify the annexes and cause them to rally around its instigator—and appoint Lokara to a much-coveted position on the Assembly.

"The agent's action will suffice," Lokara said confidently. "Even with complete failure of the agent, *Recovery*'s altered program can now function well enough on its own to fulfill the plan. Nothing will stop that ship from violating the border with all her passengers. She will be captured in our webs and all her technology and power will be ours to take. There will be war—and finally, we will have the edge over our enemies. Our triad will be the catalyst, and will grow in power, even with a damaged breeder. And Kirk, before he dies, will know this is the result of his actions, and those of his subordinates."

Srillk relaxed. "You are right about the programming, my partner."

Lokara touched its companion. "Yes. The *Recovery* itself will be our agent now." The *Skotha*'s commander turned back to the viewscreen to face the human—for what would be the last time.

"Myron, can you hear me?" McCoy murmured into the man's ear. He had hit upon a combination of anesthetics and a cortical stimulator, which worked together to produce a calm, hypnotic state in his patient. "We're heading for Tholian space. Do you know why? Can you stop the ship? Myron? Can you hear me?"

"I hear you," the researcher mumbled.

"Open your eyes, Myron, and look at this. Can you see it? Can you tell me what it is?"

Shulman opened his eyes and peered blearily at the wrinkled flimsy the doctor held before him.

"Notes," he whispered finally, letting his head loll away from it and his interrogator. "Notes. My notes. Their notes."

"Who are *they*, Myron? Tell me who *they* are."

"You know. You know. You. And Spock. And Kirk. You know. You know the three."

"How do we know the three?" McCoy asked pointedly.

"You invaded their space on the pretext of saving Kirk. You violated the territorial annex." Shulman's voice remained deep and dreamy, but grew faintly accusing. "You remained there even after being told to leave. You disregarded their laws. When they engaged you in legal combat, you returned fire and destroyed the breeder. The breeder lives, but deformed, unable to breed. You destroyed the three. You. And Spock. And Kirk."

McCoy felt a rush of déjà vu so powerful he almost lost his balance.

Territorial annex . . .

He stared at the alien writing and suddenly knew who it had belonged to.

"I am Commander Loskene. You are trespassing in the territorial annex of the Tholian Assembly. . . ."

He had been standing beside Spock on the *Enterprise* bridge.

I remember now; Spock was in command. Jim was lost in a spatial rift and we were trying to save him before he ran out of air. The effects of the unstable space were making the crew crazy, and made me fight with Spock irrationally. We almost lost the ship because of our warring. It was viewing Jim's "final orders" that snapped me out of it and made us work like the team we were supposed to be. I can't speak for the Vulcan, but I was pretty damned embarrassed by the whole thing.

He swallowed, remembering the incident vividly now. For a brief second he felt Spock's presence like a palpable thing, and could hear the Vulcan say clearly to him *"I understand, Doctor. I'm sure Jim would've just said, 'Forget it, Bones.'"* It was one of the warmest, most human things Spock had ever said to him. He was suddenly flooded by the memory of empathy and understanding he'd received from his Vulcan friend. It had been a terrible, emotional time, all of it taking place while the *Enterprise* was slowly being trapped inside the Tholian web.

This whole thing was Tholian—not accident or bad design, but revenge against him and Jim, revenge that would involve intergalactic war.

He had to tell Jim. Suddenly his patient clutched at his sleeve.

"I fought them—other ways—" the sickly man gasped.

"How, Myron?"

"I saved Angie!" Shulman's lips twitched in a pale

attempt at a smile. "I set the phaser on stun. It was the only time I got away with it. Every time after that, they made me set it to kill. I tried not to but—" He groaned and squeezed his eyes shut. "But I saved Angie."

McCoy swallowed and lied, "That's right. You saved her." He took a second to get his emotions under control, then he asked, "Myron. How can we get *Recovery* to transport everyone on board to another vessel, another set of coordinates?"

The suffering man gasped and blinked. "Universal evacuation command. Didn't want to risk *Titanic* scenario. One of the first safety margins. Even Kirk noted it. They couldn't make me rewrite that. But they made me narrow the scope. On my override codes only. My pocket." He struggled with every word.

McCoy checked every pocket in his suit before finally finding the tiny card. "Insert this in any port, and give the evacuation command and coordinates?"

Myron smiled. "Plan B."

McCoy returned his smile. This was another part of the original programming he'd preserved while the Tholian device in his head tortured him into doing what it wanted.

"What's Plan B for stopping the ship from crossing the Tholian border?" McCoy pressed.

Myron started to weep big, huge tears and the trembling began again. McCoy knew he'd asked the wrong question, but in spite of more drug manipulation, he couldn't stop the brain chip inside the scientist from punishing him.

"Can't—stop—her—from going home—!" Shulman gasped, each word sounding as if it had been torn out of him. "She—and I—are going home—together."

"The hell you are," McCoy grumbled, and administered enough anesthetic to put Shulman under completely—then ran into the next room.

Countless light-years distant, in the wavering shadow-limned shrine of Sekhet, Spock opened his eyes and let go a silent sigh as the troubling vision of Loskene, Kirk, and McCoy faded. The sensation that he sat in the captain's chair aboard the *Enterprise* had vanished as well; now he perceived only the black, glittering interior of Mount Seleya, the stone altar, the fierce, bestial image that towered above him.

Yet the conviction that his two friends remained in danger persisted—as did the sense that he had done all that he could to help them.

Irrational, Spock knew; utterly irrational. It could only mean that further effort was necessary to sever the emotional bonds.

And so, drawing a breath, he began once more to turn inward. . . .

"Have you got *Paladin?*" Josiah heard McCoy ask, as the doctor dashed up, nearly out of breath, to the diagnostics computer—now a substitute for the communications station.

Josiah ground his teeth while manipulating the tricorder and Vulcan analyzer's interphase with the diagnostic computer so quickly that Lieutenant Saed had given up trying to help him. He had to recapture that lost channel, but *Recovery* was fighting him through every line of code.

"We *had* them," Saed explained to Dr. McCoy, "but then we lost them."

"We'll get them back in a minute," Josiah promised —mostly just to reassure himself.

McCoy leaned over the console, his blue eyes bright with excitement, his words coming out in a barely comprehensible rush. "Shulman told me—this whole thing is Tholian! It's bound to be their programming. From what I could ascertain, their mating cycle involves three. Kirk has got to be told!" He thumped the console for emphasis.

"Dr. McCoy," Riley said tensely, "where's Dr. Shulman?"

"Completely under sedation and restrained, Commander," McCoy snapped back. "I know better than to leave a patient in that condition uncontrolled." He looked down at Josiah. "Look, we've got to transmit this information right away. Did you tell Kirk about the core programming?"

"We told Commander Sonak," Josiah assured him. "He'll relay it."

Unable to make any progress on communications, Josiah went back to the viewscreen and tried to get more information from the sensors. The picture on the viewscreen moved, and Josiah realized suddenly there was a third ship in the picture that had been hidden by *Recovery*'s huge bulk. He squinted. What kind of ship design was that? He'd never seen anything that sleek, that triangular—then he heard McCoy nearly strangle on an expletive.

"That—that ship!" the doctor stammered. "That's a Tholian ship! You've got to open a channel!"

"I'll do what I can," Josiah replied, straightening in his chair and swiveling it closer to the console as the small group stared in unison at the diagnostic computer's screen. He reached determinedly for the controls—

And stiffened at the sudden jolt of hot, electrifying pain that pierced his back, his ribs, his entire left side. He looked down in amazed agony to see a thin strip of metal—a piece of trim, he realized with disbelief, from a Federation shuttle—protruding from between two ribs. A bright red stain spread like an expanding sunburst on the front of his uniform.

"Oh, no," he moaned in frustration more than pain. *I don't have time for this now. . . .*

He glanced up to see the startled faces of McCoy, Riley, Saed staring at something behind him . . . at the source of the flat, mechanical voice that said, "There is no help. For Kirk, for you, there is only this—revenge for the three!"

Myron Shulman's voice, he realized, with dream-like detachment. The last word became an agonized groan . . . and then was followed by the sound of a body dropping heavily to the floor.

Riley's and Saed's faces disappeared; McCoy's loomed closer, then dimmed as the room began to spin. As he lost consciousness, Josiah's mind repeated the damnable phrase over and over:

The three! The three! The three . . . !

Chapter Eleven

ARMS FOLDED TIGHTLY in front of his chest, Kirk stood awaiting Lokara's return; the nagging sense of unease kept him from settling back into Romolo's chair. It made all the sense in the worlds to accept the Tholians' peaceful overtures; they had, after all, agreed to take part in the simulation.

Yet there was something about Lokara he simply could not trust. Perhaps it was just the veil, which kept him from seeing his opponent face-to-face; or perhaps it was simple prejudice, based on the *Enterprise*'s unfortunate encounter.

"Admiral," the communications officer called, interrupting his uncomfortable reverie. He turned and gazed at her impossibly young face, with its trace of childish plumpness at cheek and jawline.

Communications cadet, he reminded himself with a ghost of a mental smile. *All of these kids have com-*

ported themselves like a seasoned crew. Baldassare should be proud.

As he was proud, even though this was not his ship, his crew. There had been little time, ever since he had taken command of *Paladin,* to reflect on how it felt . . . but suddenly, with a sense of infinite gratitude to Romolo, to his ship, to his battle-weary crew, to the cadet staring at him, he realized that, for the first time in two and a half years, he felt *alive.*

"There's been a call from *Recovery,"* Diksen told him, her large brown eyes a bit wide as she glanced anxiously beyond his shoulder at the interior of the Tholian vessel on the screen. "Would you like to see it now?"

"Yes, on screen. Flag me as soon as Lokara hails again."

"Aye, sir."

The split viewscreen image was replaced by a dim, static-ridden picture that had been transmitted from one of *Recovery*'s medical computers—Bones had a hand in that, no doubt. He noted that McCoy wasn't onscreen, then realized he must be tending to Myron Shulman while Ngo, Riley, and Lieutenant Saed worked on the transmission.

He nodded as he heard Ngo's report about the tertiary programming, and the fact that *Recovery*'s core programming was still intact. Interesting, but . . .

He glanced over his shoulder toward the science station—it was easy, if he did not look carefully, to imagine that it was Spock huddled there over the viewer. "Commander Sonak, any speculations on who's responsible for that tertiary programming?"

The shorter, younger Vulcan shook his head. "I am totally unfamiliar with it, sir. However, knowing its basis gives us an opportunity to break its code. The computer is working on it now. If we can translate the code quickly enough, we might be able to use it to gain control of the ship before she travels into Tholian space."

"Keep me informed." He forced himself back to the command chair and sat on its edge. "Diksen, any luck getting through to the *Recovery* again?"

"Working on it, sir, but no breakthrough yet. The ship's computer seems to be able to build walls faster than we can break them down." She paused, listening, her furrowed-brow expression of distant concentration instantly recognizable. "The *Skotha* is hailing us, again, Admiral."

"On screen, Mr. Diksen," he said automatically, swiveling back to face the viewscreen.

"Forgive the delay, Admiral," Commander Lokara apologized, as the Tholian's wavering image reappeared. "I have been able to address the Assembly."

For the first time, Kirk gazed at the alien and felt a glimmer of hope.

"Don't touch that lance!" McCoy barked at Riley and Lieutenant Saed. The wicked piece of metal trim perforating the back of the padded chairback Josiah sat in protruded some six inches from beneath the cadet's next-to-last rib, and, no doubt, through his lung and perhaps a few internal organs as well. However, it was low enough to miss the heart.

McCoy couldn't believe the raw physical force the Tholian implant had been able to produce to make Shulman overcome the sedation and the sickbay cot's restraints, then throw the makeshift lance with such power. He glanced over at Shulman's still form and wondered whether the scientist was dead.

Why didn't the computer protect Josiah the way it protected Riley? McCoy fretted, but only for a minute. No doubt the computer had been unable to interpret a piece of shuttle trim as anything dangerous.

"Easy, son," McCoy said gently to the critically

wounded young man pinned in his chair. Josiah's ashen gray face wore an expression of complete startlement, but he'd said little when he was hit. "We're gonna get you out of this." He tried not to listen to his mind screaming about Tholians and communicating with Kirk and the incredible urgency they were in.

The doctor glanced over at Riley and Saed, who were crouched over the motionless scientist. "I don't want to move Josiah," McCoy said softly. "But I do want to stabilize him as much as possible. Riley, go into sickbay and wheel the cabinet I was working with in here. Most of what I need is on it. And can you tell me if Shulman—"

"He's alive," Riley said softly as he leaned closer over the unconscious man. "Breathing shallow, some eye reflex . . . no reaction to mild stimuli." He rose, keeping his gaze on Shulman as though he still didn't trust him, then finally exited.

"Can I help?" Anab Saed returned to Josiah's side, her face taut with emotions that struck McCoy as oddly familiar: concern and guilt. It took him an instant to recall where he had seen that precise expression—on Jim Kirk's face, many times in the *Enterprise* sickbay as he came to visit an injured crew member. Of course; Ngo had been her charge. She felt responsible for him.

"Your hands steady?" McCoy asked.

The lieutenant straightened with a dancer's grace to her full height. "Of course."

"Good. We'll need them," the doctor answered, as he stepped around to the back of the chair. Saed followed. McCoy took hold of the shuttle trim about six inches from the chair and touched it carefully— any move it made would be keenly felt by Josiah. "I want you to hold this steady, just like I am. Don't let it move a micrometer. Can you do that?"

She nodded, her expression growing determined, and grasped the lance behind his hands, letting him release it.

"Steady, now," he told her. "That's it."

Riley was suddenly beside him. "This everything you need?"

He glanced over the medical equipment and nodded. Taking a diagnostic scanner, he evaluated the young man's condition. The lung was pierced, the spleen nicked, and there was some foreign matter in the interperitoneal cavity from the chair. Josiah was going into shock, his temperature and blood pressure dropping. Not as bad as it could be; not as good as McCoy would've liked it.

"Josiah had a bunch of tools from the shuttle," he said to Riley. "Does he have anything that'll cut that lance?"

"In the bag," Josiah whispered. "The laser. It'll cut anything." He coughed weakly; a thin trickle of blood spilled from the corner of his mouth.

"Just stay still, son," McCoy chided. Riley was already rummaging for the tool.

"Got it," he said.

"Cut the length of that trim off," McCoy ordered, "but be careful—*don't* move the lance."

"Got it, Doc."

McCoy loaded his hypospray and moved in front of the young man. "Now, here's a little something for shock, bleeding, and some general good soup we give soldiers who get run through. It'll relieve some pain— but don't think that means you can move. Okay?" He pressed the hypo against Josiah's neck and administered a battery of drugs, pain suppressants, and electrolytes, and an artificial plasma that would replicate once it got into Josiah's body, replacing any additional blood he might continue to lose.

Hearing a clatter of metal, he saw that the bulk of

the lance had been cut and fallen to the deck; only a stump protruded from the back of the chair. He nodded at Riley and Saed, who was cleaning her hands of the cadet's blood.

Picking up a cell regenerator, he was grateful—if this terrible thing had to happen—that it had happened in sickbay. He was able to seal off some of the internal damage, but without taking Josiah into surgery where they could safely remove the lance, this temporary respite would be all he could provide. He took bandaging material from the cabinet.

"I'm going to tape you into this chair, Josiah," he said as he proceeded to do just that. "We've got to prevent you from doing any more damage by moving until we can get you into surgery. Try to be still, okay?"

The cadet's eyes were clearer, some of the raw pain gone from them. He licked his lips and said, "There's no time for that. We've got to call the *Paladin*."

McCoy drew a deep breath and looked from Josiah to the two officers. How in blazes could they do that now? Hurriedly, he started taping Josiah into the chair, stabilizing his body.

Josiah tried to lift an arm to point to the console where his equipment sat, but couldn't do it. "They're your computers. You've got to do it, Doctor. Warn the ship."

The young man was right; there was nothing more to be done. With a sinking heart, McCoy handed Riley the hypospray, and gave Saed the scanner, pointing at the readings. "If this mark dips past this point, tell Riley to give him ten more milligrams of the stimulant."

Saed nodded and watched the diagnostic tool solemnly. McCoy glanced once more at his young patient, then turned to face the cobbled-together pile of technojunk they were using to create a comm link.

He felt a moment's panic as the Vulcan analyzer glittered with symbols and words he couldn't understand. But the tricorder was still functional, and he understood that. It would help him figure out whatever he had to do. He swallowed and got to work.

They'd been trying to get through using the diagnostic computer, but the alien programming had pretty much wiped out all those pathways. He had to find another route. He thought for a moment.

Reports. He touched the tricorder, scanning the diagnostic computer's program banks. The reports program was designed to send detailed, complicated medical reports to anyone the doctor wanted them sent to—the captain, other labs, even Starfleet. He should've thought of it sooner.

He plugged into the reports program, and scanned it quickly. It looked amazingly clean. It was an obscure little program, though powerful. Could he use that to break through to the *Paladin?* He felt excited at the prospect and worked faster on parts of the machine that were long familiar to him. He manipulated the program with the tricorder and had gotten tantalizingly close to his goal when he received an indication of another transmission.

"It's closing the channel up when I send it," he told the others. *"Paladin'*s receiving another transmission, and it's intercepting us—my program is waiting its turn."

"You've got to override it and break through," Riley said. "They're probably talking to the damned Tholians!"

McCoy devised the most dire emergency code he could imagine, demanding that *Recovery* place her formidable power at his disposal to override the current transmission for the sake of saving a life. It was hardly a lie. There was a moment's hesitation. . . .

* * *

"Does your Assembly accept your explanation of the course of events?" Kirk asked Lokara.

"They are taking it under advisement," Lokara assured him. "I have reason to hope that will accept our viewpoint on this issue. I have explained how we have discussed working together to solve the problem of *Recovery*'s aberrant aggression."

Could it be possible? Kirk wondered. Could this disaster turn into a chance at dialogue with this advanced, aggressive species? *Recovery* had been quiet the whole time he and Lokara communicated. Could she be observing them? Could the pause in her flight have caused her to reconsider her mission, her purpose? Her core programming was still intact. Was it finally reasserting itself and regaining control?

"Admiral," Sonak said quietly, *"Recovery* has focused all sensors on the *Paladin*. She may be preparing to arm phasers."

Intellectually, Kirk knew what he should do, but instinct rebelled. Had the months he'd sat behind a desk so affected him that he feared to take risks when they most needed to be taken? He let out a slow breath, and finally said, "Mr. Sandover. Lower the shields."

"Aye, sir. Shields are down."

"Recovery's scans have ceased, sir," Sonak called. "She is replotting her course toward the Tholian border."

"Lokara," Kirk began, his voice edged with his new optimism, "have you any ideas how—?"

Before he could finish, the Tholian commander's image wavered, then faded; the big viewscreen began to blink madly. "Diksen?"

"Some weird emergency signal from *Recovery* is overriding everything, sir."

McCoy's bearded, anxious face filled the screen, his voice booming unnaturally. "Jim—it's the *Tholians!*

They changed the programming—planted a device in Shulman's head—they—"

Kirk's heart stopped; he spun toward the navigator while McCoy kept shouting. He heard Sonak's voice a split second before his own as both men shouted, *"Shields up!"*

Too late. In the millisecond before the blast hit, Jim realized distractedly that Sonak must have seen the discharge of the Tholian phasers in his science screen as Kirk and Lokara exchanged pleasantries and called for shields just as Jim heard McCoy's warning.

The deck beneath Kirk's feet rose like the swell of a tidal wave, pitching him in Romolo's chair as if he were on some antigrav amusement-park ride. The passive restraints kept him in but he was snapped and swung around wildly. Sonak, who'd been standing at his station, was thrown badly; he rolled, but caught himself on the railing support and clung to it with Vulcan strength.

And then the deck dropped out beneath them as the *Paladin* struggled to right herself; the crew lurched around, consoles cracked under the pressure, smoke rose into the air. Kirk heard the sound of the ship's fire extinguishers and in his mind's eye, saw once more the dreadful image: Pulver, her dark form backlit by orange fireglow, falling backward with morbid grace. . . .

The *Paladin* righted herself with a jerk; instantly, the bridge came alive with the wail of the klaxon, the chatter of damage reports. He heard Diksen responding, trying to sort through them quickly to give him a report. Sonak struggled back to his chair, then checked his station. He'd barely settled into it before the second blast caught them; this time, Kirk and his crew managed to weather it through at their stations, but he knew the Tholians were tearing them apart— an unshielded ship.

"Report!" Kirk shouted.

"Damage in Engineering," Diksen called out. "And decks five and seven . . ."

McCoy's image had disappeared, leaving now just the sight of the Tholian ship battering the hell out of them, with *Recovery* sitting behind her like a placid observer . . . as though she'd planned the whole thing herself.

"Shields, Mr. Sandover!" Kirk demanded.

"Shields are gone, sir. That was the first thing they hit."

"Fire phasers!"

Before Sandover could oblige, they were hit again, twice more in rapid volley. The entire crew was bounced around violently as Kirk gripped the arms of Romolo's chair.

"Phasers are gone, sir," Sandover reported. "We've lost . . ." He peered down at his console. ". . . all but three photon torpedoes as well."

"Arm the remaining three, and fire on my word."

"Warp engines are off-line," Sonak reported, gazing over at Kirk with a grim expression. "Three photon torpedoes may damage the Tholians, but are unlikely to defeat them."

Kirk stared at the screen knowing the Vulcan was right: They had no shields, no phasers. And *Recovery* wasn't doing a damned thing to help them. To the Tholians, it must look like the *Paladin* had run out of options.

Not all of them, if I have anything to say about it. I didn't bring the Paladin *this far just to lose her. . . .* With a sudden keen exhilaration, he drew a breath. "Mr. Sandover. On my word, drop the ship ten thousand kilometers at minus ninety degrees. Mr. Sonak, aim those photons mark four-point-five, wide scatter."

Sonak looked up from his board in surprise; Kirk

met his gaze with one of utter determination. "Aye, sir," the Vulcan said, dropping his gaze.

"Ready, Sandover . . . Fire photons!"

He turned back to the screen and saw the torpedoes flare away from the screen; the view immediately shifted as the *Paladin* plummeted down in a straight line from their previous position.

The torpedoes found their mark: the massive, gleaming surface of *Recovery*.

Like a slumbering giant roused by a stinging bee, the big ship shifted position, then swatted back hard, firing her heavy phasers in the direction the torpedoes came from. But the *Paladin* was no longer there—only the *Skotha* remained.

The blast caught the Tholian vessel dead on, crumpling her shields, physically knocking the ship back from her position.

"The *Skotha* has been seriously damaged, Admiral," Sonak reported as he leaned over his viewer. "Her shields are totally destroyed, she has no weapons, and has major damage on several decks, including Engineering."

"Sounds like she's hurt just as badly as we are," Kirk said wearily, "but she's in Federation space. Diksen, hail the *Skotha,* if you can. See if she'll surrender. Maybe we can get some answers out of them yet."

"The *Skotha* is answering our hail, sir."

The viewscreen showed the giant *Recovery* shifting from side to side as if trying to determine which of the two ships was her true enemy, as the tiny *Skotha* tilted abnormally, hanging in space. The screen flickered, then showed the bridge of the damaged Tholian vessel. The color variation on the screen quivered so much it was painful to the eyes; Kirk winced at the too-brilliant colors that strobed there.

"Commander Lokara," Kirk said to the cloaked

231

image on the screen. "Surrender, and we'll assist you as well as we can."

"Surrender?" Lokara chorused tinnily. "To you, Kirk? Perhaps you should consider this. My true discussion with the Tholian Assembly explained the chain of events that have led to this moment. They know exactly why this has all happened."

Kirk frowned, wishing he did himself.

"You see, Admiral," Lokara explained patiently, "I and my partners have always served aboard the same vessel, as is the custom of our people. While we served under Commander Loskene, the *Enterprise* fired upon us—crippling my partner, the breeder, Lanra, and destroying our future."

There was a pause as if Lokara found it difficult to speak. "But now, my partner Srillk lies dead. And the breeder, Lanra, suffers no longer. Only I am left alone, without them. But the vengeance we have lived for will continue without us. Your *Recovery* will follow its own plan, and you will not be able to stop it. Your rescue ship will enter Tholian space, be captured in a web we are even now constructing, and plumbed for every Federation secret aboard. Learn this about us, Kirk, and it will be enough: Tholians do not forgive. And we do not surrender."

Before Kirk could speak, Sonak warned, "Admiral, the *Recovery* has determined who was responsible for the photon torpedoes."

He did not say the obvious, but Kirk thought it as he stared at the behemoth on the screen:

And we have no defense of any kind. . . .

McCoy watched the battle with growing dread and was relieved when Jim's ploy worked. Riley had already given Josiah another dose of medication, and McCoy knew he had to get the young man into surgery immediately. Shulman needed intensive care, and surgery also, if there was any hope of saving him. The doctor fingered the coded cassette Shulman had given him, and glanced at his screen.

Recovery was engaged in quite a few different activities, not all of which he could interpret. But one pattern of data he understood with no problem.

"She's getting ready to move," he told Riley and Saed. "She's gearing up to go."

"Go?" Riley asked. "Go where?" Then it seemed he remembered. "You mean—into Tholian space?"

McCoy nodded. "Computers never forget their original assignment. That was the whole point of this in the first place. Make the *Recovery* violate the border, start intergalactic war."

"We've got to get out of here," Lieutenant Saed said sensibly.

McCoy shot her a wry look. "I'd say that's an understatement."

"Shields!" Josiah gasped. "Shields are up!"

"Don't worry, son. Shulman told me how to evacuate everyone and gave me his codes. *Recovery* will send us all to the coordinates Jim sent us." Then he paused, wondering if those coordinates hadn't been blasted into the vacuum of space.

McCoy moved to Josiah's side to check his readings, and suddenly realized the young man could see the screen again, and the data running across it.

Josiah blinked a few times, then said softly, *"Recovery*'s going to fire upon the *Paladin*. She'll destroy that ship. There's no way to stop her."

All four pairs of eyes stared, mesmerized, at the screen, as McCoy prayed that just this once, the cadet was wrong.

Kirk's mind raced as Sonak intoned impassively, *"Recovery* is arming phasers."

The admiral punched the arm of his chair. "Engineering? Engineering!"

"Here, Admiral," a tired voice replied.

He grinned, unable to believe his luck. Lieutenant Gambeta was still at her post, alive!

"Gambeta, shut down power on the starboard side immediately. Everything but minimal life-support. Keep everyone off communications."

The engineer never even paused at the strange request. "Power off, Admiral."

"Now shut down the port side. And the bridge. Essentials only."

Lights shut down until the crew was on emergency lighting only, augmented by the dim glow of the telltales. The soft throb of the engines that experienced spacefarers never noticed became conspicuous by its absence. Everyone grew still, stopped moving.

"Let the ship drift, Mr. Sandover," Kirk said softly. "Diksen, cut off Lokara—keep everything off that board."

The officers he spoke to nodded agreement, as if fearing that, by speaking aloud, they might elicit *Recovery*'s attention.

"Diksen, broadcast an emergency distress signal. Engines damaged, warp drive unstable, matter-antimatter unbalanced—losing life-support. Keep broadcasting until you get a reply."

The young woman's hands moved capably over the board as she spoke softly into her receiver.

Kirk took a deep breath and settled back in his chair, aware that every eye on the bridge was watching him.

I took my best shot, Baldassare. If she takes us down, it's not because we didn't try hard enough.

He could hear the creaking of their seats, the soft sound of his own breathing. He imagined that all across the ship, the crew watched viewscreens anxiously and waited. So many cadets, he thought ruefully. So many at the beginning of their careers. To end here—

"Admiral, we're being hailed," Diksen's steady voice broke through the silent reverie.

"On audio."

After a scant pause, a feminized computer voice announced, "This is the rescue ship *Recovery*. We have received your distress signal. How may we assist you?"

Kirk felt the beginnings of a grin spread over his lips. *Thank you, Myron Shulman. And thank you, Bones. The core programming really is still intact.*

"*Recovery,* we need . . . personnel," Kirk suggested, swiveling toward communications, where Reese Diksen smiled broadly, revealing teeth, as she tended her board. "Doctors, engineers, scientists—to help us repair our vessel."

"Admiral," Sonak said, his tone perceptibly more placid, "*Recovery* is scanning us—and she has lowered her shields."

Riley pointed to the tricorder. "Look! *Recovery*'s dropped her shields!"

McCoy looked away from Josiah's readouts to glance at the screen. "Looks like a good time to evacuate."

"Are we sure about those coordinates?" Riley wondered. *Paladin* had taken a hell of a pounding.

Josiah wet his lips and said, "*Recovery* will check them. She won't send two hundred people into a vacuum. Core programming."

"Right!" said McCoy. "Riley, help me."

The commander followed him over to the still form of Myron Shulman. McCoy ran the scanner over the researcher. He didn't like what he saw, but if he could get him to *Paladin*'s sickbay, he might be able to keep

235

him alive, put him in stasis—*like Angie*—until they could get to a better facility. Shulman deserved that much.

"I want him placed near the rest of us, so that he has to be transported with us," McCoy explained to Riley.

"Is that safe?" Lieutenant Saed interjected. McCoy could tell that the Security officer wasn't fond of the idea of bringing Shulman along. "He nearly killed Commander Riley, he's mortally wounded Ngo—"

"And he's single-handedly responsible for saving all our lives with this programming card"—he held it up to show her—"and for maintaining the core programming. The man's a hero, and one of the finest minds of this century. He deserves to have anything done that can save his life."

She sighed in acquiescence as Riley leaned down and scooped the man up in his arms like a child. "Damn!" Riley swore softly. "He hardly weighs anything!"

McCoy ushered them back over to the computer. "Everybody stand close. Don't move." He glanced at Josiah, who looked a little more ashen. Plugging in the card, he gave *Recovery* the evacuation command and Shulman's personal code.

Leonard McCoy never thought he would ever again so look forward to having his molecules scrambled as he did at that moment.

"Admiral!" Reese Diksen nearly shouted in her excitement, "people are materializing in cargo deck four! Dozens—no, *hundreds* of people—and a . . . *stasis chamber?*"

Kirk spun to say something to her, but Sonak interrupted.

"Admiral, the *Recovery* has transported all her personnel onto the *Paladin*. She is now completely devoid of life."

"We're getting requests for emergency medical aid, Admiral," Diksen said.

"Is sickbay operational?" Kirk asked her. As in any Starfleet vessel, *Paladin*'s sickbay was in the most protected part of the ship.

"Fully operational, sir," Diksen reported, "though its staff is busy dealing with our own wounded."

"They'll have to use triage," he commented. "Make sure the people in the cargo bay get all the help they need." He frowned as Diksen's expression grew abruptly dismayed. "What's wrong, Cadet?"

"The personnel from *Recovery* have one seriously injured party they need help with." She faltered, then composed herself and straightened, suddenly every inch the officer. "It's Josiah Ngo, sir."

He paused. "Do you want to give them a hand, Diksen?"

She wavered for only a second, then sat up straight again. "No, sir. I'll remain at my station. Sickbay reports enough hands available."

He stared at her admiringly and was about to say they'd both go down to sickbay later, when this was over—when Sonak interrupted again.

"Excuse me, Admiral, but—I seem to have made an error."

Kirk turned in genuine surprise at the confession. *"You,* Mr. Sonak?"

The corner of his lip quirked almost imperceptibly in admission. "My apologies, sir, but I reported that *Recovery* was devoid of life. According to my readouts that was true—for a moment. However, there now seems to be one lone human—a single male—aboard her."

Not Riley or Bones, Kirk prayed silently. "Can we beam him off?"

Sonak lifted a thoughtful brow. "I believe it would be safer to *request* that specific person's presence."

"Then see if you can pinpoint an identity. Diksen, open a hailing frequency to the *Recovery.*"

Myron Shulman was only dimly aware of being lifted from the deck by the strong arms of Commander Riley. He remembered feeling sheltered for that brief moment—almost comforted. He had been so tired. . . .

He felt the gentle pull of the transporter, felt his atoms disassembling—then reassembling back in his own quarters, in his own bed. He lay there, helpless, sick, in pain, yet absurdly glad to be there. This room, this bed, for the last two years had been his only home, from the moment the physical construction of *Recovery*'s shell had been completed. There had been so much work. So much work.

All destroyed.

Yet he would not weep. He'd saved the core programming. *Recovery* had used it to send everyone to safety—everyone except him.

In the moments of lucidity that had finally returned, and the vague memory of his conversations with McCoy in sickbay, he realized now what had been done to him: the Tholians had wedded him to this ship with their incredibly advanced brain device, and their unusual tertiary programming. Even as he'd struggled to overwrite the real programming of his rescue ship, the researcher in him had had to admire the Tholians' advances. Now the Federation would learn what they could from the Tholian programming.

Some of the things the Tholians had made him do had actually improved the *Recovery*. Perhaps in time the Federation would glean the good from it and improve their technology.

Whatever happened, it would all be done without him. He wondered—as many humans do when they face death—if anyone would mourn for him, or if he would be forever remembered as a traitor to his species.

He had never meant for *Recovery* to be anything more than a rescue vessel—but because of what had been done to him, he had come to think of the ship as something else—as part of himself. And now he and *Recovery* would have to bring this to an end. He didn't want to, but it was the one piece of programming he simply could not work around.

At least they would be together. He would have to trust Kirk to solve the problem he and *Recovery* were about to create. If any man could, it would be Admiral Kirk. For the first time in a long while, Myron was able to think clearly about the admiral, and realized how, even when he had opposed Myron, he had still been the scientist's ally. Shulman trusted Kirk to solve this problem somehow. It was what the admiral was best at.

He struggled to lick cracked, dry lips. "Computer—" he croaked, his voice barely audible. "Take us home."

"Admiral," Diksen reported, "the *Recovery* is ignoring my hail."

"I believe the identity of the man on board," Sonak told Kirk, "is Myron Shulman."

Kirk gazed at the screen in helpless frustration.

"Recovery has raised her shields, Admiral," Sonak warned.

Jim tensed. Surely she wouldn't fire on them now, when they were helpless, and held the entire crews from both ships. . . .

"She is once again reconfiguring her course into Tholian space," Sonak continued, then paused, frowning slightly as he noticed something on his readout. "However, her scanners are reacting to something nearby—something our sensors cannot detect—"

Kirk swiveled back toward the viewscreen, his instinct sending out alarms as loud as any red alert. He rose from his chair, training his eyes on the empty vastness of space surrounding the odd trio of the *Paladin,* the *Skotha,* the *Recovery.* "Not now . . ." he murmured. "Not now . . . !"

He spotted it at the same time Sonak reacted to the data on his science screen. The space directly above and between the two smaller ships suddenly wavered, and something vast began materializing out of the vacuum.

Like a vampire out of the mist, Kirk thought morosely, as a Klingon Bird-of-Prey solidified on the screen.

Chapter Twelve

JIM KIRK STARED with a sense of foreboding into the garish unblinking eye painted on the hull of the Bird-of-Prey. The *Paladin* now held over three hundred crew members—many of them cadets—plus over two hundred people beamed from the *Recovery*. He had felt a deep sense of relief at first, knowing that Riley, Bones, and all the others were rescued—but that relief was short-lived. The *Paladin* still had some weaponry, but she had no shields and Jim doubted that *Recovery* could be duped twice. The next time she was fired on, the behemoth would simply blow them all to kingdom come and let someone else sort them out.

And if the Klingons played their usual gambit—shoot first, don't bother asking questions at all—none of them would have a chance.

But how in God's name could he reason with Klingons?

As he turned to tell Diksen to open a hailing frequency, she interrupted with, "We're being hailed, Admiral. By the Klingon ship. They're hailing the Tholians as well."

Jim shared a look of candid amazement with Sonak. "On screen."

The image of the ungainly vessel dissolved, then coalesced once more into the ominous vision of a Klingon officer bedecked in full warrior's armor; his long dark hair and beard, streaked with auburn, spilled down onto a breastplate of black leather and dully gleaming metal. "This is Captain Qo'dar of the Klingon warship *Fury.*"

"And I am Admiral—"

"I know who you are!" the Klingon thundered; beneath his bony skull ridge, tiny, glistening eyes blazed with rage. "We have been monitoring all ships' transmissions. At first, I was convinced that this was Federation treachery, but now I know that the Tholians have staged this event to acquire a piece of advanced Federation technology!" He slammed a metal-clad fist against his console; it struck with a loud clank. "Technology they will use to conquer the Klingon Empire!"

"Admiral," Sonak called softly from his station, "the *Recovery* is showing keen interest in the shielded Klingon ship."

"Qo'dar, wait!" Kirk demanded. "If you've been observing, you know that if you fire on the Tholians, *Recovery* will destroy us all! Your shields alone are causing her to focus on you, scan your vessel—"

The Klingon turned to another officer on his bridge and growled something in his language. The officer's reply caused Q'odar to recoil angrily and whirl back toward the viewscreen. "Are you telling me to act as you do and feign helplessness, just to satisfy the sensors of an unoccupied vessel?"

Sonak's perfectly modulated voice intruded. *"Recovery* is arming her phasers."

"You heard that, Qo'dar," Kirk said quickly. "You have a choice: Keep your shields up, and be destroyed —or feign helplessness, and survive to help us outwit *Recovery.*"

The officer nearest Qo'dar snapped something at his captain. The Klingon clenched his gauntleted fists, his bronze face suffused with frustration. Finally, he shouted out a clipped command.

For an instant, Kirk dared not breathe.

"The *Fury* is lowering her shields, Captain," Sonak told him at last. "And *Recovery* is taking her weapons off line and lowering her own shields."

Aware that the Klingon must be getting similar information, Kirk turned to the warrior, searching for the right thing to say, the common ground they might use to devise a solution to this problem. For the Klingon was right about one thing—if the Tholians gained total control of *Recovery,* they would use the knowledge of the advanced Federation technology to overwhelm their neighbors—and the first to go would be the nearby Klingons.

"Captain Qo'dar," he began reasonably, "you said yourself that you've learned we are not the cause—"

"Admiral," Diksen interrupted, "the Tholians are sending out a standard Federation distress signal. They're sending it directly to—"Her eyes widened with astonishment as she swiveled to face him. "—to *Recovery,* sir."

"Damn!" Kirk swore softly, even as on the viewscreen, Qo'dar argued with his own officer. "Sonak?"

His gaze intent on his viewer, the Vulcan replied, *"Recovery* is responding, sir. The Tholians report that their ship is severely damaged, but insist they must remain aboard her for their specific life-support requirements. *Recovery* is analyzing the ship's coordinates."

"Lokara!" Qo'dar roared, shaking a fist at his invisible adversary. "I will blast you out of space before you take refuge aboard that ship!"

Sonak glanced up from his viewer to gaze pointedly at the admiral. "I believe, Captain, that the Klingons are preparing to fire on the *Skotha.*"

"Qo'dar, don't!" Kirk shouted. *"Recovery* will destroy us both and still save the Tholians. You'll gain nothing!"

The Klingon hesitated, as if Kirk's words rang too true to deny; but his face remained contorted with anger, and beneath shaggy red-black brows, his eyes narrowed mistrustfully. "You will let those skulking cowards gain access to that ship, Kirk? Better we should destroy the Tholians now, and face death ourselves than—"

"Recovery is beaming the Tholian vessel into one of her large hangar bays," Sonak intoned, leaning over his viewer, his severe features bathed in its blue glow.

The Klingon howled his rage as the *Skotha* dematerialized—so loudly that Kirk repressed a wince and nodded irritably at Diksen, who lowered the volume.

He drew a breath and with a calmness he did not feel told the Klingon, "The *Recovery* is programmed to go into Tholian space. Once she's there, it would just be a matter of time before she was captured in a Tholian power web where they could study her and reprogram her at their leisure. Destroying that one ship would have accomplished nothing."

The Klingon listening in grudging silence, then leaned closer to the viewscreen, his leather armor creaking. "And what will stop her now, Kirk? Your crippled junkheap? Or my lone warship?"

"Admiral," Sonak warned, *"Recovery* is still dealing

with the injured Tholian vessel now aboard her, but she is also preparing to restart her journey—into Tholian space."

Kirk knew *Recovery* considered *Paladin*'s problems solved by the personnel she'd transferred over. Even if the Klingon ship imitated Kirk's action—and the admiral knew better than to suggest that—the only likely response *Recovery* could have to their distress call would be to beam the Klingons aboard. He had a sudden image of a dozen battle-raged Klingons swarming through the *Recovery*'s corridors as they searched for the Tholians, and shook his head. That wouldn't stop the ship from crossing the Tholian border, and a crew of Klingons wouldn't be able to prevent the Tholians from eventually capturing and controlling the rescue vessel. He had to do something to keep *Recovery* here, something that would prevent her departure, then disable her. . . .

He took a step over to the science station and leaned over Sonak's shoulder. "Has the computer finished translating the tertiary code?"

The Vulcan straightened and released an inaudible sigh, his expression composed; but a faint crease remained between his brows. "Negative, Admiral. We need more time."

"Mr. Sonak," Kirk said softly, "if we can't find a way to control her, disable her . . ." He did not complete the sentence, but turned his gaze back toward the implacable giant on the viewscreen and finished the thought silently.

. . . *we'll have to destroy her.*

With her creator still on board.

It was an unacceptable solution; but he could not permit that ship to cross the border. First things first—to keep the vessel from leaving—

"Qo'dar, are you carrying any drones?"

The Klingon studied him a moment, then replied

warily, "You mean, the kind we use for target practice? Yes. One hundred."

"Can the drones be sent to a target, yet not arm themselves until they arrive?" Kirk asked.

Qo'dar hesitated. "If you are asking me if the drones can be used for surveillance—that is possible."

Kirk nodded, grateful for the admission. He knew that Klingons viewed automated surveillance as cowardly, preferring a more direct approach. He turned to the Vulcan. "Tell Engineer Gambeta we'll need a special shuttlecraft—one that can send out life-form readings, readings that can convince *Recovery* there are living humans aboard. And we'll need it in five minutes."

Sonak replied smoothly, "Aye, sir," and addressed his board.

"You are planning on recreating the simulation?" the Klingon asked incredulously. "Need I remind you, Kirk, that it was the simulation that nearly caused our destruction?"

Kirk held up his hands in a placating gesture. "In the simulation, *Recovery* herself was under attack. Think about it, Qo'dar—her central programming is still intact. Her responses have been appropriate when someone else is under attack. Can your drones fire on a target if they have the coordinates?"

"Of course!"

"Good." Kirk took a breath. If his next words sounded like a command he would never gain the cooperation of the honor-bound warrior. "Qo'dar—if you would please send out a stream of, say, twenty drones, a few at a time, just to give *Recovery* something to analyze until we can release our shuttlecraft . . . ?"

There was a pause, then Qo'dar grumbled a command to another officer.

Huddled over his viewer, Sonak said quietly, "The *Fury* is releasing her drones—two—five—eight—twelve . . . *Recovery* is putting her departure on hold to analyze them and determine their purpose."

"Thank you, Captain Qo'dar." Still facing his reluctant ally in the viewscreen, Kirk said deliberately, "Sonak, while there is no central command post or bridge aboard *Recovery*, there is a core brain. The schematics for its location are in *Paladin*'s computer. I want the location of that brain sent to Captain Qo'dar."

The Klingon's astonishment was plain on his sculpted bronze face.

There was a moment's pause before Sonak responded coolly, "As first officer, sir, I must remind you that that is classified information."

"Thank you, Commander," Kirk replied, without taking his gaze from Qo'dar's. "Now, send the information. Captain Qo'dar will need it." He addressed the Klingon. "If you will take this information, sir, and program the remainder of your drones with it, we might smuggle them into the *Recovery* in an unmanned shuttle—with her cooperation."

Qo'dar's expression remained one of suspicion even as the information was relayed to him. He gave orders to the soldiers around him, who scurried into activity. "I am taking your . . . suggestion . . . and acting on it, Kirk, but what good will it do to get the drones aboard the vessel? We have been told the ship confiscates any weapons brought aboard."

"That's why the drones must not be armed," Kirk insisted. "Set them to arm themselves and fire only upon reaching the target. If they're armed too early, *Recovery* will simply beam them into space. Unarmed, they're no more dangerous than tricorders, or other sensor-laden equipment."

The Klingon's eyes slitted in amusement. "Yes. Yes.

I see your plan. If the drones destroy the brain, then the ship will simply die in space. She will not cross the border and be captured by the Tholian army waiting there. We may yet confront Lokara face-to-face!" The warrior stroked his beard thoughtfully as he made a decision. "Five of my warriors will accompany the drones."

Kirk stepped closer to the viewscreen. If he didn't phrase this just right, he'd insult the Klingon's honor and everything would be lost. "Qo'dar, this plan . . . is contingent on our ability to have the drones hit the target before the Tholians inside *Recovery* can take control of her. If you send warriors over there, their weapons will be confiscated, and they themselves might be immediately confined. The chances of their accomplishing anything are slim. If anything goes wrong, their lives will be forfeit for nothing. Where is the honor in that?"

Qo'dar frowned as he considered this. "This is always the Federation way. You send in robots to do your most dangerous work. You talk and talk, saying anything you can to avoid war. You spend valuable resources on a vessel whose whole purpose is to save lives." He shook his shaggy head imperiously. "I will never understand your people."

Kirk felt Diksen's eyes on his back, and recalled their previous conversation about how the Federation must be viewed by more warlike species. He was about to respond when Sonak interrupted.

"Admiral, Mr. Gambeta reports that the shuttlecraft is ready."

"Quickly, Sonak. Release the shuttle; send its coordinates to Captain Qo'dar." He turned to the Klingon officer. "If you will transport the remainder of your drones into the shuttlecraft—?"

Qo'dar barked his orders.

"The shuttlecraft is moving toward *Recovery*,"

Sonak reported seconds later as he stared into his viewer. "Cadet Diksen, please split the viewscreen so the admiral can see what is happening."

Diksen obliged. Beside Qo'dar's image, the view of space and *Recovery*'s massive bulk appeared. Kirk watched the shuttle's activities even as Sonak reported them from his sensors.

"The shuttle has halted, and is holding position fifty kilometers from the rescue vessel. According to sensors, the shuttlecraft holds two humanoid passengers —and now contains eighty Klingon drones. *Paladin*'s sensors report that they are surveillance devices, nothing more. *Recovery* has noted the shuttle's activity."

"Qo'dar, the twenty drones that are floating in space," Kirk suggested, "have them surround the shuttlecraft and fire upon it. Two, three times, light hits, that's all we'll need. Be sure they don't fire on *Recovery* herself, or either of our ships."

The Klingon nodded and snapped orders to his crew.

Suddenly, the small flock of drones suspended in space turned and swarmed the tiny shuttlecraft. Quickly, three of the drones blasted the ship randomly.

"The shuttle is issuing a standard Federation distress call, Captain," Diksen called out.

"Good," Kirk murmured to himself, waiting for the ship to dematerialize and be brought into *Recovery*'s womb. No one moved or spoke for seconds, but nothing happened.

"Kirk?" Qo'dar growled.

Jim turned to Diksen questioningly.

"Distress signal still being sent, sir," she reported.

"What's happening?" the admiral asked the air. "Why isn't she getting beamed aboard?"

He imagined he heard a faint edge of disappointment in Sonak's voice. "Sir, it seems that *Recovery* is not convinced that there are life-forms aboard. Her sensors are more sophisticated than ours—"

Suddenly, Qo'dar shouted another command to his crew, and the Klingons aboard the *Fury* scrambled to obey. Kirk didn't like what he supposed they were being ordered to do. "No, wait!" he implored, but it was too late.

"Captain," Sonak reported, "five humanoids have just beamed aboard the shuttle."

Before he could protest Qo'dar's move, Kirk watched the shuttlecraft dematerialize and disappear from the viewscreen.

"The shuttlecraft is now aboard *Recovery,* Admiral," Sonak assured him.

"Now you will see how a Klingon faces death, Terran!" Qo'dar boasted, waving his clenched fist. "And the Tholians will see it as well. But I have taken your advice. My warriors have gone unarmed; a Klingon warrior is weapon enough."

Kirk swallowed, and forced himself to say, "Good luck to your brave warriors, Qo'dar. May they succeed in their mission."

"Captain," Sonak remarked, *"Recovery* has raised her shields and has departed for Tholian space on impulse power."

Suddenly, the viewscreen blinked sporadically and Kirk turned to find Diksen working frantically at her station. "What is it, Diksen? What's happening?"

"It's *Recovery,* sir," the cadet told him, never taking her attention from her work. "She's breaking in—forcing a transmission on us."

"Let it through, Cadet."

The distorted image of Lokara once again faced him across the screen. Qo'dar was gone.

"Sensors indicate this transmission is being sent simultaneously to the Klingon ship," Sonak told Kirk.

The screen showed the bridge of the damaged Tholian vessel. The color variation on the screen quivered so much it was painful to the eyes, and Kirk winced at the too-brilliant colors strobing there.

"Kirk!" Lokara exhorted in a multioctave cascade, "I have control of *Recovery*'s communications. Soon I will control the ship's brain. Meanwhile, *Recovery* will follow its own plan, and you will not be able to stop it. This vessel, and all the weapons and knowledge aboard it, will belong to the Tholian Assembly."

"Commander Lokara." Kirk forced a reasonable expression and tone, uncertain whether the alien would even understand the subtleties of human expression. "You're condemning your people to a long, protracted war—"

A burst of muffled, mechanically distorted sounds came over the speakers. Lokara's veiled image turned as it consulted its console; meanwhile, the sound intensified.

"Sonak, what's happening?" Kirk demanded.

The Vulcan raised a quizzical eyebrow. "I believe, Captain, that is the sound of Klingons who have located their objective."

As he spoke, the noise became distinguishable as the impassioned shouts of Klingon warriors on the kill.

On the screen, Lokara moved swiftly, jerkily, apparently adjusting controls to no avail. Kirk wondered if the Klingons had taken laser tools to cut their way into the ship. Would *Recovery* let them do that?

"Kirk!" the Tholian shouted at the screen, with rage rendered comically shrill by the mechanical voice distortion, "this is your treachery again!"

The viewscreen flashed, and Lokara was gone, his image replaced by the dark, looming figure of Captain Qo'dar. "You dare to give Kirk the credit?" he boomed. "Those are Klingons at your door, Lokara!

You may as well invite them in—since *Recovery* will protect you no longer!" Then he shouted an order to a subordinate.

"Captain, the drones have found their target," Sonak said, "and have armed themselves and fired immediately. The *Recovery*'s brain is effectively destroyed. She was unable to achieve warp, and is traveling on inertia at impulse velocity. Shields are down."

Kirk did not allow himself the luxury of relief; the situation was not yet resolved. "Mr. Sandover, can you get a tractor beam on that ship before she's out of range? We've got to stop her from crossing that border."

Sandover turned toward him, his normally pale skin flushed beneath his freckles with excitement and alarm. "Captain, if we try to put a tractor beam on something that big in the shape we're in, she'll pull us apart!"

Kirk realized he was right, and turned to Diksen. "Hail Qo'dar! His ship's in good shape. Maybe they can stop her momentum."

Suddenly, the Klingon was on half the viewscreen, even as beside him, *Recovery* moved farther and farther away. "Your communications officer relayed your request, Kirk. I'm sorry, but that vessel is too large for us to affect." Qo'dar paused a beat, then said gruffly. "We will have to destroy her."

With Shulman still on board. "No," Kirk countered. "Your men, Qo'dar—"

"It is every Klingon warrior's dream to die in battle, Kirk. My men will roar their way to death in joy."

"Mr. Sonak," the admiral called, with a sinking sense of failure. He knew even before Sonak responded what the Vulcan's answer would be.

"Still no success in breaking the tertiary code,

Admiral." Sonak paused. "You should know, Admiral, that there are no longer any human life-form readings aboard *Recovery.*"

So Shulman was gone; but there were still five Klingons and the Tholians aboard her. He stared at the sight of the rapidly receding vessel on the screen, then said heavily, "Mr. Sandover. Arm all phasers. Load torpedoes. Fire all on the *Recovery* on my order."

"On your command, Kirk," Qo'dar said, with a respect that made him gaze back in gratitude—a feeling he had never thought to feel toward a Klingon. "Know that my warriors will welcome it."

"Mr. Sandover," he said softly, bitterly, "fire all weapons."

The Klingon captain uttered a hoarse monosyllable. On the viewscreen, dazzling photon bursts emerged like hurtling supernovae—from *Paladin,* from the *Fury*—and converged on the retreating vessel just as the rays of both ships' phasers burned into her hull. *Recovery* rocked from the concussion, and began to drift off course—damaged, but not destroyed.

The Klingon cursed. "What a ship this is!" he spat, and Kirk realized his complaints were admiration. "Had this been a Klingon vessel—!"

The viewscreen flickered once more and Diksen called out, "Transmission from *Recovery,* Captain," and he gestured for her to pull it in, get it on screen.

It was Lokara, its image so grotesque and distorted, it took a second for Kirk to realize the Tholian had lost its visor and stood revealed before them. He got a brief impression of shimmering golden skin shot through with rainbow sparks, of sinuous, waving tentacles . . . but the picture was so wavering, so bizarre and canted sideways that Kirk could not clearly describe the alien even though he looked right at it. The shouts of the Klingons had not dimmed; if anything, it sounded as if they were nearly beside the beleaguered Tholian.

"It is over, Kirk!" Lokara babbled, in a cacaphony of voices grown grotesquely shrill. "Over, forever. I told you—Tholians never surrender!"

Then the grainy, broken-up, but unmistakable image of a Klingon warrior loomed behind Lokara. As the Klingon grappled the Tholian in a deadly embrace, Lokara screamed and slapped a writhing golden appendage down on the console before him.

The viewscreen exploded in searing white incandescent light. Kirk raised a hand, momentarily blinded, until Diksen closed the channel and returned the view to darkness of space and the smaller image of the drifting *Recovery*.

"Admiral," Sonak called out, "the Tholians have caused their ship to self-destruct. This explosion has caused a warp-core breach aboard *Recovery;* a second explosion will follow in seconds. Without shields, we do not have the ability to withstand the blast—" He broke off and peered at his viewer, one brow lifted in puzzlement.

Before Kirk could ask for an explanation, Qo'dar once again shared the viewscreen with the image of *Recovery*.

"Hold on, Kirk! Hold on, with all your might!" the Klingon roared.

He stared at the commander's shaggy image, uncertain whether the Klingon was gloating or mocking him; the *Fury,* after all, was well shielded and would no doubt survive the blast.

On the screen beside him, poised just before the border of Tholian space, within sight of the fleet that waited to claim her, *Recovery* exploded.

It was eerie in its silence, as the massive ship dissolved into a blaze of light and hurtling debris.

Kirk watched helplessly as the shock wave rolled toward them, unimpeded in the vacuum of space.

"Hold on," he said uselessly to his crew. His mind spun with a million thoughts in the blink of millisecond—Bones was here, aboard this ship, yet he hadn't had a chance to see him, and now it was too late—Diksen, with her whole career in front of her, modeling on him, and now she would die—Sonak, a fine scientist who would make an excellent first officer —Gambeta, Ngo, Riley and his wife, Sandover—all who'd worked so hard, pushed so much, followed his every order—all of it to end like this?

I'm sorry, Baldassare. Sorry that I couldn't tell you myself about your gallant crew . . .

The shock wave hit hard. Kirk felt his body torn by the force as he rocked in his chair. He heard the alarms, saw Sandover's station burst into flames, watched the helmsman battle to extinguish it, even as the bridge was buffeted. Someone grunted in pain behind him; he heard fabric tear, synthetic and metal break and splinter. The *Paladin* was coming apart.

And this was how it would end—

He shut his eyes, felt the power of the blast tear through him, through his ship—then ebb and subside, even as the vessel rocked like a wind-tossed cradle and started to restabilize. In amazement, he opened his eyes. His crew was scrambling to put out fires, responding to emergency calls from all over the ship.

They had survived. But how—?

He turned to Sonak.

"I had no time to tell you, sir," the Vulcan said, straightening his uniform, "but the *Fury*—extended her shields around us at the last minute. We're badly damaged—we'll have to be towed to the nearest starbase for repairs—but we still have life-support, and the ship is holding together."

Kirk turned toward the viewscreen that was now

nothing nothing but static and white noise. "Diksen, hail the *Fury*—" He paused and swiveled back toward the cadet's comm board. "Diksen, are you all right?"

He could see her hands trembling from where he sat, but she squared her shoulders and said, with only the slightest quaver, "My board is fine, sir. Hailing frequencies open. I mean, I'll raise the *Fury,* sir."

The viewscreen came back on as she manipulated the board, and soon Qo'dar filled it with his dark presence.

"I see you did as I suggested, Kirk, and held on. You survived the blast. Too bad. That means one more Federation ship to deal with." Qo'dar struggled to maintain an expression of disdain, but couldn't quite manage to hide a slight smirk of satisfaction.

"You extended your shields, Qo'dar," Kirk accused. "Don't deny it. You deliberately tried to save us, a Federation ship! What will the Klingon High Command say about that?"

"They cannot address that which they never hear of, Kirk. As far as I know, you are not in the habit of willingly communicating with them. We both achieved what we wanted—even if our goals were different. No doubt you would have rather talked the *Recovery* into surrendering."

"And you would have preferred she fought back against your warship," Kirk commented wryly.

Qo'dar threw back his head in a raucous, good-natured laugh.

"I hope your warriors died gloriously," Kirk offered sincerely.

The Klingon's merriment faded. "And I regret we could not have saved your rescue ship. It was an honorable experiment."

"Captain," Diksen said softly, "we're being hailed by a Federation vessel who's responding to the distress signal we broadcast earlier. They . . . are concerned about the Klingons' presence, sir."

Kirk nodded. "Captain Qo'dar, one of our own ships is coming to our aid. But your assistance will not be forgotten. Perhaps, someday, in the future—"

Qo'dar only chuckled. "You think in the future, someday, Klingons will be like you, and will sit and talk and talk, Kirk? I hope not! I, too, dream to die like a warrior!" With a sharp command in Klingon, Qo'dar closed communications, and the viewscreen returned to the image of ever-brilliant stars and space—and countless pieces of debris floating away in gravityless vacuum, all that remained of the rescue ship *Recovery*.

I'm sorry, Myron. More sorry than you'll ever know. He sagged back in Romolo's chair, more exhausted and more exhilarated than he had been in two years.

"We're being hailed by the *Cavalry,* sir," Diksen reminded him as the Klingon ship warped away.

Kirk swung around to grin quizzically at her. "The . . . cavalry?"

"Aye, sir. The captain of the *U.S.S. First Air Cavalry* is hailing us."

He chuckled, remembering the hubbub surrounding that name when the ship was christened. But the First Air Cavalry had been a famous fighting unit in history and deserved the acclaim, and all the resources that the huge starship offered were desperately needed by the *Paladin* right now.

"On screen, Diksen."

When the familiar visage of Captain Marie Childress appeared, with Ambassador Sarek standing beside her, Jim allowed himself a broad smile.

"Marie! You're a sight for sore eyes. As are you, Ambassador." He enjoyed watching Sarek raise one eyebrow ever so slightly in the blandest display of surprise. "How did you get here so fast?"

"Jim, several ships were stationed in the neighborhood of the simulation," Childress answered, "simply because of the proximity of the Romulans, Klingons, and Tholians. We heard about the *Recovery*'s breakdown and have been chasing you ever since. There are a few more ships tailing us, and several stayed to assist the *Starhawk*."

"Is Captain Romolo with you?" Kirk asked hopefully. He wanted nothing more than to tell Baldassare —in front of his crew—just how valiantly they'd served their "stand-in" captain.

Captain Childress shifted in her seat, her brown eyes searching Sarek's face. The ambassador lowered his gaze for the briefest of instants; when he raised it again, his eyes and voice were somber. "I'm sorry, Admiral. But I'm afraid that Captain Romolo—did not survive the attack on the *Starhawk*. To you, and to the entire crew of the *Paladin*, may I say—I grieve with thee."

Kirk could say nothing—could only exhale abruptly, as though the wind had been knocked from him. A moment of silence passed, and then Sarek said, his pitch rising ever so slightly with curiosity:

"Captain Akhmatova was critically wounded and is still in sickbay. She wished me to relay a message to you. . . ." He paused. "She says to tell you that she knows what to do now. She says—tell Kirk Baldassare made the right choice. The fourth choice."

"The fourth choice," Kirk repeated, too stunned by the news to make sense of the words. And then his conversation with Akhmatova returned to him.

"I figure I've got three choices: accept the promotion and be kicked upstairs; refuse it; or retire and be done with it." Baldassare Romolo had made the fourth choice, the right one: he had died in action, as a captain on a starship.

A small sound behind him caused him to glance

over his shoulder. At communications, Reese Diksen sat stone-faced, staring at her board, her fists clenched in fury.

With a sigh, he turned back to the screen.

"Marie. This crew is hurt, hungry, and exhausted. Many of them will need to beam over directly onto the *Cavalry* for medical care. We need a relief team— especially for the bridge crew—and lots of hands."

"I'm sending my best, Jim," Marie assured him. "You should be off that bridge within the hour."

He nodded his thanks and thought, *There's got to be some Saurian brandy somewhere on this vessel. Once I locate it, all I have to do is find Bones . . .*

Epilogue

ABOARD THE *PALADIN,* Kevin Riley settled down against the all-too-inviting bunk with a gusting sigh. The events aboard *Recovery* had left him feeling exhausted and years older; after a brief exchange with Admiral Kirk, he had returned to his guest quarters to clean up and change from a uniform spattered with Josiah Ngo's blood. The admiral had looked as weary as his aide, his uniform likewise blood-smeared. But unlike Riley, Kirk had seemed rejuvenated by the experience, and Kevin had no doubt that the admiral would make good his promise to procure a starship of his own.

But at the moment, Riley could not bring his tired mind to contemplate it. He was due now for a long rest. His body ached for it; yet even as he lay, unwilling, unable to move, against the bunk's soft firmness, he contemplated rising. Anab and he would not be aboard the *Paladin* for long. He wanted to seek her out, to see her alone, removed from the insane backdrop of the *Recovery,* before duty and space separated them again.

He lay there some moments, fatigue warring with desire, and when the door at last chimed softly, he smiled to himself and rose.

"Come."

The door slid open to reveal Anab—as always, to Riley, breathtaking in her dark beauty, her elegance— smiling shyly, her uniform also now clean of Ngo's blood. She ran a hand over her close-cut hair and lingered in the entryway a moment, unsure of her welcome.

"Come in, please," he said easily, and gestured toward a chair. "I was just thinking about going to see you."

She crossed to a chair and sat in front of him, crossing her long legs as he settled onto the bunk. "I came to apologize, K.T."

He blinked, sincerely unable to figure out what she referred to, and gave a short laugh. "For what?"

"For the way I treated you on *Recovery.* I couldn't accept that you'd changed. You have, you know. You're not the man I left."

He felt a faint surge of warmth on his cheeks and realized, to his amazement, that he was blushing like a cadet. "Oh . . . well—I guess I *have* changed. In some ways, at least. But . . . let's face it, Anab. You had a point. I make a rotten Security officer."

He said it so ingenuously that she laughed aloud, and he joined in with her.

"I know," she said, smiling, her teeth a pearly half-moon against red-brown lips; and then she suddenly grew somber. "You almost got yourself killed. Twice—once because you saved me. I wanted to thank you."

"You did the same for me. Remember?"

"I remember." She lowered her face for an instant, then raised it shyly, looking up at him from beneath long, dark lashes, and released a sigh. "I really came because I miss you, K.T. I couldn't leave without letting you know—even though I had to leave to do what I wanted with my life—that I still care." Her voice grew suddenly soft, so that he had to lean forward to hear. "It's not like I can just stop loving you."

Her words pierced him just as that first sight of her in the *Paladin*'s briefing room had; but this time, there was sweetness with the pain. "I know." He leaned forward further, and touched the hand that rested in her lap. "Being apart . . . hasn't really changed the way we feel, has it? I've just . . . learned to get used to it."

She took his hand, gently, and again lowered her face; this time, she did not look up. "I wish . . ." she whispered. "I wish there were some way we could be together."

A year before, a month before, perhaps even the day before the events aboard *Recovery,* he would have prayed to hear those words. But now he let a long silence pass between before he answered, lightly:

"We can't. Because I've learned something: I'm not cut out for active duty in space. There's no reason to blame myself—not everyone belongs aboard a starship. And I've learned that I don't."

She looked up at him and said bitterly, "And I do."

"And you do." He stroked her cheek softly with the back of his hand. "I really see that now."

Another silence passed; and then she asked, "So you're going to stay with Kirk? In San Francisco?"

He paused, remembering Kirk's determination as he went to demand a better assignment from Nogura.

Seeing the exhilaration on Kirk's face now, he suspected he knew the precise assignment the admiral would demand.

Just as surely, he knew that he was not meant to accompany him.

He gazed beyond Anab, at a far distant point somewhere in his future, and murmured, "I don't know. . . ."

McCoy sat by Josiah Ngo's bed, waiting patiently for the young man's lids to flutter. He should be coming up right about . . .

The eyes under the dark lids rolled, the lids blinked. Josiah glanced around warily from beneath a fringe of brown-black lashes.

"You're okay, son," McCoy said kindly. "You're coming out of cell regeneration. You've been under quite a while. How do you feel?"

Josiah tentatively raised a hand and touched his chest, then patted it more firmly.

"It's gone," McCoy reassured him. "You came through surgery just fine. You've been in cell regeneration for over two days. You'll be out of sickbay in two more, so we can use this bed for someone who really needs it."

Josiah nodded, still dazed. McCoy lifted a glass of cool water to his mouth and let him have some. "We—we on the *Paladin?*" the cadet croaked, his voice rusty from disuse and probably the remnants of blood in his trachea.

McCoy nodded. "We started your surgery in sickbay and were ready to close up when you gave us some trouble—" He shook his head, remembering the boy's blood pressure dropping, all the vitals going zero, as though the kid had just suddenly given up. "We had three doctors—including myself—working on you. Once we got you through the worst of it, we brought you here for cell regeneration and recovery. And you've been doing fine. You haven't been critical for the last twenty-four hours. You'll be dancing by tomorrow."

Josiah shot him a skeptical look, but managed a wan smile. "Lieutenant Saed and Commander Riley? Reese?"

"All safe." The doctor grinned at the thought. "Your friend Reese'll be coming to visit you soon."

"Did you—ever get to have that drink with Admiral Kirk?"

McCoy looked solemnly into his patient's dark eyes. "No, 'fraid not. Jim hasn't been free to talk— and you and I were in surgery. But I'll get with him, soon as he gets everything on *Paladin* squared away." In truth, he'd been hesitant about seeing the admiral again. The events with *Recovery* had only served to underscore the fact that Kirk belonged on the bridge of a starship, and the doctor wasn't so sure he could hold his tongue and keep from telling Jim so.

At the same time, he yearned to see his old friend once more. *But what's the point of rehashing old times?* he thought bitterly. *They can never come again. . . .*

Josiah nodded, then blinked sleepily. Regen patients never could stay awake for long. "Hey, Doc— you did it. You got that call through. You're a doctor —and a computer expert!" In spite of his condition, Josiah managed a brief grin.

"A temporary condition, I'm sure," McCoy reassured him. "Now, go on back to sleep." He dimmed the lights and within seconds Josiah had obeyed him, allowing him to leave the room quietly.

Outside the private quarters, McCoy rubbed a hand over his tired eyes. He felt about three hundred years old. His first nap had only been a few hours ago; he had felt compelled to be there when Josiah had his first conscious moment after the surgery. Now he wouldn't have to worry about the boy waking up terrified on a strange ship, without anything recognizable around him.

It was time for him to take his own advice now, and get some sleep. He moved wearily two doors down and entered the quarters that had been assigned to him. As he crossed the threshold, he saw a shadow, and, still jumpy from all the violence he'd experienced on the *Recovery,* he froze, poised for flight.

A figure stepped out of the shadow, then asked the computer to brighten the lights.

McCoy blinked, then stared at the tall, dark specter. "Angie?" he whispered hoarsely.

"Leonard, are you all right?" Angelina Mola moved to him with the same fluid grace he remembered. It was a hallucination, he knew, probably part of post-stress syndrome and lack of sleep. But it was so good to just *see* her again. "Didn't they tell you, Leonard? Didn't you hear? Oh, *Dios,* poor dear, what a shock. Just what you didn't need."

She took his hands and hers were warm, the same warm, long-fingered, strong hands that could move so agilely in any surgery, so assuredly in any emergency. McCoy could do nothing but gape at them in wonder.

"The *Recovery* preserved me perfectly," she explained, "and maintained the stasis chamber exactly the way she was supposed to. My chamber—still fully functional—was beamed aboard the *Paladin* with the rest of you. They brought me up while you were still in surgery on the young cadet. I have a new, artificial heart"—she thumped her chest—"complete with a five-year warranty! If it fails, I get my money back! You've been so involved with your case—I guess, after a while they just forgot to tell you. I'm so sorry. It must've been like seeing the dead."

As she spoke, his eyes filled; he had to blink rapidly

to clear them. "More like seeing a saint. Angie, it's so *wonderful* to see you—!" He embraced her, hugging her to him, and she returned it, her arms strong.

Swallowing the emotions, he pulled back and said gently, "Have they told you—?"

"That I was the only one so . . . lucky?" She closed her eyes for a moment; grief slackened her features. "Chia. Nassar. Monique. It's so hard to believe. And *Myron* . . . For him to die as he did, such a gentle soul taking so many with him . . ."

McCoy shook his head, as though trying to negate the horror of it. "He—he was so proud, Angie. So proud that he'd saved you. I thought you were gone forever, but I humored him. He died believing that he'd saved you on sheer will alone. He saved us all, in the end."

She opened dark, lustrous, intelligent eyes, so full of pain that he was forced to look away from them. He let go a long, tremulous breath and continued: "When we materialized in the cargo hold, only a few of us knew where we were. There was so much panic by then. Some Starfleet people were with me, and they had the force of will to get everything under control pretty quickly. Then I told anyone who would listen in the cargo hold how we'd gotten there—that Myron had saved the core programming. It took some fast talking but—by the time they brought Josiah and me to sickbay, they had started a service for Myron right there in the cargo hold. There were ten men from Zotos Four who'd worked with him over the years and they were saying a—a *kaddish* right there. I wish I could've stayed for it."

"You haven't spoken yet with Kirk," she said knowingly.

He shook his head. "The *Paladin*'s a mess, hanging together with spit and wire. Jim's really the captain with Romolo dead, and has been too busy for something so personal. And I was in surgery for—I don't know, it feels like days. . . ."

He looked up, remembering something. "Angie, did they tell you—all of it?"

She lowered her gaze and suddenly looked her age—shrunken, old. "Yes. Myron's death. The loss of *Recovery.*"

He knew the two deaths were, in many ways, of equal value to her.

"Leonard, the advances we'd made on that ship—all lost."

"It can't all be lost, Angie! Myron's data exists other places. The things he created can be reproduced."

She shook her head. "In time, some of it, no doubt, will be. But *Recovery* is a lost dream. You can't know the effort it took to get the original built, the money, the politicking, the resources, the staff. And now there's no Myron Shulman to pull it all together. He *was* a genius, Leonard, and his creativity and inventiveness is gone forever."

The aged, stately woman looked at him squarely. "The FDRA will not be the only organization to suffer in this. The Federation will feel it. This setback will slow down technological development. The loss of *Recovery* will taint many activities, many discoveries. The investigations alone will go on for years."

She was right, he realized gloomily.

"Of course, if another individual," she said cagily, staring at him, "with popular clout, with the savvy to think on his feet, and the respect of Federation higher-ups brought the proposal to them—"

His eyes widened. "Keep talking like that, lady, and I'm gonna have to check you for brain damage. Forget it, Angie. There's no way I'd have the patience to even try all that wheeling and dealing, and—after what I've been through, I don't even know if I could believe in the project myself. Some things—might be better off left to rest in peace." He looked away from her guiltily, avoiding her disappointed gaze.

He shook his head again, talking more now for his own benefit. "That joyride on *Recovery* was my last bit for God and country. The only way the Federation's ever gonna get me to work for them again will be to forcibly draft me. And that's a promise."

The two old friends stood silently in his chambers for a long, long time, holding a memorial service of their own.

"It's pretty amazing, Admiral," Riley was saying the following morning as they walked through the *Paladin*'s battle-scarred corridors, "that with all the chaos going on, the scientists managed to save all the data they'd brought aboard from Zotos Four."

Kirk had been surprised by that information himself. "They worked damned hard for it, which made them very cautious. Not only did they have it stored in the *Recovery*'s main computer—where it was destroyed when the ship was—but they kept duplicates of all the computer work on cassettes right on their bodies! So when they were beamed aboard *Paladin*, the data all came with them. Good thing they were wary of the new ship."

The last two days had been nonstop, minute-to-minute stress as a thousand decisions had to be made about *Paladin*'s repairs, crew transfers, data transfers, and *Recovery*'s survivors. Food was a catch-as-catch-can situation, and sleep was worse. Jim couldn't remember when he'd had the latter, but it had been in a chair somewhere, a quick catnap, then back to the grind.

He'd never gotten to talk to McCoy. He'd tried to get to sickbay, but in spite of Captain Childress's reassurance, he hadn't left the bridge for hours. By the time he did get free, Bones was deep in critical surgery on Josiah Ngo. The two were transferred onto the medical vessel while Jim was working with the engineers on the warp-drive realignment. He never even knew about it till it had long passed.

He was relieved, at least, that Kevin Riley was once more by his side.

"Admiral." Riley's tone grew suddenly formal; his pace slowed. "If I could have permission to speak freely, sir . . ."

Kirk raised an eyebrow. "I always expect you to speak freely with me, Riley. You know that."

He grinned sheepishly, revealing a flash of white teeth in the midst of golden-brown beard. "Yes, sir. I have the feeling that you've made some decisions—being out here again. I can see it in your face. The whole time I've been here with you—you've been, well—it feels just like when we were on—"

Kirk held his hand up. "No. Not quite like that. I'm taking *Paladin* home. She may be decommissioned, since she's taken quite a beating, but if she is, I'll be part of the decision. I owe that to Baldassare. And I'll take her on her last trip. She deserves that. But—you're right about the decisions. I've already sent my reports to the old man. And my request."

Riley's expression grew sly. "You mean, your demand."

Kirk smiled and inclined his head, a gesture that allowed the truth of the last remark. "Nogura will see it that way—but he can't deny me now. Not after this." He glanced at Riley. "I want the *Enterprise* back. And I'll get her. No more being distracted by Nogura's promises to make the admiralty into something it's not."

"I believe you, sir."

Kirk grinned saucily. "Want to come along?"

Riley shared his conspiratorial smile briefly; then his boyish countenance grew somber. "I know I said earlier that I'd follow you, sir—but . . . my time aboard *Recovery* has made me think twice about serving aboard a starship again." His shoulders lowered as he released a small, silent sigh, and Kirk watched a glimmer of uncertainty and guilt cross his features. "I don't belong with you there, sir—but I meant what I said about not pushing someone else's papers. I have no desire to serve at headquarters without you."

The two men stopped walking; Kirk turned toward him thoughtfully. He'd always felt that Riley's destiny lay somewhere beyond a desk at Starfleet Headquarters; he'd hoped that it would be with him, aboard the *Enterprise*. But if that was not to be . . .

He spoke swiftly as inspiration struck. "Kevin . . . I spoke with Ambassador Sarek today. He lost two of his closest aides in the attack on *Starhawk*. If you're interested, it could open up a whole new career for you—in diplomacy. Interested?"

Riley brightened. "Yes, sir! The time I assisted you in diplomatic troubleshooting was the best part of the job. That is, if you think—"

"I'd be happy to recommend you to him."

"Thank you, Admiral." He let go another sigh and grinned. "Thank you. Frankly, I was worried about how you'd react. I'll be sorry to leave you. You've helped me more than you can know."

"As you've helped me," Kirk said softly. He extended his hand; the two men clasped palms warmly.

"With your permission, sir." Riley straightened. "I'd like to contact the ambassador as soon as possible. . . ."

"Go right ahead, Kevin. We'll catch up with each other later." He let go of Riley's hand and watched with a sense of nostalgia as his aide—his *former* aide—strode confidently away from him down the hallway.

By the time he reached the turbolift, Kirk was no longer sure where he was going. They'd certified the ship safe for travel—as long as she didn't exceed warp four—and now they were finally under way. Maybe this would be a good time to find some empty quarters and actually try to sleep horizontally for a few hours. The lift opened, and Reese Diksen stared at him in surprise.

"Captain Kirk, I mean—Admiral, I mean—" She stopped stammering and collected her thoughts. Stepping out of the lift, she started again. "Admiral. Nice to see you. Everything all right?"

"For the last ten minutes," he assured her. "Where are you heading?"

"My quarters. They're on this floor."

Without discussing it, the two of them started walking together. "I could use a little advice on that subject, Diksen," he remarked.

"Excuse me, sir?"

"Any ideas where I can bunk tonight?" It suddenly occurred to him how she might take that and he almost blushed. He'd asked her in all innocence, since, after all they'd been through, he'd come to view her as a fellow officer—a comrade-in-arms—not an available female. But, in truth, she was.

She mulled over the questions, and her expression never showed any discomfort. "I take it you'd rather not stay in the captain's quarters."

"Correct," he said too quickly. Romolo's ghost would haunt him as it was. He wouldn't get a wink of sleep in the dead man's bed.

"Well, actually," she suggested helpfully, "the quarters next to Sonak are empty, sir, up on deck two—unless someone's appropriated them because of damage on other decks."

But that was unlikely, he knew, since so much of their crew had been transferred to the *Cavalry*. Diksen had stayed. As had Saed. Ngo, he had no doubt, would have stayed had he not been wounded. . . . A glimmer of guilt assailed him at the memory.

As though she'd heard him thinking about Ngo, she said, "I heard that you recommended Ngo for the Medal of Valor. I think that's wonderful, sir. If he gets it, he'll be the first cadet ever to earn it in action."

Kirk smiled slightly. "Oh, I don't know. He may actually be just *one* of the first cadets."

Diksen's brows furrowed; then, as if she'd finally figured out what he was suggesting, her ears burned a furious red.

He had to laugh. "There'll be enough medals to go around after this, Diksen." Then he grew serious. "I remember how I gave you the chance to leave the bridge, to be with Josiah—and you stayed."

"I couldn't have helped him. I could've helped you."

Kirk nodded. "You did help me. Through the whole thing. You show a lot of promise, Diksen."

She held a breath, then let it out with control and faced him. "I'll remember what you told me. I'll never forget my ambitions."

He looked at her attractive, youthful face, saw all the hard choices coming before her—and envied her for it. "I'll remember, too. I promise you."

Her eyes widened. "You—you're going back to space?"

"I'm going to fight for it." He grinned. "Want to come along?"

"Yes, *sir!* Absolutely!"

"That's a deal, Diksen. It won't be communications, this time—"

"That's okay, sir. A captain has to know how to run everything on her ship!"

Laughing, he continued, "And you can bring Ngo along, too. I'm thinking of talking to Lieutenant Saed, as well." He was already planning on his staff, he realized. Could he pull his old crew off their new assignments? Would they come with him again? He'd talk McCoy into it somehow, despite all the doctor's grumbling that he'd had enough of the Fleet.

But Spock . . .

The presence of his Vulcan friend had been so real at times during this mission, he had almost heard his voice. But Spock was on Vulcan, studying *Kolinahr*. That was one relationship he would never enjoy again.

Then he remembered Sonak.

"What deck were those quarters on again, Diksen?"

A few minutes later he approached the rooms the cadet had told him about. The doors slid open to reveal a puzzled Vulcan on the other side. "Admiral Kirk? Can I help you?"

"Sonak! Forgive me. I must've confused the room assignments. Diksen said there was an empty one, but I could've sworn it was this one."

"There has been an error, sir. These are my quarters. But I can show you a vacant one." The Vulcan walked down the corridor with Kirk, just one door from his own. The doors opened onto a clean but empty room, with a bunk neatly made—an inviting sight.

"Thank you," Kirk said. "It's been a while since any of us have had adequate rest," then, he amended, "that is, any of us humans."

Sonak merely quirked an eyebrow.

"Since I have this chance, Commander, I wanted to thank you for all the help you've given me—"

To his surprise, Sonak interrupted. "It is illogical to thank me for my help, Admiral, when I failed in the two most critical functions I needed to perform in our confrontation with *Recovery*."

"Failed?"

"I could not decipher the tertiary code quickly enough to gain control of the vessel," Sonak reiterated calmly, "nor did I determine the Tholian Lokara's intent to fire upon us until it was too late to raise the shields. If you will remember, sir, it was my recommendation to lower the shields."

Kirk nodded, recognizing the sense of defeat the Vulcan felt, even if he never expressed it. "Mr. Sonak, you will find in your career that sometimes the most logical decisions don't always work out. Not even Spock could've translated that code quickly enough to stop that ship. And our lowering the shields probably kept *Recovery* from doing to us what she did to the *Skotha*. I'm satisfied with your decisions and your actions. I may be a mere human—"

Sonak nodded all too willingly.

"—but I know a good science officer when I see one. I'm hoping to get another vessel, to go back on active duty in space. If that happens—would you serve with me?"

Sonak drew himself up into that tall, stately Vulcan stance and met Kirk's gaze. "I would be honored to serve under you, Admiral, on any vessel."

Kirk nodded, knowing Sonak would not extend his hand as Riley had. "Thank you, Mr. Sonak. A good rest to you."

As Sonak left him in the empty room Diksen had correctly told him about, Kirk collapsed on the bed and stared at the ceiling. It didn't take long for him to realize, as his eyes moved back and forth in the dim light, that sleep would evade him, as he couched all the arguments he would have to use on Admiral Nogura to get his way. But he had made up his mind how it would end. The events aboard the *Paladin* had brought home too keenly the memory of what he had been—and what he was determined to be again.

J. M. Dillard

*No more double-talk, Heihachiro. This time, I won't
back down. You'll either have to give me a starship or
drum me out of the Fleet.*

And not just any starship. Sooner or later, he would
be back in space—back aboard the *Enterprise*—
where he belonged.

In the midst of his reverie, the door chimed softly;
he sat up, ordered the lights on. "Come."

He steeled himself, half expecting Diksen, or another *Paladin* officer, with news of some other forgotten
task, some detail that demanded his attention before
he could rest. Or perhaps it was Riley, with news of his
meeting with Ambassador Sarek. . . .

The door slid open, revealing a lean figure, its face
hidden in shadow. For a fleeting moment, the visitor
remained silent; Kirk frowned, opening his mouth to
speak, but before he could, the figure moved . . .

Slowly, leisurely, raising an arm to lift something
dark and gleaming in its hand. A flask, Kirk realized,
and as the light glinted off the amber liquid inside, he
said, with a grin:

"That had better be Saurian brandy."

"Damn straight," McCoy said, stepping into the
light.

Deep within Mount Seleya's cold heart, Spock
opened his eyes.

Outside, Vulcan's sun burned relentlessly in the
desert sky, but inside Sekhet's dark, windowless
shrine, shadows leapt, quivering, in the silent gloom.
For days he had meditated, motionless and undis-
turbed, without drink, without food, determined to
break the bonds that connected him to Kirk and
McCoy.

And at last in the middle of his vigil's third day, the
stubborn conviction that his friends were in danger
eased.

He lifted his gaze to Sekhet's stone visage before

him, and observed the play of light and dark over her fearsome face as he recited the customary prayer of thanks.

Yet even as he whispered the ancient words in an ancient tongue, a strand of doubt wove its way into his consciousness. The sense of danger to his friends had vanished; but did that truly mean all bonds were dissolved? That his friendship with these two was forever consigned to the past?

Spock completed his recitation, then turned and made his way back through the great archway, out into the passageway. At the spiraling stone stairs, he paused.

Faintly, as though from a far, far distance, someone, something brushed his mind.

Jim Kirk?

He hesitated, softening his breathing, quieting his thoughts to better understand the source of the transmission.

Leonard McCoy?

But the sensation disappeared as abruptly as it had come.

He dismissed it as the aftereffects of the fast and meditation, no more. He had completed the ritual of Sekhet; he would have to trust that all ties now were truly severed, and that he was prepared to undergo the ritual with the High Master.

Spock drew a breath and began slowly to climb the stairs with an odd sense of destiny, of moving toward the unknown future. . . .

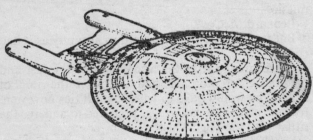